Peril in the Cotswolds

By Rebecca Tope

THE COTSWOLD MYSTERIES

THE LAKE DISTRICT MYSTERIES

THE WEST COUNTRY MYSTERIES

Peril in the Cotswolds

REBECCA TOPE

Allison & Busby Limited
12 Fitzroy Mews
London W1T 6DW
allisonandbusby.com

First published in Great Britain by Allison & Busby in 2017.
This paperback edition published by Allison & Busby in 2018.

A CIP catalogue record for this book is available from
the British Library.

10 9 8 7 6 5 4 3 2 1

ISBN 978-0-7490-2199-3

Typeset in 10.5/15.5 pt Sabon by
Allison & Busby Ltd.

The paper used for this Allison & Busby publication
has been produced from trees that have been legally sourced
from well-managed and credibly certified forests.

Printed and bound by
CPI Group (UK) Ltd, Croydon, CR0 4YY

Dedicated to Luke
with thanks for helpful input

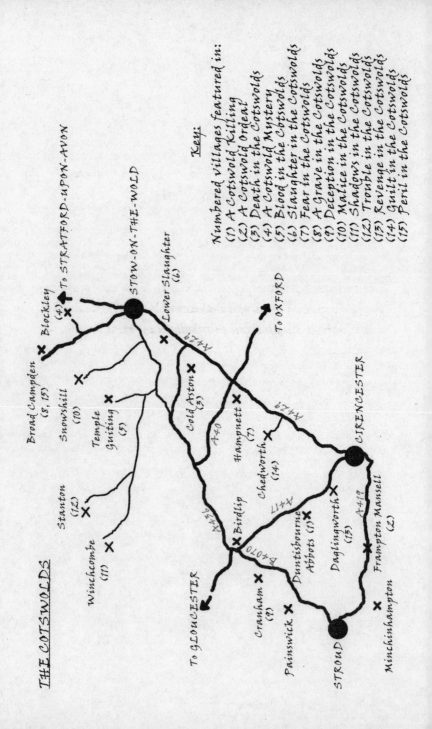

THE COTSWOLDS

TO STRATFORD-UPON-AVON

Broad Campden (8, 15)
Blockley (4)
Stanton (12)
Snowshill (10)
Winchcombe (11)
Temple Guiting (5)
STOW-ON-THE-WOLD
Lower Slaughter (6)
Cold Aston (3)
Hampnett (7)
Chedworth (14)
Birdlip
Cranham (9)
Painswick
Duntisbourne Abbots (1)
Daglingworth (13)
Frampton Mansell (2)
Minchinhampton
CIRENCESTER
STROUD
TO GLOUCESTER
TO OXFORD

A429
A40
A436
A417
A419
A429

Key:

Numbered villages featured in:

(1) A Cotswold Killing
(2) A Cotswold Ordeal
(3) Death in the Cotswolds
(4) A Cotswold Mystery
(5) Blood in the Cotswolds
(6) Slaughter in the Cotswolds
(7) Fear in the Cotswolds
(8) A Grave in the Cotswolds
(9) Deception in the Cotswolds
(10) Malice in the Cotswolds
(11) Shadows in the Cotswolds
(12) Trouble in the Cotswolds
(13) Revenge in the Cotswolds
(14) Guilt in the Cotswolds
(15) Peril in the Cotswolds

Author's Note

Liberties have been taken with the village of Broad Campden to suit the requirements of the story. The houses described might appear very similar to actual properties, but are in fact invented.

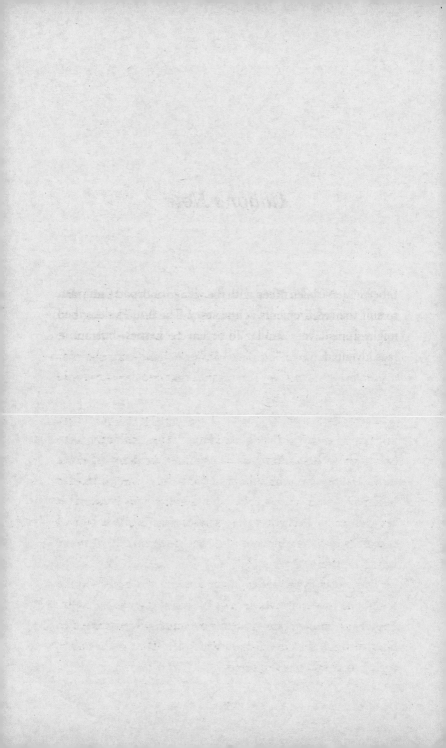

Chapter One

'For heaven's sake, Heps, get out of the way,' pleaded Thea, feeling ashamed of herself even as she spoke. The dog had one leg in plaster and could hardly be expected to move quickly. Combined with her physical handicap, she was also in need of constant reassurance that one day she would be able to run and jump again.

But it was the first day of the spring school term, and the household was in chaos. The children were every bit as demanding as the spaniel, in their different ways. Stephanie was adamant that only one particular headband was acceptable, and Timmy was making it very clear to everyone that school was a place full of torturers and criminals, and it was indefensible to make him go there.

Drew was in the room at the back of the house on the telephone to a man whose wife had died during the night. Sounds of family conflict were very much not permitted to filter through the closed door, which left Thea on her own, trying to attend to every need.

'She can't help it,' said Stephanie, leaping to the dog's defence. 'Don't shout at her.'

'I wasn't,' said Thea, with a strong sense of being unjustly accused. 'But I can't move with her at my feet all the time. How can I find your headband if I can't even go into the hall without kicking the dog?'

'You can't *kick* her!' protested Timmy, his face full of horror.

'No I know I can't. That's why I'm stuck here, and you're going to be late for the bus.'

It was obvious that Timmy thought this an outcome devoutly to be wished. 'Here it is, still in my bag,' Stephanie discovered. 'It must have been there for *ages*. Since we broke up last term, in fact. It smells.' She sniffed at the strip of blue satin. 'Pooh!'

'Why? What else is in there?' Thea asked warily. She had a sneaking feeling that she had simply left the bag unexamined for two and a half weeks. 'Let's have a look.' She pulled out a plastic bag containing the mildewed crusts of lunchtime sandwiches and a furry apple core. 'Could be worse,' she muttered. 'The smell's just your trainers. You haven't needed them over Christmas.' She turned to the small boy. 'What about you, Tim? What's been left in your bag all holiday, I wonder?'

He tipped the mini-rucksack upside down and nothing whatsoever fell out of it. 'I emptied it in my room,' he said, 'on the first day of the holidays.'

'Well done, you,' she approved. 'I'm glad one of us has got some sense.'

The child made no reply, but merely sighed.

'Where's Daddy?' asked Stephanie.

'You know perfectly well he's on the phone.'

'I want him to kiss us before we go. It's a new term – it's special. Timmy wants it as well.'

'The bus goes in two minutes. You've got to go *now*. You can't miss it on the first day – they might give your seats to someone else, and then I'd have to drive you every morning.' Thea had worked hard to get permission for the children to travel on the school bus, despite living under the requisite two miles away. Timmy had seemed terribly young to be consigned to such a form of travel, but his sister promised to watch out for him, and the previous term had seen them collected and returned without mishap, five days a week.

It was in no way her fault that Drew was unavailable to kiss his children goodbye. That she was getting the fallout from it was inevitable and not unduly burdensome. She felt no resentment about it. But she noticed it, just the same. She noticed everything, from the way everyone automatically assumed she would step into the role of general family organiser, to include everything from meals, clothes, housework, timetables and health matters to the absence of space, either physical or emotional, for her to be herself – whoever that might be. Thea Osborne had mutated into Thea Slocombe, and the new person was often hard to recognise.

She had spent half her life as Osborne, having married young and been widowed twenty years later. Drew Slocombe had come along quite out of the blue, here in Broad Campden. They had fitted together like magic, knowing – as they afterwards insisted – from that first

11

day that they would end up as a couple. Now they were married and she had become a replacement mother for the two children, their own mum having died not too long ago. It had taken her a foolishly long time to accept that she was well and truly a stepmother, with everything that label entailed. While the fairy tales dealing with the subject held virtually no overt relevance to the new-made Slocombe family, the daily detail, the ever-present sense of responsibility, had been a slowly burgeoning shock. It was so far from the future she had imagined for herself that she was still not entirely convinced that it was real.

The children had been gone for three minutes when Drew reappeared. Having waved to them from the doorstep, Thea was sitting with a mug of tepid coffee thinking of nothing. Drew glanced around the kitchen, made a little face of regret and bent to scoop Hepzibah into his arms. 'How's our patient this morning?' he crooned. 'Does it hurt, I wonder?' He stroked the animal gently as she flopped awkwardly on his arm. A cocker spaniel, with all her weight at the front end, she was never easy to carry. Drew had only recently begun to do it, apparently feeling a need to demonstrate his affection for her.

'She's getting lumpy,' he observed, pulling at a section of matted hair over one haunch. 'Ought to have a haircut at the poodle parlour.'

'Put her down,' said Thea. 'You missed the children. They were hoping for a goodbye kiss.' *And so was I*, she added silently. Not goodbye, but good morning. As far as she could recall, Drew had not so much as looked at her since the alarm had gone off at seven-fifteen.

12

He very carefully let the dog slide to the floor. 'That was a funeral,' he said. 'Completely out of the blue. He wants it on Monday next week.'

It was currently Tuesday. 'Is that a problem?' she asked.

'No, not really. It means more work for Andrew, which'll please him. In fact, he's going to be flat out for the rest of the week. We've got Miss Temple on Friday, and three separate lots of people want to come with trees on Saturday.'

'In January? Is that sensible?'

'Apparently you can plant bare-root things during the winter, so long as there's no hard frost. I didn't think I should argue.'

'No.'

'Are you okay?'

She sighed. 'Oh, yes. First day of term. Tasks left undone. Stephanie's schoolbag hadn't been emptied since the end of last term and we couldn't find her headband. It was in the bag, which was quite smelly. My fault, obviously. And I still don't understand the system for school dinners that they're doing now. It's going to be a nightmare.'

'I used to do their packed lunches every day. I did it for about two years. You get into the swing of it. Buy stuff in bulk – that's the secret.'

'I know the theory. But now it's cooked dinners for two days and sandwiches for three. How will that work? And the obesity police will check everything I give them and hold them up to ridicule if there's a Wagon Wheel.'

'I've got to give a talk to the local radio people this afternoon. I mean – they're going to come here and ask questions and then broadcast it a few hours later. I wanted to think up something that sounded really up to date and innovative.'

'Have you made any notes for it?'

He shook his head. 'All I can think of is what's wrong with our field. It would never have been chosen as a burial ground by anybody who knew what they were doing. It's too low-lying, too shady and too far from the church.'

'You can make all those things sound like advantages if you try. It's working out well enough, isn't it?'

'It could be a lot better,' he persisted. The field had been left to him, along with the house, by a woman who had embraced the concept of green burials shortly before she died. Remaking her will in Drew's favour must have felt like an act of supreme generosity as she did it. The house was certainly a valuable gift by any standards. But the field was a distance away, the planning permission slow and complicated to obtain, and local attitudes still hovered on the fence between acceptance and rejection of such a business in their midst.

'Say something about New Year resolutions, and giving some thought to making a will, and keeping everything simple and affordable for the family,' she suggested.

He pulled a face indicative of scepticism and impatience. 'It doesn't sound very positive,' he objected. 'I get the feeling I should be aiming much more for the aesthetic side of it. How every grave can be individually designed, to reflect the person's character.'

'More of those embroidered felt shrouds, I suppose. I don't know why it is, but I can't take them seriously.'

'People like them,' he said vaguely. 'But they mostly change their minds when they hear the price.'

'Drew . . .' She had no idea what she was going to say. She felt tired, with nothing to look forward to. Christmas was over, with a stack of greetings cards on the windowsill and a large bag of crumpled wrapping paper behind the sofa all there was left to show for it. She had been intending to smooth out the paper in the hopes of using it again. The cards were too fresh to throw away, but were entirely useless. She remembered her grandmother cutting them up for labels the following year, and entertained the idea for a brief moment. But there were too many of them, and they would only create clutter in the intervening eleven months.

'What?' For the first time that day he looked into her face. 'What's the matter? You're not really okay at all, are you?'

'Oh, it's nothing in particular. I'm just a bit frazzled. It's the sixth of January – isn't that supposed to be a national day of depression or something?'

'Is it? Sounds barmy to me. Like a government edict to be miserable.'

'It's probably next week, now I come to think of it. But you can understand it. Short days. Too much family jollity. Overeating and drinking. No wonder everybody feels a bit sick.'

'I don't. I'm looking forward to a promising new year. I hate to say it, but I really am counting my blessings.'

'You're disgusting. What happened to worrying about your talk and providing innovations for your customers?'

'I wasn't really worried; just thinking aloud. It'll be fine when it comes to the point. After all, everybody who'll be interested is going to be over eighty, in all likelihood, and quite happy with something traditional.'

'Traditional? What's traditional about being buried in a shallow hole in a field with a tree for a memorial? No church, no hymns or fancy flourishes. No, my love, your customer base is the mavericks of this world, and you know it. Not every eighty-year-old is a conformist, anyway. Especially these days.'

He smiled at her, patient as always. 'Depends how far you go back through history, I suppose. I'm thinking nineteenth-century tradition. I agree with you, if we're talking twentieth. And the twenty-first has still not decided what it thinks about anything.' Drew's innumerable virtues – tolerance, patience, benevolence – had not faded or changed in the months since their marriage; Thea's awareness of her own imperfections had intensified as a result. The imbalance made her search for flaws in him. Surely nobody could be as perfect as he often seemed to be? And wouldn't it be impossible to endure if you turned out to have married a paragon?

One of his characteristics was to address discomfort or discord head-on. 'I am very far from perfect,' he regularly assured her. 'I'm afraid of lots of things, lazy, unobservant, impatient of trivia . . .' His list would generally fizzle out at that point. They both knew, but did not mention, that his greatest and most serious failing was in his relationship with his son. Timmy had been an intruder into the cosy family circle of Drew, Karen and Stephanie. He had brought noise and worry and inconvenience in his wake. A fractious baby, demanding at first and then all too dreadfully *un*demanding as he seemed to grasp the limitations of the situation. His mother had almost died when he was still a toddler, and never fully recovered her health. The deficiencies that he endured from that time on could be glimpsed in his eyes, from time to time. Thea suspected that the other children at school could see it, and punished him accordingly for his frailty.

And she herself found it hard to give the child what he craved. She substituted – as Drew had done – an undue emphasis on the superficial. He was given his favourite foods, electronic toys, the right clothes and shoes – as far as finances would allow. His school progress was closely monitored.

'Oh, well,' said Thea, after a silence. 'Better get on. The dog hasn't been out yet. She must be bursting.' Taking Hepzie for a walk had been reduced to a brief hobble to a corner of the garden, where she would obediently relieve herself. The broken leg had been the result of a farcical accident as Drew had been unloading two newly constructed coffins from his van. The dog had been sniffing interestedly at the fresh woody scent, jumping up at the exact moment that Drew lost his hold, and the whole thing slid to the ground on top of her. A sharp corner caught her femur, and despite the relative lightness of the coffin, the impact on the soft body was disastrous. 'I swear I heard the bone crack,' Drew said miserably, as they waited for the vet to diagnose the damage. Thea had heard the canine screams through two closed doors, and rushed to see what had happened. It had been Christmas Eve. The whole family piled into the car and dashed to the vet, who had to be summoned from a party. The resulting bone-setting and plastering had been traumatic and expensive, and Hepzie became a heroine in everybody's eyes. Drew, however, managed to avoid censure for his carelessness, except in his own conscience.

Now two weeks had passed, and everyone was growing impatient for the plaster to be off and normality resumed. The dog had tipped over into middle age: her coat was less glossy and her eyes more rheumy. As Drew pointed out, there were matted areas all over her body, where the soft feathering had turned into felty lumps. Thea knew she would be forced into regular trimming, losing the shaggy animal she loved, and replacing it with a streamlined version that looked completely different.

'Come on, then,' she said now to the dog. 'Let's get you some fresh air. We'll go down the lane a bit for a change. You can manage that if you try.'

She opened the front door, and waited for Hepzie to limp through it. Three-legged progress was not supposed to be such hard work, she reflected, thinking of a number of dogs permanently reduced to such a state, which she had seen running as fast as any fully equipped animal. 'Come on,' she said again. 'We'll go into the field a little way.'

But before they had even got down the short path between the door and the little lane they lived on, a man had interposed himself, standing solidly in their way.

Chapter Two

It was Mr Shipley, a seldom-encountered neighbour from the other side of the lane, his property a handsome old house set at an angle on a gentle rise. Broad Campden consisted of gentle rises and dips, with generous patches of green on all sides. Meandering little roads, a narrow footpath and a sporadic little waterway gave it a jumbled spontaneous sort of atmosphere. No hint of deliberate design could be detected in its layout.

Mr Shipley had harrumphed mildly when Drew and Thea had first met him, expressing doubt as to the desirability of living opposite an undertaker, but since then had given relatively affable greetings from a distance, and no more than that.

'Morning,' he said.

'Oh – hello. Did you want to see us about something?' It was quite obvious that he did. His expression was severe.

'I did, as a matter of fact. I have a piece of business to discuss with your husband.'

'Ah. Well, he's just in there. I've got to take the dog out

for a bit. Go ahead. Just open the door and give him a shout.'

This informality clearly startled the man. 'Well . . . well, all right.' He nodded. Thea knew quite well that he expected her to perform a proper introduction, turning back and summoning Drew. But the dog came first, and she saw no reason to involve herself with whatever the man might have to say. The best guess was that he had a dead or dying relative requiring a woodland burial; the other end of the spectrum was a threat to make a formal complaint over excessive noise, obstruction or nuisance arising from funeral operations in the little road.

The walk with the dog took twenty minutes, during which Thea made much of the cool wintry light and the fresh breeze. January was predicted to be quiet and fairly gentle, with no snow and only moderate frost at times. She enjoyed the passage of the seasons, the reliable cycle bringing such extreme differences in the landscape that she could barely remember what trees looked like in full July leaf. She was conscious of the good sense in remaining in the present moment as far as possible. There before her was a stretch of English grassland bordered by skeletal trees, and beyond that a tranquil landscape of undulating hills in all directions. It was ancient country, inhabited for millennia by workers on the land. The Romans had taken to it wholesale, and then later the feudal lords had readily colonised it. Much of this history had been recorded in surprising detail. And once into the nineteenth century it would appear that almost every person and every square foot of ground was noted in some archive somewhere. Famous families had lived here in their grand houses, employing legions of workers indoors and out. Broad Campden, despite being a recognised settlement boasting significant buildings for well over four hundred years, had been slow to come to wider notice, its own brief climax occurring in the 1900s with the Arts and Crafts Movement selecting it and Chipping Campden as favourite locations. The Essex House Press, a famous weaver and a very old Norman chapel all successfully put the two villages on the cultural map.

Thea considered herself to be an amateur historian, regularly falling into short-lived obsessions with small aspects of the past. Canals, craftsmen, footpaths, woodlands all in their turn fed her curiosity about the area. She was trying to arouse a similar interest in Stephanie and Timmy, especially where canals were concerned. There were tunnels, abandoned locks and derelict bridges to discover, all with their own dramatic stories – and the children were finally taking a gratifying interest. 'You should have been a teacher,' said Drew. 'It's brilliant the way you've got them to take notice.'

Hepzie finally showed signs of involvement with the scents and sounds around her, and began her customary zigzag pursuit of rabbit or squirrel with the heavy plaster held well out of harm's way at a strange horizontal angle. Thea wondered whether the leg would ever look normal again, even when released from the cast.

They meandered back to the house, with Thea in a better mood after her fix of natural beauty. None of her complaints had any real basis: Drew was a miraculous find, and his children were far more amenable and contented than they might have been. She just hoped the Shipley man would have gone before she reached home.

As she left the field and headed up the unpaved track leading back to the house, she could see him going back to his own house. 'Praise the Lord,' she murmured. 'What good timing.'

Drew was in the kitchen washing up when she went in. 'What did he want?' Thea asked him. 'Was it good news or bad?'

'Neither. It was something quite peculiar. Well, it's good news, I suppose, that we're sufficiently accepted to be included in a village concern; bad news that there's something sinister going on that we're expected to take notice of.'

'Sinister? What, for heaven's sake?'

He dried his hands, and put the kettle on. 'Sit down for a bit and I'll tell you.' She obeyed, with a sense that here at last was something to enliven the day. Drew made coffee before starting his report. 'Okay. So – did you know there was a couple living in one of those tall houses opposite the church called Hilary and Graham Bunting? Retired. The one with honeysuckle round the door and a little flower bed at the front. It had lots of gladioli last summer.'

'Vaguely.' She nodded. 'Didn't everybody have good gladdies last summer? Even ours weren't bad.'

'Never mind them. The thing is, there've been ructions between Hilary and Graham: shouting matches that could be heard as far as the pub one way and the new houses the other. It's disturbing the peace and spoiling the ambience and generally causing annoyance.'

'What – worse than us?'

'Very much so. We're paragons by comparison. The thing is, some people think it's all due to Hilary being under terrible strain because her sister's dying, and others think it's because Graham has always had a bit of a gambling habit, but in the main they all just want it to stop. There's a petition.'

'Oh, no. Did you sign it?'

'He didn't bring it with him. They're still arguing about the wording.'

'Have you ever heard shouting matches?'

He shook his head. 'We're probably too far away, unless it's extremely loud with the door open and a carrying wind. I don't think I've ever even seen either of them.'

'So we're not affected at all?'

'Not really.'

'It's a witch hunt,' she said flatly. 'A lot of intolerant old villagers turning against a couple who've got some domestic trouble. Like medieval times.'

'It might be that, but Mr Shipley did seem genuinely concerned. He said they'd discussed all kinds of solutions: calling social services, for one; consulting a doctor; having a quiet word with that community police girl who everybody likes so much. But they all run smack against the Data Protection Act or whatever it is. You can't intrude on a person's privacy even if it's obviously in that person's best interests.'

'They could try reading the Buntings' emails or tracking where they go with their mobiles,' said Thea sourly. The surveillance society, which everyone else appeared to accept without a murmur, still outraged her. 'Or fixing a CCTV camera to a lamp post outside their house,' she added for good measure.

'They couldn't without good reason, as you know perfectly well.'

'So what happens now?'

'He isn't sure. I think he was hoping I'd take on the role of a sort of secular vicar and call in for a quiet word.'

'And offer them a cut-price funeral while you're at it? I'm sure that would go down beautifully.'

'Don't be sarcastic. I said I couldn't possibly invent a pretext that would be remotely credible. Besides, I don't even know them.'

'Haven't they got any *friends*? What's the matter with these bloody villages where nobody knows anybody?'

'I thought you liked the villages.'

She sighed. 'I do, mostly, but they're not exactly sociable, are they? Maybe a few are, and I'm sure there are little groups of chums here that we haven't found out about yet, but I haven't seen much sign of communal garden parties or anything. Even at Christmas, nobody invited us for sherry.'

'Nobody invites undertakers to sherry, except other undertakers. I thought I'd explained that. And you're a bit notorious yourself. They're afraid that if they get too friendly, you'll start ferreting out old murders in their family that they'd rather not think about.'

'Oh, pish,' she said.

'Pish?'

'I've been reading some lovely old detective novels from the thirties, and people quite often say "Pish". I've decided to use it myself.'

24

'Okay.' He seemed lost for anything more to say, until a new idea occurred to him. 'Mr Bunting plays bridge, for money, according to Mr Shipley. There's a club in Blockley. That seems to be what's meant by his tendency towards gambling. Did you ever play bridge?'

'No, but my dad taught us whist, and I don't think it's very different. I have often rather fancied it.' She smiled. 'And I like Blockley. It's got everything a little town should have. Are you suggesting I join the club and spy on the old chap? I might be up for that. It could be my new year hobby. I was trying to think of something different I could take up.'

'Not if they play for money.' He shuddered. 'You'd bankrupt us in no time.'

'Besides, they probably don't want learners.'

'Fortunately. Why don't you get a disk for the computer, or download something to teach you how to play?'

She pulled a face. 'Because that wouldn't be half as much fun.'

Again, he seemed stumped for words.

'Anyway, thanks for updating me on what Mr Shipley said. Heps had a better walk than usual. She's going to be fine again once the plaster's off. It'll teach her to stand clear another time.'

'I can guarantee it won't happen again,' he said fervently. 'I never want to hear screams like that for the rest of my life.'

She treated him to her most forgiving smile. 'You can't defend against accidents. Isn't that the *definition* of an accident?'

'You can be careful.' Drew was on the whole a careful

person, which sometimes irritated his wife. Thea had a reckless streak that had led to a range of good and less good consequences. She was driven by curiosity more than the average person, wanting to know the end of every story and the reason for every action. This could cause her to intrude into private lives and ask outrageous questions. But she did share with Drew a habit of voicing her feelings. This, she often thought, was the key to their relationship. So long as nobody hid anything, they'd be fine.

'You know – I could probably think up some excuse to go and visit the Buntings,' she suggested slowly. 'They do sound interesting, and maybe in need of a friendly face. I could say' – she paused – 'I was thinking of starting a plant-swapping club. Or looking for people to answer a survey about bats or water voles or something.'

'Or a book group,' he offered.

'No. Absolutely *not* a book group. There are far too many of them already, and I never want to belong to one.' She took a breath in preparation for an extended rant, which Drew quickly aborted with a flip of his hand.

'Okay. I forgot you didn't like them,' he said. 'Plant swapping sounds quite sensible.'

'It's not. Stop humouring me. I can think of something better, given a bit of time.'

The phone then rang again, and Drew's work day began in earnest. Thea made herself more coffee and applied herself to the matter of the warring Buntings. By half past ten, she had a firm plan, and ten minutes later she was putting it into action.

* * *

26

The house was set well back from the lane, on the junction with the tortuous road that ran through the village. An expanse of bumpy grass filled the space between the row of houses and the small lane that ran down to the Slocombes' house. The front doors opened directly onto a barely visible path, but the one in question had broken with convention to create a very small flower bed under one window. Thea was reminded of the village of Stanton, where a similar arrangement occurred. No pavements in Broad Campden – walkers took their chances, getting muddy and splashed in winter, and brushed by impatient tourists in cars in the summer.

When she rang the bell, she was cheered to hear a dog barking inside. Drew had not mentioned a dog, probably because he had no idea it existed. It sounded quite large, and Thea set herself to guessing what breed it might be.

After a lengthy interval, the door opened cautiously. A woman's voice was heard to say, 'Back, Biddy. Get back, will you? Who is it? I'm trying not to let the dog out.'

'I'm sorry. Can I help?'

'Wait a minute. I'll put the lead on her. I've got it here.' Finally, the door opened fully, and Thea stood face-to-face with a tall woman of about sixty, holding a sandy-coloured mutt with long hair and a very long-suffering expression. In fact, the woman and the dog both gave an impression of exhaustion, as if they'd just come back from an extended walk.

'I am so sorry to bother you. It's nothing at all important. My name is Thea Slocombe. I live just a little way down there.' She pointed accordingly. 'My husband's the alternative undertaker. We do the green burials in

27

Mrs Simmonds' field. I expect you know about it.'

'Of course. What do you want?' The question was uttered without any aggression or hostility, a simple request for an explanation.

'Actually, it's nothing at all to do with funerals. It's really a project I've decided to take on, to do with local history. I know there's a strong link with the Arts and Crafts Movement here, but I can't find very much detailed information about it. I thought perhaps if some of the residents got together and pooled everything they know, we could come up with a booklet or something. I don't know for sure, but I have the feeling you've lived here quite a long time.'

'Oh! I suppose we have. Twenty-four years is a long time. But Ashbee was here a century ago or more. And surely there must be all kinds of books and other material already available. I can't believe there's a need for anything else.' She hesitated, evidently considering the matter more closely. 'I don't think there is very much about Broad Campden specifically.'

Thea was forced to bluff. 'Perhaps not,' she agreed. 'But I'm sure there's more than people realise.'

'Possibly. It *would* be nice to look at the Coomaraswamys a bit more. I've always liked the sound of them.' She smiled faintly.

'Who is it?' came a strong male voice from inside the house, saving Thea from an embarrassing dilemma. She was unaware of the Coomar-whatsits. 'Have you had that door open all this time?'

'Sorry, dear.' The woman looked at Thea, from the six

or seven inches advantage she had on her visitor. 'Would you like to come in? My name is Hilary Bunting, as you probably know. This is Biddy. She belongs to my sister. We're just minding her for a while.' The weary face clouded, and Thea remembered a reference to a sick sister. 'We're no good with dogs, I'm afraid. She really isn't having a very nice time.'

Thea had been a house-sitter until she married Drew. She had taken charge of numerous dogs and other animals in their own homes. She knew a lot about their needs and anxieties. She definitely recognised a confused and pining dog when she saw it. 'Has your sister gone on holiday? When does she get back?' It was a small piece of dishonesty, but it seemed unwise to admit that she knew otherwise.

'She's in hospital. Nobody can say when – or whether – she'll be able to go home.' She raised her chin bravely. 'Well, of course we do know if we're honest with ourselves. There's no chance of a recovery. We're all just waiting for the end now.' A tear swelled at the corner of one eye.

'Oh dear! That must be such a worry.'

'Hilary!' The man's voice bellowed again from close by. 'Who are you talking to?'

'Go through,' the woman ordered her visitor. She closed the front door, and ushered Thea ahead of herself and Biddy. 'The door on the right.'

Curiosity was mixed with a thread of trepidation as Thea entered a room that felt like the lair of an angry animal. A man was sitting in a deep armchair, holding a newspaper open on his legs. He had a strong grey beard and black-rimmed spectacles, giving an impression of a man in disguise. Only his nose could be properly inspected. 'This is Mrs Slocombe,' said his wife. 'She wanted to talk about local history.'

'What?' The man's voice remained just as loud as when he was calling across the room and down the hallway. 'Did you say local history? Of all the idiotic things to come bothering people with, that takes the biscuit.'

'Don't shout, dear,' the woman said.

'Am I shouting? I can't help it. You know I can't.' The decibels reduced only slightly for this. Thea wondered what bizarre medical condition caused a person's voice to emerge unnaturally loudly. The man clearly wasn't deaf, which could have accounted for it. It did, however, explain the alarm in the village, assuming conflict and rage where it might not exist. Plus, it would surely be intensely disturbing for the wretched dog.

'I think you can try a bit harder,' said Mrs Bunting. 'You know what that therapist said. There's no organic cause for it. You just have to learn to stop it.'

'I *do* try,' he said like a sulky child. 'The point is – aren't we expecting the Taylors any time now? Didn't you tell them eleven?'

'I did, but they're always late.' She turned to Thea. 'Our friends from Blockley are coming for the day. Graham plays bridge with them on Tuesdays. Morning and afternoon, with lunch in the middle.' She smiled. 'It gives me a chance to get on with my own little jobs in peace.' The smile grew warmer. 'We could have a chat about your history project, if you like.'

Thea realised how very ill-prepared she was for such

instant enthusiasm. She was also suddenly inspired by the whole hasty idea. She was, after all, genuinely interested in the Ashbee story, and did actually suspect that there was scope for it to be revisited, for the edification of local people and visitors alike. 'Well, it's all very embryonic at the moment. I was basically just canvassing opinion, to see if anybody might be interested.'

'I *am* interested,' said Hilary. 'It sounds really intriguing now I think about it a bit more. And I'll talk to Rachel about it. I know she'd be keen to join in as well.'

Voices outside diverted them, and before she could ask who Rachel was, Thea was holding Biddy while Hilary Bunting went to welcome the Taylors. There had to be three of them, Thea reckoned, to make up a table of bridge with Graham. And sure enough, there they were – two women and a man, taking up most of the space in the hallway. The lady of the house looked harassed and indecisive. 'I'll go,' said Thea. 'Maybe I could come back when you've got a bit of time.'

'This afternoon,' said Hilary breathlessly. 'Two o'clock. Is that all right?'

'Absolutely,' Thea assured her. She was openly inspecting the new arrivals, trying to work out whether she had seen any of them before, during her visits to Blockley.

'Oh, excuse me,' gasped Hilary. 'This is Barnaby and Sally Taylor, and Sally's friend Rachel Ottaway. This is Mrs Slocombe,' she concluded the introductions.

Barnaby Taylor was broad and silver-haired. His skin was reddish, his expression bland. 'Pleased to meet you,' he said carelessly. The woman standing close to him had to be his wife, Sally. She had a long grey ponytail, was slim and dignified, and did not smile. The third person – Ms or Mrs Ottaway – was much more animated. She gave a little laugh and held out her hand. 'Slocombe?' she repeated. 'The funeral people?'

'That's right,' said Thea, taking her hand. 'You've heard of us, then?'

'Very much so. My father's booked one of your graves. He's ninety-seven, and bright as a button. You might have to wait a while yet for the business.' She laughed again. 'You should have seen his excitement when he read about you. Said he thought it was an act of Providence, because it's so exactly what he's wanted for ages.'

'That's very nice to hear,' said Thea, instantly liking this woman. Five new people in a morning was riches indeed. More so, because at least one of them seemed to approve wholeheartedly of her and Drew.

'Thea's trying to start a new interest group, looking at the history of the Arts and Crafts Movement here,' Hilary said. 'I said you'd be sure to want to get involved.'

'Me?' said Thea's new friend. 'Just try to keep me away. That's exactly what this place needs.'

32

Chapter Three

She and Drew sat down together for a very basic lunch, shortly before one o'clock. His morning had been uneventful, going through the schedule for the coming days with Andrew, paying a few bills. He was avid for Thea's findings at the Bunting residence.

She gave him as much detail as she could, pleased to have his attention. 'The man seems very strange. He shouts all the time, even though he's obviously not deaf. She tells him not to, but that doesn't make much difference.'

'Is he angry?'

'Hard to tell. He might be. He was quite rude to me, actually. Is it some sort of brain damage, do you think?'

'I suppose it's possible. Must be very hard to live with.'

She thought about it. 'He *is* bossy. She hadn't been two minutes in the hallway before he wanted to know what she was doing. The dog must hate him.'

'Dog?'

'Biddy. She belongs to Hilary's sister, who's in hospital. Actually, both the things Mr Shipley told you about them are true. Her sister's ill – dying, in fact – and he plays bridge. He must be addicted, because he's not just in the Blockley club, but has people over to play every Tuesday.'

'That's nothing. I had an aunt who played regularly four times a week, come what may.'

'Gosh. Anyway, I'm going back after lunch to see Hilary and talk about the Arts and Crafts Movement. I'll have to do some quick research in a minute. I never thought she'd take it up with such gusto. I have no idea what happens next. I burbled something about writing leaflets for visitors, but I expect the museum in Campden does plenty of that sort of thing already.'

'Listen to you – Campden! You sound like a real local.'

'Nobody says "Chipping Campden" every time. It's far too cumbersome.' She shook the interruption aside and went on, 'But it does seem reasonable to claim some special status for Broad Campden in its own right, where the Arts and Crafts stuff is concerned.'

'Broady, surely?' he joked.

'Stop it. Although I wouldn't be surprised. I'll have to ask someone.'

'Good idea.'

'To finish my story, I have to tell you that Mrs Taylor's friend, Rachel, strongly approves of green burials, and thinks we're the bee's knees. She's the nicest of them all. She lives in Blockley.'

'All very symmetrical,' he said obscurely. 'I mean – two sets of a man and two women. The Bunting man and the Taylor man,' he elaborated patiently. 'Two triangular relationships. Any offspring that you noticed?'

'Must be some, but they didn't get a mention.'

'I'm sure all will soon be revealed this afternoon.' He stared at the wall for a moment. 'Doesn't it strike you as slightly odd that she jumped at your idea so quickly? I know you can be very persuasive, but wasn't she a bit *too* enthusiastic? Wouldn't most people ask more about it, or say they'll think about it, or something? She sounds as if she was desperate for something to fill her empty life.'

'She wasn't enthusiastic at first. But you're probably exactly right. She might have lost all her friends because of her shouty husband, and is taken up with the dog and worry about her sister, rapidly going mad with it all. Then I come along, offering an absorbing distraction. No wonder she seemed relieved. I felt as if I'd saved her from something. And, I might remind you, this is almost exactly what we planned. It's what I was angling for, and the mission was accomplished.'

'A bit too well,' he insisted.

'Not if I get googling right away.' She went to the laptop, which was the family's only access to the internet, and began tapping keys. 'Here!' she said triumphantly, two minutes later. 'There was a woman weaver, Ethel Coomaraswamy, married to a Sri Lankan philosopher. They lived right here. We ought to concentrate on them, at least to start with. I love that name, Coomaraswamy,' she repeated the word sensuously, making it sound like a song. 'Ethel must have been English. Doesn't it make you feel nostalgic for those sunny days? I'm going to have a lovely time finding out more detail. Had you ever heard of the Coomaraswamys? Hilary knows about them. I had to pretend I did as well.'

He shook his head. 'Ignorance prevails, I'm ashamed to say.'

'We're as bad as each other.'

Drew brightened. 'You know – there's no shame in it, after all. You can say you know hardly anything beyond the basics, and the two of you can find out more together. That would be a lot better than you giving her a lecture.'

'I think she already knows more than I could hope to tell her. But it wasn't meant to be just the two of us. I wanted to get a proper group going.'

He gave her a searching look. 'Since when? I thought this all began – only a few hours ago – as a way of getting to know the Buntings and see if they warrant the concern of the whole village.'

'Yes, but now I've thought of it, I like the idea of involving some other people. It would rehabilitate the Buntings at the same time. Besides, all this stuff about Ashbee and his arty friends is hugely interesting. I can't think why it's taken me so long to get into it. It's what Broady's famous for, after all.'

'Please don't say Broady,' he begged. 'At least not where anyone can hear you. I only said it as a joke.'

She laughed. 'I bet you 50p it's common usage already.'

'I accept your wager,' he said with a little bow.

'I'll ask my new friend Hillie. She's sure to know.'

When she went back an hour later, having wished Drew the best of luck with his interview, she took with her a notebook and the laptop. But she was met by a much less welcoming woman. 'Oh Lord – I forgot all about you,' Hilary gasped when she finally answered the doorbell. 'It's all in chaos here. My sister's in a coma. The dog's jumped over the wall at the back and disappeared. Graham yelled at Rachel for making the wrong bid and said she was a terrible player. I can't talk to you now, after all. Sorry.'

Thea just stood there, eyes wide. 'How did all that happen in just a few hours?'

'It just did. Everything comes at once – isn't it always the way?'

'Are the Taylors still here?'

'Rachel's gone looking for the dog. The others went home ten minutes ago. I don't suppose they'll ever come back,' she finished with a groan. 'I knew it was all too good to be true. I was so *cheerful* this morning. And then when you turned up it was another nice hopeful thing. Honestly, I've been so depressed for months now, and I really thought it was going to get better. At least it looks as if we'll be getting the gutters cleared sometime this week,' she added. 'They've been full of leaves for months.'

It seemed a funny thing to add to the list of much more major worries, but Thea understood the way such things could work. 'I could go and help look for the dog,' she offered. 'I'm really sorry about your sister. Which hospital is she in?'

'The John Radcliffe. It's the best place; everybody says so. And it's not too awful to get to from here. I just hope Biddy hasn't tried to run home. That's Burford, by the way.'

'That would be bad,' Thea agreed. 'Let's hope not. She's probably just very lost and bewildered, poor thing.'

'Well, if you've got time, it would be terribly kind of you to have a look round. You seem to be good with dogs.

Rachel is as well, and Biddy does know her. But it'll be dark in an hour or two. What if she's out all night?' The expression on Hilary Bunting's face was haggard with worry and guilt. 'I'll never forgive myself.'

'Give me your phone number and Rachel's,' said Thea efficiently. 'Then we can all keep in touch. If one of us finds her, we'll need to tell the others.'

'Of course.' Hilary extracted a new-looking mobile from a nearby handbag and read out the numbers. 'I can never keep them in my head,' she said. 'I used to be so good at that sort of thing.'

'Nobody but me memorises them any more,' said Thea. 'Tell me your landline number and I'll remember it. Here – let me give you mine as well.'

Hilary did as suggested, and then produced a thin leather belt. 'Take this to use as a lead. I gave Rachel the proper one. I was going out to look myself, but Graham wants me to stay here.'

Thea waited for an explanation for this demand, but none came. At least, none beyond the shout that Thea realised she'd been expecting. 'Hilary! Where are you?' The booming voice echoed around the house, carrying hints of insane rage, or perhaps a fairy-tale ogre. *I'll grind your bones to make my bread*, started running through her mind, making her smile.

'He *does* shout, doesn't he?' she whispered.

Hilary rolled her eyes, but didn't smile back. 'I've got to do something about it. He's getting worse.'

'Poor you. Well, let me go and look for the dog. Would you like me to take her home with me, if I find her? I'll phone you first, of course. But it looks as if you've got enough to cope with already.'

The woman's face lightened. 'Oh – would you? That would be *wonderful*. But first we've got to find her. She's a nice dog, you know. Caroline adores her. She's had her from a tiny pup.'

'We'll find her,' said Thea, with unwarranted confidence.

Outside it was a still day – chilly but not bad for January. Darkness would fall soon after four o'clock, and a beloved domestic pet would be ill-prepared for a night outside. Having ascertained the direction in which Biddy was last seen headed, Thea set off on her search. As she climbed the rising footpath to the south of the village, she was reminded of earlier desperate quests for absent animals consigned to her care. The most memorable had ended badly, and she thrust the memory aside. Biddy's escape was definitely not her fault and she could do nothing but good in volunteering to look for her. It might almost be seen as atonement for her irresponsible actions in the past.

In the months that she and Drew had lived in Broad Campden she had grown familiar with the footpaths that converged on the village from all directions. No fewer than six were marked on the map, and the presence of the little settlement as the clear hub where they met made it plain that this had once been a place of significance.

Biddy had, it seemed, gone southwards towards Blockley. This was Thea's favourite track, used by herself and Hepzie now and then. It was the worst option for a solitary dog, however, being close to the road. Visions of Biddy being crushed under the wheels of a speeding four-by-four filled her mind, before she shook herself and changed the horror for a scenario where a benevolent driver stopped and gathered up the bewildered dog. She should have asked whether Biddy had a microchip, which would quickly identify her if taken to a vet or the police.

Another path ran south-westwards, on higher ground, doubling back to meet the first one at Blockley. It was a bigger track, more frequently used, and might have more appealing scents for a lost dog. After a moment's thought, Thea opted to investigate that one, which entailed traversing the village street as far as the pub, and then turning left onto the path.

The track was narrow and stony, with a new-looking stone wall running alongside it. On the other side a field contained a substantial flock of sheep. Was Biddy tempted to chase them, Thea wondered. These would very likely be heavily pregnant and vulnerable to damage. But they seemed placid enough, showing no signs of a rogue dog having bothered them. Further on, through an old gateway with a broken-down gate that no longer served as a barrier, the path abruptly changed character, running alongside a great sweep of ploughed acres, bordered by small trees. It had a lonely atmosphere, especially in winter. Nothing moved or cried. Leafless brambles showed little sign of the abundant fruit they had doubtless produced three or four months earlier.

She should have Hepzie with her, she realised, as assistant dog-seeker. While there was no chance that she would be of any use hampered by her plaster, it would have been nice to have the company on the lonely hillside. Not many – in fact, not *any* – walkers fancied a stroll on a January afternoon.

Especially not in the middle of the week. Biddy would be free to gallop unimpeded across miles and miles of open fields and small patches of woodland until she dropped from exhaustion and sore feet. Would she really try to get home to Burford? Did homing instincts work that well? She thought almost certainly not. But to get there you would indeed have to go through Blockley, and then Stow, and then . . . an easy journey by car, yes, but a very considerable expedition on foot, for man or beast.

How far should she go in any one direction? Where was Rachel? And only then did Thea think of telling Drew what she was doing, and checking that he would be available to receive the children when they came home from school.

It was a habit that neither of them had fully acquired: that of constantly monitoring each other's movements. When he answered, it was with only the most casual interest.

'Hey – I'm out in the wilderness searching for a lost dog, in case you're wondering. I won't be back for the kids, so I hope you can stay put for a bit?'

'No problem, except I've got to remove that lady who died in the night, at some point.'

'Did she die at home?'

'She did. And he's in no great hurry. But I ought to go today sometime.'

'Today's almost over.'

'I know. I should have done it by now, but Andrew's gone to Cirencester to collect some rocks and I've got to wait for him.'

'Rocks?'

'Big lumps of granite for grave markers. One of the

41

tree people wants a rock as well. And that's sure to start a trend. We saw these cheap, so Andy's gone to get them.' He explained with his customary patience, giving no hint that he wanted to know why she was in search of a lost dog. She was not deceived.

'It's the dog the Buntings were minding. It ran away. Hilary's in meltdown, so I offered to look for it. I can come home if you need me. You should do that removal. It looks bad if you leave the poor woman dead in her bed all day. Is somebody doing the necessary?' She meant *laying out*, but nobody said that any more, according to Drew.

'The GP will have done a bit. It's not far away. I can wait a while. What are your chances of actually finding the dog?'

'Minimal, probably. It might be trying to walk home to Burford.'

'Good luck, then,' he said cheerfully. She rang off, unsure how to feel about the conversation. Drew had no reason to be worried, after all. He had responded promptly, updated her on his own obligations – but she detected an underlying lack of interest in what she had to say. In fact, it had not lain very far below the surface. He was blatantly *not* interested, and that was hurtful.

'Biddy!' she yodelled, as loudly as she could. 'Where the hell are you?'

'Steady on,' came a voice behind her. 'You'll wake all the hibernating hedgehogs, making a noise like that.'

42

Chapter Four

A man and a dog were standing there, perhaps ten yards away, giving her a careful examination. Thea wondered how she had failed to hear footsteps on the stony ground. 'Hey – that's Biddy,' said Thea. 'Thank goodness.'

The dog did not twitch at the sound of the name, but instead pressed against the man's legs as if alarmed. 'You what?' said the man.

'I'm sorry. I'm looking for a dog that ran away. I've only seen her once. She looks like that.' She stared at the cringing creature. 'Same colour, anyway. Biddy?' she repeated enticingly.

'This is Percy. Male. I've had him for nine years.'

'Sorry,' said Thea again. 'How embarrassing. Have you seen a loose dog, by any chance?'

'Nope. Do you want to explain the whole thing?'

'There's nothing much to tell. The dog escaped from the woman who was looking after it. I only met it for the first time today, but I hate to think of the poor thing lost out here so I offered to look for her. She doesn't live here, you see, so she has no idea where she is.'

'Have you got anything that smells of her?'

'Pardon?'

'So Percy can have a go at finding her. He's quite good at it. But he needs some help to get started.'

Thea pulled the leather belt from her pocket. 'I don't suppose this does. Her usual lead is with someone else who's looking for her. It's hopeless, really.'

'Get the lead, and the place where she was last seen, and I bet you Percy can find her.'

Thea felt weak, but hope buoyed her up. She phoned Rachel, who turned out to have gone back to the Bunting house empty-handed. 'I'm handing the lead back and going home,' she said crossly. 'It's getting dark, and I'm exhausted. I can tell you the dog is nowhere between here and Sedgecombe.'

That was the direct way to Blockley, which Thea's instinct had first suggested as the most likely way Biddy would go. 'Oh dear. I don't blame you for giving up, but it does seem a pity. There's a man here who thinks he might be able to find her. Can you hang on until we get to you and find something of Biddy's so his dog can get her scent?'

'The lead's here. Do you really need me?' said Rachel.

'No, not really, if the Buntings are there.'

'They are. Well, I suppose I can wait a bit. How far away are you?'

'I must be about ten minutes away,' said Thea. She turned to the man. 'Are you sure you've got time?'

'No problem,' he said.

'See you soon,' Thea told Rachel.

She and the man set off towards the road. 'My name's Ant, by the way,' he said.

'Ant? Short for Anthony?'

'Antares, actually. It's a star.' He said it wearily, making it clear it was something he had to say virtually every day. She turned sideways to inspect him more closely: mid thirties, fair-haired, tall. Nicely spoken and polite. Perfectly Cotswolds, in short, except for his name.

'Right. I'm Thea. Not short for anything. Do you live round here?'

'Not far off. How about you?'

'Just over there.' She waved vaguely. 'It's been quite a complicated day.'

'I did rather get that impression. So let's see if Percy's still got his old talents. He used to do competitions, but we've let that go lately.'

They hurried down the slope to the village centre, where Thea led the way to the Buntings' door. Rachel was waiting for them, the dog lead in her hand. 'I've been given the job of dealing with you, before I go home,' she said ruefully. 'Graham's too embarrassed to be seen with me, or something. I got told off for my bidding this morning.'

'So I hear. This is Ant. And Percy. Percy's a tracker dog.'

'Antares Frowse,' said Rachel with studied carelessness. 'I remember you. You've got a sister called Aldebaran.'

'Had. *Had* a sister. She died.'

'Good God. When? How come I never knew that?'

'She went to America, and was murdered in Texas by a psychotic gunman. It didn't attract much attention here. It was five years ago now.'

'I'm appalled. Your poor mother! She and I used to get the same train to London, about a thousand years ago. Then she had babies and we lost touch, more or less. I remember you from those big Christmas parties she used to organise in the barn. Do you still live in that place?'

He nodded. 'New owners now. We're banned from the barn these days.'

'Oh?' The woman cocked her head, clearly wanting to hear more.

'I'm afraid I don't remember you. Have you got kids my age?'

'No kids. I'm Rachel Ottaway, if that means anything to you.'

He shook his head. 'Not really. Deb would have remembered. She took more interest in Mum's friends than I did.'

'Why did she go to America?'

'Horses,' he said shortly. 'It was just meant to be for six months while she worked on a ranch.' He took a deep breath. 'I think we still believe she's alive over there and will show up again one day. Now let's get back to the business in hand.' He gently took the dog lead from her and ran it past Percy's nose, saying, 'Seek, Percy, *seek*.' The dog tilted its head and sniffed the lead. Then it sniffed the ground and looked at its master. 'Was it here that Biddy ran off?'

'I think it was the back, actually,' said Rachel. 'We can go round here, look.' The end-of-terrace house had a paved walkway to the back garden, which they followed through a wooden gate and over a large lawn. At the bottom of the garden there was a stone wall about four feet high.

'She's a steeplechaser, then,' said Ant. 'How are we going to get over that?'

Thea suddenly realised that she was expected to follow the tracker dog for an indefinite time, until Biddy was found. This seemed to her to be beyond the call of duty. 'Er . . .' she said. 'I think I ought to be getting home. The children must be back by now. They'll be wanting their tea.'

'Ye'll be wanting yer tay,' said Ant, in a bad Scottish accent. Only Rachel laughed. Thea looked at them both blankly. 'Sorry – that's a Radio Four joke,' said Ant. 'You must be too young for it.'

'You're way younger than me.' She looked at Rachel, who was considerably older than either of them. 'Aren't you going home? You said you were exhausted.'

'I might as well stay. I've been restored with a cup of tea.'

'Look – he's got the scent!' said Ant to Thea. 'You can go home, if you must. Is there anybody in this house? Whose dog *is* it, anyway? What happens if we find her?'

'That's rather complicated,' said Rachel. 'I'll stick with you and explain as we go.' She gave Thea a look of mild reproach. 'I'll call you if we find her.'

'Thanks,' said Thea.

'Come on, then. Can you vault the wall?' Ant asked.

'Watch me,' said the woman, who was tall and agile enough to achieve the manoeuvre, with the assistance of a nearby metal bucket. Ant lifted his dog over and then followed with a graceful swing of his legs worthy of a gymnasium. Thea lingered to watch all of them, the dog following an obvious scent towards an open gate. She waited until they were out of sight into the next field, and then waited another thirty seconds, wistfully regretting her domestic obligations. There was so much she wanted to discover about these new people who lived nearby and might become firm friends with a modicum of encouragement.

But Mr and Mrs Bunting were still there in the house, conducting some obscure marital business that kept them from joining in the hunt for the animal that was their responsibility. The back door was right there, and it was surely only polite to go in and give them an update. So she did. With a perfunctory knock, she opened it, and called, 'Hello?'

At least Graham Bunting wasn't shouting. In fact, everything was deadly silent. 'Hello!' she repeated. 'Are you there?'

Husband and wife were suddenly in the kitchen doorway staring at her. 'What are you doing in here?' demanded the man. 'How dare you?' His voice was as loud as ever, and Thea quailed. At the same time, she wondered how he would sound if he was saying something nice. To bellow 'I love you!' into his wife's ear would be far from romantic. 'Pass the salt' or 'Turned out nice again' would also come over as aggressive if uttered at maximum decibels. It would be unbearable, all day every day.

There had to be something wrong with him. Most likely his throat, or larynx. Some hollow space formed where it shouldn't, making an echo or reverberation and thereby increasing the volume. Surely there was some kind of muffling procedure available, if that were the case? Hilary ought to insist that he go for it, as a matter of urgency.

'Did Rachel tell you about the man and his tracker dog? They've gone over the fields at the back, looking for Biddy. I would have gone as well, but I'm needed at home. I'm sure they'll find her. Could you be kind enough to phone and let me know if they do? I *have* spent the last hour on the search, after all. I feel quite involved now.' She spoke calmly, looking from one face to the other, refusing to be intimidated. 'Has there been any more news of your sister?' she asked then.

Hilary shook her head. 'She's just the same, but I know it's bad. They didn't say so directly, but it's clear she isn't going to wake up. Her son is with her and they've said they're just going to do the palliative care now. They'll move her to a different ward.'

Thea's idea of the John Radcliffe was of a high-powered establishment that dealt with the complicated and interesting end of the medical spectrum. It was not known for its low-tech treatment of dying patients, waiting for a slow and gentle conclusion to a life. 'Will they send her to a hospice or somewhere, do you think?' she asked.

'Too late for that,' boomed Mr Bunting. 'Why do you think they'd do such a thing, anyhow?'

'I don't know, really. It's just not what they're famous for.'

'People die in every hospital,' the man said. 'They couldn't just reject her on that account.'

'No, but—' She wanted to say, but your sister might be blocking a bed needed for someone they could save. But what did she know? Her experience of hospitals was minimal and out of date.

'I'm taking a turn with her tonight,' he went on. 'We've got a rota worked out. Her son's exhausted, poor chap, but he insists someone should be by her side right around the clock.'

'Gosh!' said Thea faintly. 'That's a big commitment.' Privately she wondered at such dedication. Through Drew, she had heard a dozen stories of dying people waiting for the moment when their relative slipped out to the loo before expiring in peaceful solitude.

Graham Bunting just hunched his shoulders, and Thea felt dismissed. 'Well – I should go. My husband has been interviewed for local radio this afternoon, and it's being broadcast at six. I ought to be back to hear it with him.' Given that it was only just past four, and the walk home would take barely a minute, this was a frail excuse for leaving. But Hilary seemed to take it for what it was.

'Six? The local station? We might tune in to that, then. A local celebrity, after all.'

Thea smiled, relieved that relations seemed to be holding up. 'Hardly. But he's usually quite interesting, I must say. Bye, then, and good luck with Biddy.'

And then Hilary said what Thea should have already guessed was in her mind. 'It doesn't really matter now, does it? If my sister dies without waking up, she'll never know the dog was lost.'

Thea's heart lurched with shock. 'But . . . but what about the poor thing being frightened and lost? Hungry, as well. Think of the dog!' She would have added words such as *callous* and *heartless*, given another moment. But then her phone trilled in her pocket and she had to speak to Drew.

By six o'clock, the children had been fed and Drew's new customer collected from her home, with her weeping husband pleading for just a few more hours in her company. They had been married for fifty-six years, spending barely a night apart. Drew and Andrew had felt cruel as they gently performed the final and absolute separation. He told Thea

50

about it, briefly but feelingly. It cast a melancholy atmosphere over the whole family, as they slumped briefly in the sitting room, entirely forgetting Drew's talk on the radio.

Hepzie circled the family in search of attention and sympathy. She had had a very boring day with Drew, who left the back door open and told her to sort herself out if she needed to relieve herself. Stephanie, as usual, was her best hope. The little girl wriggled herself comfortably into the softest armchair and then gently hauled the dog onto her lap. 'She's got *lumps*,' she announced, during a comprehensive stroke of Hepzie's entire body.

'Don't you start,' snapped Thea. 'I can't do anything about it while she's in plaster, can I?'

Nobody replied, but four faces gave her to understand that snapping was uncalled for. 'She's lucky to have a nice home with all of us,' Thea went on. 'That poor dog who's lost has nobody to love her now her mistress is dying. Even if they find her, she won't have much of a life.'

'We can adopt her, then,' said Timmy, as if it was obvious. The story of Biddy had occupied much of their teatime, with questions and expressions of concern from the children.

'I'm not sure Hepzie would be too pleased about that,' said Thea.

But Drew knew better. 'You're joking! She's always been fine with all those assorted creatures you've been employed to look after these past few years. Hasn't she?'

'Not always,' said Thea, mindful of a few occasions where conflict had erupted between dog and dog. 'There's a lovely Alsatian in Stanton who might have something to say

51

on the subject. And you can stop playing devil's advocate. You're the last one to want another dog.'

He smiled ruefully. 'There's some truth in that,' he admitted.

'Oh – we've missed listening to your interview,' Thea said, at seven-fifteen. 'Wasn't it going to be on at six? That's what I told the Buntings.'

'There's a podcast of it. We can listen any time we like.'

'Oh. Okay.' Thea, true to form, had not willingly got to grips with podcasts and iPlayers and Listen Again. Never especially committed to the radio, other than for background company, she worked on the principle that if you missed something you missed it, and that was that. But Drew had shown a degree of enthusiasm for the various means of catching up, and she had acquired a working knowledge of it all, impressed in spite of herself at how simple it could be.

And then it was bedtime for the children, with Drew reading the stories and Thea restlessly trying to process the events of the day. Frustration bloomed as she remembered her brilliant Arts and Crafts project, as well as the unfinished business of Biddy. The potential friendship with Rachel, and perhaps Hilary if she could escape her noisy husband, was far from certain to proceed. All was up in the air, and Thea Slocombe, formerly Osborne, did not like that one bit.

So she told Drew she was just going to pop round to the Buntings again, to see if the dog had shown up.

'No,' he protested. 'You can't do that. It's half past eight. Why don't you just phone them?'

'I don't know their landline number, and it seems wrong to use the mobile. They might be waiting for a call from the hospital. It would be intrusive.'

'So would a knock on their door.'

'I thought I could peep through the window and see if I could see the dog. Look, it's barely two minutes' walk away. It's no big deal.'

'Thea, if I was a properly old-fashioned husband, I would forbid it. You would have promised to obey me, and I could exert my rights. As it is, I'm just asking you not to do it. Nothing's going to happen between now and tomorrow morning. You can go there at a civilised hour – I suggest about 10 a.m. – and be a good neighbour. But there is no reason to go now, other than idle curiosity. You can't possibly do any good, and are almost certain to annoy them.'

'Oh, pish,' she said. But she did as he wanted, in the interests of harmony and in the knowledge that he was, as usual, perfectly in the right.

Next morning, some – but by no means all – of her curiosity had worn off. The children were no more efficient in getting ready for school than they had been the previous day, and Timmy was even more convinced that the world was out to get him. A new graze on his knee was cited as evidence. But it was a dry day with glimpses of the sun, and Hepzie was definitely happier than she had been for weeks.

'Okay, then,' Thea called out to Drew, at ten o'clock. 'I'm just popping round the corner to the Buntings.'

He put his head out of the office. 'They didn't phone, then?'

'You know they didn't. I think a bit of curiosity is

justified, don't you? Anything might have happened.'

'And probably did,' he said with a tolerant smile.

She walked along the little village lane – not quite a street, given the lack of pavement, and certainly not as significant as a road. There was really no word that adequately described the almost accidental conjunction of tracks that had come together at this spot, and given rise to a settlement that was now of very doubtful utility. Expensive properties, no shop, one pub and a scattering of venues for quiet holidaymakers – it hardly qualified as a community at all. Even the village hall was a token hut hidden away down a narrow path and seldom used. The only life she saw on her short walk was a man on a long ladder, three houses away from the Buntings', fishing dead leaves out of a gutter.

The curtains were drawn across the window of the downstairs front room, which they had not been the day before. That seemed ominous to Thea – perhaps it was an old-fashioned sign of mourning for Mrs Bunting's sister, although she didn't think anyone had done that for about eighty years. Well, sixty, she amended. Victorian habits had persisted far into the twentieth century, after all.

When she knocked on the door, nobody came. With that strange sense that everyone had experienced but could never articulate, she knew for sure that the house was empty. Graham and Hilary had gone out – probably to the hospital in Oxford, and she had missed them. *It's Drew's fault*, she thought crossly. *He should have let me come last night*. The absence of a barking dog was a worry.

Biddy had not shown up, then. She was still either running southwards, or quivering, cold and hungry, under a hedge somewhere. Other alternatives were possible, admittedly, but Thea preferred the two most dramatic on the list.

'No answer?' someone asked at her elbow. She turned to face Rachel, the bridge player and dog hunter.

'Nope. I wanted to ask about the dog.'

'We found her!' came the incredible reply. 'Ant took her home with him. He's quite a lad, isn't he? I got to know him pretty well while we were tracking Biddy. I'll tell you all about him, if you like.'

Thea was once again bemused by the rapid turn of events. 'So where are they?' she asked, indicating the silent house. 'They haven't opened the curtains.'

'Good question. Graham phoned last night and said he hadn't meant to snarl at me yesterday. He was quite sweet about it, actually. I came over to cement our reconciliation. I need to go down to Bristol later in the week, so this was my only chance.'

'Does he shout on the phone as well?'

'Pretty much. He can't help it. It's some bizarre brain thing. They've tried all kinds of remedies, but nothing works. It only came on about six months ago.'

'Bizarre, indeed,' said Thea. 'Well, we should go, I suppose. Why don't you come back with me for a coffee, and you can fill me in about Antares the star.'

'Thanks. That'd be great. But just let me . . .' She was trotting round to the back of the house before finishing the sentence. Automatically, Thea followed her. The back garden was deserted, no birdsong or rustling undergrowth to suggest a rural retreat. The Buntings clearly believed in artifice over nature, with woodchips covering any naked earth and the grass tamed beyond all reason.

'Keen gardeners, then,' said Thea.

'Not really. They have a man one day a week who does it all.' Rachel tried the back door. It opened invitingly and both women walked cautiously through it.

'Hello?' called Rachel, just as Thea had done the day before. But this time, there was no expectation of the two outraged faces appearing in the doorway. The silence was palpable. 'There's nobody here,' said Thea's new friend.

'No,' agreed Thea. 'So we should go. Funny they've left the door unlocked, though. That seems out of character.'

'They're in a state, with everything that's going on. Graham is actually quite fond of Caroline, to judge by the way he talks about her. They all go on holiday together most summers.'

'What happened to her husband?'

'Oh, the usual. Much the same as happened to mine. Everything falling apart once you hit fifty or thereabouts. I think the word "boredom" best sums it up. I must say, I've come to the conclusion that the ones who stick together are the dull ones. I've had a really great time since my divorce.'

Thea processed this in silence. Any mention of divorce frightened her, as it had done all her life. None of her siblings had endured a broken marriage, nor her parents. They were all committed to the idea of couplehood, she supposed, and were quietly proud of themselves as a result.

They were standing in a large kitchen, which had apparently not been modernised for some time. A row of white goods lined one long wall – washing machine, dishwasher, fridge – flanked by a big chest freezer. There would have been a good case for creating a utility room, thought Thea, instead of cramming everything in here. There was no table, but a small breakfast bar and numerous cupboards with glass-fronted doors. Worktops, double sink and an electric cooker filled most of the remaining space. There was only one door leading into the rest of the house.

In short, Thea found it singularly uninteresting, except for one curious detail. Packs of slowly defrosting food were laid out on one of the worktops. Meat, ready-meals, ice cream and bags of vegetables were all clearly desperate for a sub-zero temperature, like fish gasping to be returned to their water. 'Look at that,' she said.

But Rachel had already noticed the anomaly. 'Must have been clearing out the freezer,' she said. 'And got called away in the middle of it. Maybe we should put it all back.'

She went to the chest and heaved at the lid. 'It's stuck,' she said. 'Have they locked it for some reason?' She fiddled with a small key that was in a lock on the handle, and tried again. Still it wouldn't budge. 'Come and help,' she urged.

Together, they got it open, against some incomprehensible resistance. Inside, only an inch or two from the top, was the naked body of a woman, her face a blue-grey colour, the eyes – oddly red-rimmed – wide open, the cheeks glazed with ice.

Chapter Five

Thea was sick. She threw up on the kitchen floor without shame. Rachel had uttered a scream and slammed down the lid. Both were shaking, teeth chattering, as if they too were inside the freezer.

'Oh God, oh God, oh God,' said Rachel. 'Did you see what was in there?'

Thea saw no reason to answer that question. Wasn't it obvious?

'It was Hilary. In the *freezer*.'

'Open it again,' Thea managed to say. 'We have to make sure she's dead.'

'Of course she is. Didn't you *see* her?'

'Even so.'

This time the lid came up easily. 'Why was it so difficult to open before?' Thea asked. Had the woman been holding on to it somehow? Had she been locked in? Or what?

'It's to do with relative temperatures,' said Rachel, with due authority. 'If you put something warm in there, it makes a sort of vacuum, and there's resistance.'

'Oh.' She didn't understand the concept at all. 'A vacuum? Really?'

'Something like that. I had it all explained to me once.'

They were deliberately avoiding the main point, and Thea suspected they both knew it. But the moment came when they had to direct their joint gaze on to the terrible frozen thing that had been a living woman. The naked flesh was nothing like meat, or a human body. It was pale grey in colour, except for the face that had a blue tinge. The legs were folded sideways. The freezer was roughly four feet in length, and nearly three feet deep. Not all the original contents had been removed. Packets of chips, peas and bread peered from around and beneath the body.

'But *how* . . . ?' spluttered Thea. 'I mean – did she die in there, or was she already dead?'

'We have to call the police,' Rachel realised, as if this came as a real surprise to her. 'Nine-nine-nine, I suppose.'

'Look at the mess I've made.' Thea eyed her own vomit on the kitchen floor, and was belatedly ashamed of herself. 'Let me clean it up before they get here.'

'Maybe you should leave it. They'll think signs of cleaning are suspicious.'

Rachel's recovery had been quicker than Thea's. 'Oh, yes. Maybe.' She frowned at her own thick-headedness. The world had begun to wobble beneath her feet, and she barely knew which way was up. 'I can't think straight,' she complained. 'And this isn't the first time I've had to call about a death. Why am I so useless now?'

'Have you seen a body in a freezer before? Or anything half as ghastly?'

'Not that I can think of.' It was true. There had been bodies in living rooms, and fields and ponds, but nothing so deliberately gruesome as this. 'It's her *nakedness* that's so dreadful,' she burst out. 'Can we cover her up with something?'

'There's this.' Rachel took a green dressing gown from the back of a chair, where it had been folded and draped.

'Thanks.' Thea arranged the garment like a sheet over the bare flesh, then watched as her companion made the call to the police, giving the address clearly and repeatedly to the person in Birmingham or Manchester or wherever the call centre might be. Campden caused considerable difficulties, it seemed, with its inaudible 'p'.

'There's a dead woman here,' Rachel said, with only a minimal flutter in her voice. 'Oh yes, I'm sure. There's really no doubt at all.'

And yet, Thea thought with alarm, perhaps there *was* a slender chance of reviving poor Hilary Bunting. Didn't people's bodies recover miraculously from extreme cold from time to time? If they could warm her up, perhaps her heart would respond, and everything get started again. With this thought, she went to the electric socket on the wall and pulled the freezer plug out. At least the poor woman wouldn't get any colder.

'Actually, she's in a chest freezer,' Rachel was saying. 'I suppose somebody must have put her there.'

It sounded ridiculous, and certainly not a story that a first responder was likely to believe. Was the person taking it calmly, or assuming it was a hoax? Thea felt helpless, wishing she had been the one to make the call.

And where was Graham Bunting, the husband?

'We should try to get her out, shouldn't we?' Thea asked, when Rachel had finally finished talking to the bemused operative.

'I don't think we can, even if that was a good idea. They'll want everything left as we found it.'

'I know – but what if she could be revived? What if we've been standing here doing nothing when we might have saved her life? You hear about that sort of thing happening, don't you?'

Rachel gave a long exasperated exhalation. 'Not this time. She must have been in there all night. See how defrosted the stuff on the side is. That would have taken hours and hours. It's winter, and the house isn't very warm. I wonder what's happened to Graham?'

'He must have done it, surely. Who else? He'll have run off to South America or somewhere by now.' Thea was feeling very much out of control, afraid of her own uselessness, as well as the thought that there might be a crazy killer close by. 'Unless he's still hiding upstairs,' she added with a shudder.

'He's not. Don't be silly.'

'We should go out to the front and wait for the police, then. They'll want to ask loads of questions and we'll have to explain what we were doing here, trespassing in someone else's house. And that sick . . . I wish I could clean it up. It's embarrassing.'

'It's the least of anyone's worries. God, poor old Hilary. It's grotesque, isn't it? What a way to kill somebody. Do you think she knew about it and pushed at the lid before she died?' Rachel watched Thea's face closely as if checking that she was paying attention.

'Like being buried alive,' said Thea. 'Her hands don't look damaged, though. Wouldn't they be bruised or broken if she'd beaten on the lid? Maybe he drugged her first. That wouldn't be quite so gruesome.'

'He? You really think Graham did this, do you?'

'Who else?' said Thea simply.

'I don't know. Why would he? They were happy enough.'

'You never know, though, do you? They didn't seem all that happy to me. And he does seem a bit . . . volatile, maybe. He could have just lost it.' She rubbed her forehead, as if trying to push her thoughts straight. 'But we saw them both only yesterday. How could anything so terrible happen so quickly?'

'This looks planned to me. As if it was brewing for a while.'

'Did you say he phoned you last night? What time was it?'

'A bit before six, I think. He was being quite friendly, funnily enough. Wanted to patch things up with me after being so horrible about my bridge playing. When he yelled at me I told him I wasn't going to come any more. We did have quite a spat, actually. He said Hilary was upset to think the Tuesday bridge might not happen any more.'

'And what did you say?'

'I was still a bit frosty with him. I know I'm the weakest player. It gets quite intense at times, and I don't enjoy it very much.'

Thea tried harder to gather her thoughts. Somebody had done a terrible thing, here in her own home village. Somehow she had persuaded herself that despite all the crimes and killings she had encountered over recent years in the Cotswolds region, nothing would impinge on her and Drew in Broad Campden. Now, it seemed, there was peril close at hand, and this realisation was hard to bear. That, she supposed, was why she was still shaking, standing outside with a woman she barely knew. It occurred to her to wonder – was this woman everything she appeared to be? Had the entire discovery of the body been staged, with her, Thea, as an innocent witness? The suspicious thoughts came automatically, born of a gradual loss of trust in people she didn't know well. Too often they had turned treacherous, hostile and even homicidal.

She badly did not want to spend hours being questioned by the police. There were so many things she had seen and heard in the past twenty-four hours that they ought to know about: the dog, the bridge party, the dying Caroline and the very helpful Ant with his tracker-dog Percy. But she had no desire to be the person to explain it all to them. 'Just find Graham Bunting,' she would say to them. 'That's all you need to do.'

But was it really going to be that simple? Murders mostly *were* simple, of course. The husband or lover did it nearly every time. And everything pointed to the loudly critical and controlling Graham this time, too. Her thoughts whirled untidily and contradictorily as she waited in the cold. When at last an ambulance arrived ('Did you ask for an ambulance?' she asked Rachel, who shook her head dumbly), she just went on standing there, barely reacting. A man and a woman jumped out of the vehicle with their inevitable self-important briskness, and asked where the patient was.

'She's dead. There's no need for you,' said Rachel. 'See for yourself. Round the back. In the kitchen.'

'Show us, please.' They evidently feared some sort of ambush at the rear of the house: gunmen lying in the shrubbery, a pit full of spikes to fall carelessly into.

Rachel led the way, and Thea trailed behind, knowing she would regret missing the looks on the paramedics' faces when they saw the corpse if she stayed where she was.

The yawning lid of the freezer drew them like a magnet. They looked in, stepped back, then looked at each other. 'Blimey!' said the woman.

Thea smiled. Sometimes it was the only word to use. Whatever its origin, it covered situations like this quite excellently.

They looked again. 'Better leave her,' said the man. 'For the police.'

'There was no need for you to come,' said Rachel again.

'Have to be sure.'

'Well, *be* sure, then. Take her pulse. Check for breathing, why don't you?' It was Thea who lost patience with them, as she so often did lose patience. The world was so very full of dimwits, jobsworths, the hesitant and the unreliable. The mendacious and the obstructive. The unimaginative and the self-obsessed. The list went on growing, and she really did not think it was her fault if she found them annoying.

'Calm down, madam,' said the man, thereby increasing her fury. 'You've obviously had a very nasty shock. We can take it from here. Perhaps if you and your friend went back outside . . .'

'Come on, Thea,' said Rachel. 'I can hear a car in the road. It might be the police.'

It was. The usual patterned car containing two uniformed officers had pulled up close to the grass verge that fronted the house and its neighbours. And suddenly there *were* neighbours in plenty. The sight of an ambulance had drawn them to their doors and windows, in belated realisation that a drama was unfolding at the Bunting house. The man cleaning the gutter came down from his ladder and stood at a little distance, eyes wide.

Despite considerable involvement with the police over the past three years or so, Thea did not recognise either of the officers. She was better acquainted with the senior detectives than the lower ranks – but she did wonder whether they knew who *she* was. Not just because she'd been witness, sleuth and all-round busybody on several occasions, but because she was now married to a local undertaker. While Drew was not one of the mainstream traditional operators, he had been called to bodies by the police quite a few times. If the deceased person had made it clear that they wanted one of Drew's funerals, then Drew would be the one called to attend to the body.

But these men did not have her name and barely glanced at her. They asked for Rachel, and spoke exclusively to her. Thea was unaccustomed to being sidelined in such a way, and stepped back in confusion. Could she just *go*, then? Could she slide away, leaving everything to the other woman, who did after all know the Buntings and showed every sign of competence and balance?

When Rachel began to lead the policemen around the

side of the house, Thea hung back. *They don't need me*, she thought. *They haven't even asked who I am.*

But then one of the men looked back. 'Were you here when the body was found, madam?' he asked. He gave her a searching look, sympathy and concern showing on his face. *I must look awful*, she thought.

She nodded. 'Yes, I was.'

'We'll need your details, then.'

'Okay. Then can I go home? I live just down the lane past the church.'

'Give us a few minutes, all right? One thing at a time, eh?' His easy kindness was disarming. Thea felt a startling desire to push her face into his chest and cry. 'You'll be in shock,' he added.

It was ridiculous. She was married to an undertaker, for heaven's sake. How could the sight of a body reduce her to such jelly? When these policemen realised who she was, they'd think less of her. They'd be scornful. She struggled to gain control. 'Thanks,' she said. 'It just took us completely unawares. You just don't expect . . . I mean, she's in the *freezer*.'

'Let's go and see, then.'

The paramedics were still hovering in the kitchen, one holding a phone, the other running water in the sink. Was it possible that even a professional was in need of a settling drink? They greeted the police with evident relief. 'Not seen one like this before,' said the ambulance man.

Shock was electric in the air as the two newcomers peered at the frozen face, and then looked around the room. Six people were arranged as if for a John Osborne play. A kitchen-sink drama, thought Thea wildly. 'That was me, I'm afraid,' she said, pointing at the mess on the floor. 'We thought you might not want us to clean it up.'

Rachel had gone very quiet. She stood tall and pale, her eyes darting from side to side, from face to face, one hand at the base of her throat. Then she spun round and quickly went out into the garden. There she doubled over and retched, but nothing came forth.

The ambulance woman followed her, and put a hand on her back. Thea dithered, watching but not trying to join the pair in the garden.

'You all need to go outside,' said the kind policeman. 'This is officially a crime scene. Nobody is to touch anything. I need a full account of your movements since you got to the house.' He looked at Thea, and then Rachel. 'There'll be someone from CID here soon.'

'And a police doctor and forensics and SOCOs,' said Thea with a sigh. 'I know the routine.'

'Oh?'

She explained as best she could, and suddenly she was elevated to being by far the more interesting of the two witnesses. Rachel's malaise kept her at a distance, anyway. Thea provided her contact details and a basic summary of how they had come to find Hilary Bunting. She knew well enough that the whole story would have to be told again in much greater detail. 'I barely know them,' she added. 'I met them for the first time yesterday.'

'But you live here? You're virtually neighbours.'

'Not really. We're not close neighbours. And people don't socialise very much around here. We know the two other families with primary-age children, and our immediate neighbours vaguely – but we'd never met the Buntings.'

'And Mrs Ottaway?'

'She's a friend of the Buntings. I only met her yesterday as well. I don't even know whether she goes by Ms or Mrs. She lives in Blockley.'

He looked at a notebook in his hand. 'She said "Mrs" when she called this in.'

Thea blinked. She had not registered that part of the phone call at all. She really must have been in a state of total shock, she supposed. What an odd thing, when she'd always been so calm and capable previously.

'She knows other friends of the Buntings as well. They all play bridge together.' Why did it feel treacherous to reveal such harmless information? As if she might be incriminating Rachel and her friends. Then she realised, she was indirectly hoping to do just that – by making it clear that she herself had no motives, no axes to grind, no reason whatsoever to wish harm to either Mr or Mrs Bunting. She was pure unadulterated innocence, with nothing at all to feel guilty about – except for being sick on the nice clean kitchen floor.

Then a familiar voice was heard from the front of the house. A very loud voice, asking questions. 'What the devil's going on here? Has something happened? Where's my wife?'

Graham Bunting came round the house at a trot. 'What the . . . ?' he spluttered. 'Has there been an accident?' He glared round. 'Rachel? What's the matter with you? There's an ambulance outside. Where's Hillie?' His voice raised to an even louder pitch as he yelled, 'Hillie!! Where are you?' His beard jutted from his chin and his heavy glasses looked to be steaming up. He was like a figure from a Victorian children's book: the wild man of the woods, or the shipwrecked mariner with a casket of treasure. Something uncontrolled about him made him incongruous in this respectable English setting. But the loss of control had little violence to it; rather it was unbearably desperate, imbued with the pathos of what they knew and he – apparently – didn't. What violence there was was that of a cornered animal, or a cow separated from her calf.

Everyone stood frozen, watching him. The policemen had both turned pale and wooden. Their training might have lightly touched on possible scenarios where calm consideration had to be given to distraught relatives in receipt of dreadful news, but the reality could not hope to match even the most intensive role-playing.

'Er . . . Mr Bunting?' said the kind one. 'Could we perhaps go into another part of the house? Through the front door? The kitchen isn't . . . That is, you can't . . .' He put a hand on the man and steered him back the way he'd come. Or tried to.

'What do you mean? Has there been a fire or something?' He managed to peer through the kitchen door for a moment, glimpsing the scene inside. He went rigid at the tableau that met his gaze. Thea supposed it amounted to an open freezer lid, officers beside it and a green dressing gown covering something inside it. At the very least that's what he would have seen.

There must have been a hundred questions surging

through the policemen's heads, but they remained admirably controlled. 'We just need you to come indoors and sit down,' said the one who had yet to address Thea. He was slight, and fair-skinned, and spoke with a Birmingham accent.

'Why can't we go into the kitchen? I want to see exactly what's in there.' Graham's voice had sunk to something that to him must have felt like a whisper, but was still as loud as a normal person's when speaking to someone across a room.

'We'll explain it all to you in a moment, sir.'

Thea felt again that she was superfluous. She was not even observing events properly. She hadn't noticed the policeman phoning for reinforcements, or the ambulance pair leaving on another job. She heard the woman say, 'We've got a shout down in Moreton,' but didn't register the significance. Rachel was sitting on a damp garden seat. Graham Bunting was the main focus now, and quite right too.

Even if he was a murderer, he had to be treated with due consideration. And he *was* a murderer, surely? Wasn't that obvious?

And yet – if so, why had he come back? And how did he manage to look so bewildered and pathetic? And if he hadn't killed Hilary, then who had?

Chapter Six

She got back to the house and Drew and Hepzie just before noon. He was in his office with Andrew. When Thea went through to them, they both gave her looks full of patient interest that did nothing to conceal the fact that they felt she had interrupted something important.

'I've got a family coming in a minute,' said Drew. 'They want a burial early next week.'

'Another one?'

'Right. A lady from the hospice.'

Bodies did, of course, have to be stored on the premises in advance of their burial. Alterations had been made somewhat hastily to the garage attached to the house, with additional paved areas for the hearse and the van used to remove bodies from the place of death. It had all been accomplished within the constraints of local planning regulations, as well as respect for the sensibilities of neighbours. A trolley wheeled the corpses from vehicle to cool room invisibly through a newly made rear entrance. But it was all on a small scale, and there was no space for more than two bodies at a time.

'Doesn't that make three?' asked Thea.

'Unfortunately, it does. We'll have to do some juggling. That's what we were discussing just now.'

'What do you have to juggle with?' She was willing to continue this conversation for as long as it took, in no rush to explain what had happened that morning. It felt like a kind of heroism to hold back on her own concerns while her beloved husband attended to his. But then it occurred to her that he might feel reproachful, once the tale was told, so she jiggled a little to indicate that she had something to say.

'We might have to ask the Cirencester people to help us out. I did ask them, a while back, if we could use them as overflow if it came to the crunch. But with Miss Temple going on Friday, I think we can swing it. She'll be coffined up on Thursday, and can tuck in somewhere.' He was looking at her face, for the first time since she'd come into the room. 'Did something happen?' he asked.

She pulled her thoughts away from the image of an inhabited coffin sitting somewhere in the house. The hallway, perhaps, or a corner of the kitchen? 'You might say that,' she confirmed. 'I've just come from a crime scene. Looks like a murder.'

He narrowed his eyes, suspecting a poor joke. 'You do look a bit ravaged,' he observed.

'So would you, if you'd seen what I have. I was sick.' She couldn't decide whether this was a matter of shame or pride. Neither, probably.

Andrew Emerson, their employee, had been sitting with his back to the door, and after a swift glance when Thea came in, had returned to the same position, removing himself from the discussion. But now he turned again and looked at her worriedly.

'Not in sleepy Broad Campden?' he said, half-humorous, half-wary.

'It's Hilary Bunting. We found her in their big chest freezer, stone dead.' And then she splurged the rest of the story, such as it was. It only took a few more sentences.

'And you think the husband did it?' queried Andrew.

'I did think so, although he seemed totally bemused when he turned up. And *why* would he turn up like that if he'd done it?'

'Smokescreen,' said Drew, who was fond of this idea. 'Throwing suspicion off by acting innocently. Oldest trick in the book.'

'I'm sure there must be older ones than that,' flashed Thea, feeling oddly defensive. Drew was being irritating. 'And when have you known anyone actually do that?'

He raised his eyebrows. 'Unlike you, I have seldom found myself in a position to judge the actions of a murderer. I can't say never, of course. I've had my share, but a very small share, compared to yours.'

'Oh, Drew.' The tears she had wanted to shed on the kind policeman now began to flow all over her husband. She was in his arms, her face against his shoulder, regardless of the embarrassed Andrew. 'I was so *shocked*. I was *sick* on the *floor*. I couldn't stop shaking. I was an absolute *mess*.'

He rubbed her back and murmured soothing noises at her. Slowly he pulled her off so he could see her face. 'What's this all about?' he asked her gently.

'I'm not exactly sure. I think I thought all that was over and done with. I thought it was to do with the house-sitting, and it could never happen again. It feels so scary, so *dangerous*, this time. I mean, she was there in her own kitchen, stuffed naked into her own freezer. It could happen to anyone. Maybe there's a lunatic living in our midst, a monster who seems just like any ordinary person.' She was babbling, almost hysterical. 'And besides all that, I really was minding my own business. I wasn't being nosy. Was I?'

'Only a bit,' said Drew with an affectionate laugh. 'We can blame Mr Shipley for that. He started it.'

'Yes! He did, didn't he?' She pulled back to look into his face. 'Maybe *he's* the killer in our midst. It was all part of a clever plan.'

'Good grief! You two!' Andrew complained. 'I never know when you're being serious.'

Andrew had been a farmer until TB in his cattle had driven him out of business. He had lost heart completely until Drew rescued him by offering him casual low-paid work as his assistant. Having sold the farm at Chedworth, paid off his debts and moved with his wife and teenage son to Blockley, he found himself to be surviving quite nicely. The wife found herself a job; they grew large quantities of vegetables, used bicycles wherever possible and regarded themselves as truly blessed. 'But I do miss the cows,' he would sigh, almost every day.

'Oh, we're always serious,' said Drew cheerfully. 'It just doesn't always look like it.'

'I haven't been interviewed yet,' said Thea. 'They'll be wanting to ask me lots of questions.' She wiped her face with a hand that felt as if it needed a good wash. 'I hope it's Gladwin.'

Sonia Gladwin was a detective superintendent, mother

of twin boys, Tyneside born and bred, and a thoroughly decent person. Unorthodox at times, ignoring edicts as to priorities and protocols, she had repeatedly permitted Thea to get closer to murder investigations than was usual. The other senior members of the team appeared to tolerate her without any great enthusiasm. Thea suspected that her blithe intelligence made them feel dim and bumbling at times.

'We haven't seen her for a while, have we?' said Drew, who had only met the detective fleetingly. 'Are you sure she hasn't moved on to a new patch?'

'I think I'd have heard.'

A small cough from Andrew alerted Drew to the need for a return to business. 'Let me make a couple of phone calls, and then we'll have a sandwich or something. I'm hungry,' he said.

'I don't think I can eat,' said Thea. 'I feel all churned up. I might manage a cup of tea.'

'With loads of sugar in it, for the shock,' said Drew.

'Yuk!'

But ten minutes later she was drinking it exactly as described, finding it remarkably pleasant. Drew had been a nurse in his younger days and possessed skills that regularly came as a surprise. He could diagnose childhood ailments and injuries; produce appropriate medicines, including ordinary items from the kitchen cupboards; rub sore areas with precision and monitor digestive processes with absolute accuracy. It was like living with an angel, Thea commented once. 'Makes a change from a saint,' he had quipped. But she had assured him he was one of those as well.

* * *

When a detective sergeant she had never seen before came to the door at half past one, Thea was unreasonably disappointed. Then she reproached herself: why should she warrant the attentions of a superintendent, anyway? The senior investigating officer, whoever it might be, would be busy with Graham Bunting and perhaps Rachel Ottaway. He or she would be issuing orders to the team – find out as much as you can about the marriage, the background, the family, the bridge club, the dying sister and even the errant dog. Thea Slocombe could be of no help with any of that. All she did was tag along behind the person who found the body. A bit player. Only slightly higher up the list than Ant and his valiant Percy. If they were on the list at all, of course. Why would they be? Somehow, she felt they were part of the picture, but could give no proper reason why.

She took the unfamiliar man – who had said his name was Forrest – into the front room and offered him tea. He declined, and took out a neat little notebook, which made her think of the electronic gadget favoured by Gladwin. 'Start from the beginning,' he invited her.

'I'll try, but I'm not sure where that is.' Was it the previous day, when she had first knocked at the Buntings' door? Or that morning, when she had gone there again? 'Today, I suppose. I went to the house at ten o'clock, and the curtains were drawn.' She went on to describe the arrival of Rachel Ottaway, their ingress through the back door that opened directly into the kitchen. The food defrosting on the worktop. The struggle to open the freezer lid. 'Why wouldn't it open?' she asked. 'Rachel said it was to do with a vacuum caused by putting something warm in there.'

The man blinked. 'I have no idea,' he said.

'It might be important. It would give some clue as to how long she'd been in there. If Rachel's right, then she must have still been a bit warm. She didn't *look* warm.'

'I'll make a note,' said Detective Sergeant Forrest.

Thea said nothing more. The significant part of the story had now been told. If the police suspected Graham Bunting – and how could they not? – there was nothing Thea could usefully contribute to their pursuit of evidence against him. Her customary tendency to intrude herself into the investigation, following up hunches and paying intrusive calls on potential witnesses, did not appeal to her at all on this occasion. She *lived* here now. She could not afford to alienate local people who would be her neighbours for the foreseeable future. When working as an irresponsible house-sitter there had been little hazard in stirring up ancient animosities, or putting herself in the role of straight-talking amateur sleuth. Now it was all completely different.

'How long have you known Mr and Mrs Bunting?' he asked.

'I told you – only since yesterday. I'd never even seen them before.' Ruefully, she realised that the start of the story, and her testimony to the police, would have to include the visit from Mr Shipley and the apparent concern of many villagers.

'So why did you go to see them yesterday?' came the inevitable question.

She did her best to explain, without casting anyone in a bad light. 'We don't know Mr Shipley very well, so it was a surprise when he tried to get us involved. And I think Mr Bunting's loud voice makes everything sound much more alarming and aggressive than it really is.'

Forrest raised both eyebrows. 'Or perhaps not,' he said.

She wondered whether anyone else would have supplied this information about village concern, if she had not. Very possibly the answer was negative, although surely the people in the houses close to the Buntings would have revealed that the couple were noisy, and often seemed to be fighting. Then she wondered why that bothered her. Why did she feel protective towards Graham Bunting, when he had shown little or no sign of friendliness towards her? He didn't seem to be a very nice man. Because she remembered his face when he'd come home that morning to find his garden full of officers of the law and paramedics. There was a very long way between not being very nice, and being a deliberate murderer.

'And Mrs Ottaway?'

'What about her?'

'How long have you known her?'

'Oh – the same. Although I saw more of her yesterday. She seems very . . . *brisk*. But friendly. She knows the Buntings far better than I do. Mr Bunting wasn't very nice to her when they were playing bridge yesterday, but I think they've made it up again now. She's reasonably public-spirited, too. We went off on a dog hunt together.' She shook her head. 'I'd forgotten all about that until just now.'

'Whose dog were you hunting?'

'Hilary Bunting was looking after it for her sister. She was making rather a mess of it, actually. Then it ran off, and Rachel and I volunteered to look for it. And a man called Ant. He found it in the end, and took it home with him. Rachel told me that this morning. I suppose I thought the whole problem was solved, so I didn't need to bother any more about it.'

The sergeant tapped his teeth with his pen for a moment, before concluding that the dog could have no relevance to the case in hand, but Thea was having second thoughts.

'Who's going to have her now?' she worried. 'Poor Biddy. She's going to be horribly confused.'

'Mm,' said the man unfeelingly.

Thea lapsed into silence, thinking of the many confused dogs she'd encountered in recent times. People kept dogs, thereby shouldering a responsibility that they were not always equal to. She regarded herself as a kind of dog magnet, falling into involvement and concern without any conscious intention. But not this time – Biddy was definitely not in any way her problem.

'Okay, then,' said Forrest, a minute later. 'Thank you very much. I'll leave you in peace now.' He paused. 'You had a nasty shock. Are you going to be all right?'

'Oh yes, thanks. My husband's very good with that sort of thing. He'll make sure I'm okay. After all, it isn't the first time.'

'No. So I understand,' he said with a little smile. It was oddly disconcerting to discover that even this unfamiliar sergeant knew who she was, and how she had been involved and connected with police work several times in recent years. 'But it's never easy, is it?'

'No,' she said, thinking that his words were ludicrously inadequate to describe the impact of murder in all its dreadful forms. 'And this one was the worst. I was so scared. I haven't felt like that before – or hardly ever.' She remembered a week in snowy Hampnett when she'd been frightened, alone, and cut off for days with a body and a miserable old dog. 'This one goes deeper somehow,' she finished falteringly.

'You never know how it's going to take you,' he said, with his eye on the door. The interview was over and he had others on his list, she presumed. She saw him out with a sense of abandonment. She felt hollow and vulnerable and not a bit like her usual self.

The children would be home in an hour or so. The bus dropped them about two hundred yards from the house, and they walked down the little lane unescorted. But even in a tiny peaceful English village, where traffic was discouraged from using the branching tracks that led from the main road to outlying properties, one or two people had looked askance at the fecklessness of letting them take such a risk. Stephanie was *nine*, Thea wanted to shout, and Timmy not much younger. Forgetting the vanishingly minuscule chance of anyone abducting them, there was very little else that could go wrong. They could dodge the very occasional – and very slow – cars. If one of them fell over, the other could shout for help and be heard from the house. So far as Thea could see, there was nothing else that could possibly happen. And yet she determined to go and meet them on this unsettling Wednesday, when somebody had committed a most sinister murder.

Drew and his assistant had gone off to collect the new

body, having discreetly interviewed the family while Thea entertained the police detective. Parking outside had become complicated, with two extra cars. Everything in Broad Campden felt cramped and enclosed, even in winter when the leafless trees did at least reveal some open vistas. In summer the place had a secretive atmosphere, with vegetation concealing entrances and making the lanes seem even narrower. As with numerous other Cotswold villages, it was not on the way to anywhere, unless you happened to go from Blockley to Chipping Campden. This in itself felt like a mistake, sending travellers on a looping little road that many a motorist must have found confusing. But then they would become diverted and enchanted by the unusual sight of thatched roofs atop the honey-and-cream stonework of the cottages. Thea always remembered Drew telling her about Maggs Cooper's instant response to the original mention of Broad Campden – 'That's where all the thatched roofs are,' she said, or words to that effect. Both Drew and Thea had been profoundly impressed. Neither of them had ever even heard of the place until summoned there by a burial and a house-sitting commission respectively, resulting in their first encounter.

She made herself the tea that Detective Forrest had refused, but she did not add sugar to it. The cold, discoloured face of Hilary Bunting remained in her mind's eye, insistent and hideous. What would it be like, she couldn't help wondering, being shut in a dark, airless freezer? Had the woman still been breathing – had that somehow caused the vacuum that kept the lid so tightly shut? And did that mean the victim wouldn't have been able to heave it open, if she'd been conscious? Stories of children dying inside fridges came to mind. Had the same weird chemistry taken place on those occasions? Heat transfer or something? No – it must be more complicated than that. She wished she'd been taught better science at school. She'd enjoyed physics, but found chemistry impenetrable. She could google it, probably, but wasn't sure she wanted to know the details.

Then it was past three o'clock, and she went to get her coat and then to meet the school bus. Hepzie was more than happy to go with her, despite her disability. The three-legged gait was getting quicker, Thea noticed. By the time the plaster was off, it would be second nature, and the dog would have to relearn how to walk normally.

Stephanie and Timmy tumbled eagerly off the bus at the sight of their stepmother and her spaniel. It was mostly the dog, Thea realised ruefully. But it felt good to be part of a little family, with the distractions and normality that came with it. No time to agonise over murder and the hatred that surely went with it.

She made a big thing of encouraging accounts of the school day, the plans for the term ahead, the odd thing that appeared to be happening to Timmy's teacher, Mrs Allsop. 'She's always red in the face,' the child reported. 'And her legs are fat.' Thea had heard that the woman was pregnant, and smiled at Timmy's focus on the less obvious side effects of the condition.

'She's having a baby, stupid,' said Stephanie.

'I know *that*, but why does it make her all red?'

Nobody offered an answer to that little mystery.

The day drifted to a close, with Drew back by four, and Thea preparing a favourite meal in the form of 'sausage bake'. She believed her mother had invented it back in the seventies, but Drew said it was known across the land. In any case, everyone loved the bloated sausages in the thick tomatoey and oniony sauce, with plenty of herbs for good measure. 'And anyway, it's not a "bake", is it?' Drew had said more than once. 'It's actually a casserole.'

'Oh, shut up,' said Thea and Stephanie in unison.

The children were in bed by eight, tired from the school day. Drew had successfully appealed to a traditional undertaker for an emergency overnight place in one of their fridges, having changed his mind about leaving Miss Temple in a corner somewhere, and delivered the latest body accordingly. The sense of being gainfully employed was deeply satisfying, to the extent that Thea's experiences of the morning did little to dent his complacency.

This was not altogether to Thea's liking. Had she not boasted to the Forrest man that her husband was good at dealing with shock and stress? Now here he was, virtually ignoring her in her hour of need. But he had lit the woodstove, dimmed the lights, and created a cosy nest on the sofa. Hepzie was cuddled against him on one side, and he patted a space on the other, inviting his wife to join them, when she came down from reading to the children.

'You look very snug,' she said.

'I am.' He gave her a look that told her he had noticed the edge in her voice and was not going to dignify it with any sort of response.

Drew's softness had worried her at first. Would he allow her to manipulate or even bully him, if her own less admirable qualities asserted themselves? Would he perhaps make her even sharper, as a reaction to his own easy ways? But the worry had soon evaporated. His subtle way of holding up a mirror to her moments of impatience or intolerance was highly effective. Without a hint of criticism, he helped her to see that there were other ways to behave. While far from transformed, she did hope that she had mellowed just a little. Moments from the past few years continued to haunt her – she had been close to cruel once or twice, and certainly rude. There were people she would not like to meet again, knowing they were unlikely ever to forgive her for the things she had said to them.

She pressed close to him and did her best to relax. Drew would keep any evil away, by the very goodness of his character. Even if murder had come to the heart of Broad Campden, they could repel it. Outside, a wind had sprung up, cold and hostile. They could hear it rattling one of the upstairs windows. The woodstove was not drawing properly. The curtains were tightly closed. And still Thea was listening for footsteps on the path, a knock on the door. Or worse – a stone through a window. It had all happened before, and she had been forced to be strong and independent, like it or not. Nothing was genuinely safe in this world: her husband Carl had died in his car; Drew's wife Karen had been shot in the head; a coffin had fallen on her dog. There was peril on every side, and only an idiot would deny it.

Chapter Seven

Thursday was still windy. When Thea took the dog out, there were swirls of dead leaves dancing in the corners of the garden. Next door's big fir tree was tossing wildly. If it carried on like that, it might well blow over and land in the Slocombes' garden, jeopardising the precious hearse, which was parked close to the fence. A proportion of the garden had been sacrificed to the demands of the funeral vehicles, as well as the path to the new mortuary. Planning permission for the modest conversion had been provided unnaturally fast, perhaps because the council members could not face a prolonged debate about dead bodies.

Thea was content to wait for any developments concerning the death of Hilary Bunting to come to her. She was not tempted to go searching for news, perhaps because the clear assumption had to be that the husband did it. There might well not be very much of an investigation at all. The whole thing would be wrapped up, with general regret and a degree of horror, after the man broke down and confessed. He might plead diminished responsibility, or the onset of a red mist followed by a foolish attempt to conceal the result of his rage.

But questions persisted. Did the Buntings have any offspring? How was sister Caroline doing? Was Rachel coping with the shock she'd gone through? And – the most persistent of them all – did Graham Bunting *really* kill his wife? Could anyone put on such a persuasive act as he must have done the previous day?

Hepzie was limping across the surviving patch of lawn, her long, black ears flapping in the gale. She had her head up, and a doggy grin was spread over her face. 'Oh, Heps,' Thea sighed. 'You are sweet.' The dog had been a constant companion through the very dark days following Carl's sudden death. She had accompanied Thea on numerous house-sitting commissions, getting herself into mischief at times, and providing much-needed comfort at others. For Drew to cause her more damage than on any other occasion was both ironic and alarming. Nothing was truly safe if an empty coffin could break a dog's leg.

'Come in, then,' Thea told her pet. 'We might go into the field later on, if the wind drops a bit.' She stooped to stroke the soft head. 'And it's not long now till that plaster comes off. You won't know yourself then.' Hepzie wagged her long, feathery tail and gave no sign of impatience.

The children had gone for their bus. Drew was already on the phone to someone about a funeral. There was very little for Thea to do other than a spot of tidying in Timmy's bedroom. Stephanie kept her things neat, taking great pride in doing so. Her little brother covered every surface in stones, comic books, fantasy figures, and small squares of plastic that contained crucially important electronic games for his device. The stones were a beloved collection, waiting for the day when someone bought the child a polisher so their true glory could be revealed. Drew kept warning that he knew for a fact that such machines were impossibly noisy and expensive to run.

Tidying involved little more than straightening the duvet and picking up discarded clothes. Most of them could be worn again before needing a wash, so she piled them onto a chair and looked around the room. It was large by modern standards, with plenty of space for a table, chest of drawers, set of shelves and two chairs – as well as the bed. The chairs had found their way there a month previously, when Timmy had flu, and both Drew and Thea had sat with him through one long feverish evening. Afterwards, Thea wondered why she had felt so compelled to share the vigil with the child's father. No real answer had been forthcoming, other than a need to be at the heart of things. 'That's you,' said Drew. 'That's what you do.'

Now she looked out of the window, which was at the front of the house. Trees and roofs and natural undulations filled the space between this house and that of the Buntings, but still she stretched her neck to try to see it. Off to the north it lay, or a little north-west, perhaps. There were no straight lines in Broad Campden, points of the compass wavered confusingly, with roads and footpaths taking their own meandering ways from one place to another. Houses sat at crooked angles to the lanes that led to them; gardens and parking areas evolved haphazardly as the need arose.

And there was a woman coming down the winding

little road, visible only in snatches until she reached the Slocombes' gate. Rachel Ottaway, carrying a canvas bag, wearing a blue scarf and long leather boots. She must have left her car up by the church, or on some other rarely available spot. Parking in the village was seldom easy, as Drew's clients regularly observed.

Thea ran downstairs and opened the door. 'I saw you from Timmy's window,' she said breathlessly. 'How are you? Come in. Shall I make some coffee?'

'Me? I'm perfectly all right. Why shouldn't I be?'

'Well . . .' For a moment Thea wondered whether the events of the previous day had all been a dream.

'*You're* all right, aren't you?'

'I suppose I am,' said Thea, in some surprise. 'I hadn't really thought about it.'

'Of course you are. Shock doesn't last very long. People like us just dust ourselves down and get on with our lives. Coffee would be great, thanks.'

Thea led the way into the kitchen, where Hepzie expressed delight at having a visitor, and Rachel studiously avoided looking at the crumbs and splashes that were still on the table from breakfast. 'Look what I found in my landing bookcase. I remembered what Hilary said about your new society, and thought this might be a good place to start.' Rachel rummaged in her bag and produced a hard-backed book. The cover depicted a fuzzy old photograph of boys wearing cloth caps and doing something that looked like an outdoor gym lesson. Legs bent, arms outstretched and expressions registering effort on their faces. Thea took it and gave the strange image a long examination.

'*The Simple Life*,' she read aloud. And then, 'Oh – I see!' She had noted the subtitle – *C. R. Ashbee in the Cotswolds*. 'Gosh!'

'I thought it might give us a good start in our local history studies,' said Rachel. 'It's full of good stuff.'

Thea had turned to the flyleaf, which spoke of 'utopian social history', among other things. 'Gosh!' she said again. 'That's brilliant.' She put the book down on a clean part of the table and busied herself with the coffee. 'Is instant all right?' she asked. 'The real thing's such a palaver, isn't it?'

Rachel waved a careless hand, and then adopted a dreamy expression. 'I was really into all this Arts and Crafts stuff, ages ago. Must be twenty-five years, at least. I kept most of the books. It would be wonderful to go back to it.' She sat down at one end of the table, and eyed Hepzie with a distracted glance.

'Yes, but . . .' said Thea with a frown.

'Oh, you're worrying about that business yesterday, aren't you? It was dreadful, I know. But life goes on.'

'And shock wears off,' muttered Thea as she passed Rachel a mug of coffee. Wasn't it preposterously *quick* to be forgetting poor Hilary and carrying on as if nothing had happened?

'Yes, it does,' confirmed Rachel. 'And I see no reason to waste time. I agree with you when you say that Chipping Campden has almost forgotten its heritage, and Broad Campden has never taken much notice of it in the first place.'

'Oh, by the way – do you ever call it Broady? I bet Drew 50p that people do.'

'Sorry. I think you've lost money there. I've never once heard anybody say that.'

'But they say "Chippy",' Thea persisted.

'That's short for Chipping *Norton*, not Campden.' Rachel gave her a look that suggested mild contempt for her failure to grasp these nuances. 'Anyway,' she proceeded firmly, 'I think we should make some leaflets and try to assemble a group for discussions. It only needed somebody dynamic like you to move in to get things going. I can't tell you how pleased I am.'

'Yes, but . . .' Thea tried again. How to explain that it had been little more than a careless pretext with which to approach Hilary and Graham Bunting? Her own historical studies had lapsed at about the same time as Rachel's, apart from a few flurries of interest over the years. The flare of enthusiasm that had gripped her on Tuesday was now sullied by Hilary's death and all the worry and grief that came with it. 'Are you sure there isn't something going on already in a history society somewhere?'

'Just go and have a look at the museum, if you're in any doubt. They've never even *heard* of William de Morgan or Ethel Coomaraswamy.'

Thea was startled. The woman had just named the two individuals that she herself found the most interesting. At least, de Morgan's wife Evelyn had attracted her curiosity during a house-sit in Cranham, and she had subsequently learnt that the couple had visited the Campdens a number of times in the early twentieth century. Had Rachel Ottaway been eavesdropping somehow? 'How did you know I had a thing about the de Morgans?' she demanded.

Rachel grimaced. 'I guessed, actually. That business in Cranham was in the papers, if you remember. I recognised your name.'

'Which is different now.'

'Not your first name. It didn't take a genius to work out it was you.'

Thea took a deep breath, and changed the subject. There were suspicions burgeoning as she tried to make sense of Rachel's stream of startling remarks. 'How well did you know Hilary?' she asked, with determination. 'Have the Buntings any children? Is there any news of Caroline?'

'Oh, stop it. Why can't you just leave it alone and let the police sort it all out?'

'I wish I could. I am trying to. It's true I was a house-sitter, and have been involved in violent crime quite a few times, and everybody says I'm nosy and thick-skinned and so forth. I didn't feel I had much choice, most of the time. But now all that's behind me, and I just want to help Drew with his business and the children, and forget the past few years. It's more difficult than I thought, though.'

'*His* children?'

'Wasn't that in the papers as well?' Thea snapped crossly. 'We were both widowed. Stephanie and Timmy lost their mother nearly two years ago. I have a grown-up daughter in the police.'

'I see. Well, fair's fair. I can tell you that the Buntings have two sons, in their thirties. One spends most of his time in Japan, and the other's a teacher in Kent somewhere. Neither one is married, or has any kids. I don't think they'll be too devastated by what's happened to their mother, from what I've gleaned. It sounded to me as if their Aunt Caroline got more of their attention than their parents did. She's got one son of her own.'

'You know Caroline, do you?'

'Never met her. Hillie used to talk about her all the time, that's all. Graham seemed to dislike her in a mild sort of way, most likely because his sons were so fond of her. But that all changed when she got poorly. He's been very devoted since then. I shall never understand that man. Anyway, Caroline's probably dead by now.'

The careless tone was chilling. *Do I ever sound like that?* Thea asked herself worriedly. She sincerely hoped not. 'Do you think Graham was just getting back from watching her die, yesterday?' It was a distressing idea. Had the poor man returned home with the ghastly news, only to walk into something even more desperate? Or was he a scheming murderer, callously arranging an alibi for himself in the form of a dying relative? Two sisters dying on the same day, or very close to it, surely had to be significant. Was there family money involved? Did somebody's son stand to inherit it all, depending on which woman died first? Suddenly, the whole business acquired an interesting new aspect. 'So Caroline has a son. Is there a husband?' she asked, without noticing that Rachel had not yet responded to her first question about Graham's movements.

The silence persisted, and when Thea looked at the woman's face, she saw something unfriendly in it. 'You really can't leave it alone, can you?' she said. 'It's like a disease with you; a morbid disease. You certainly found the right man to marry, I'll say that much. Plenty of dead bodies to take an interest in. Personally, I prefer to avoid the subject of death as far as I can. And for the record, since it's obviously so important to you, Caroline has been divorced for ages.'

It felt like an attack. Sentences that began with 'You' usually did. Nobody liked to be told about themselves, especially by an uninvited stranger. 'Yes, well, most people agree with you,' she said mildly. 'It obviously springs from fear, which is quite understandable. Death is terrifying, and there's no getting around it, however much you try to dodge it.'

Rachel picked up the Ashbee book in one hand as she drained her coffee with the other. 'I can see I've timed it badly. You'll need a few more days to get this business out of your system. Pity.'

'Well, it *does* feel a bit . . . insensitive, somehow. But I really am keen. Don't give up on me. I need a new interest.'

'You could learn to play bridge.'

'I don't think that would suit me.' She forced a laugh. 'Although I might give it a try sometime.'

'You think you're too young for it,' Rachel accused. 'A game for people trying to ward off dementia.'

'Not at all,' lied Thea. 'But for now, I'll stick with local history. Less competitive, for one thing.'

'That's true.' Rachel gave a grudging smile. 'You're no fool, I can see that. I used to come across people like you when I was working. Delving into corners, following non-existent threads, convinced they'd solved some ancient mystery. Happened all the time.'

'Why? What was your job?'

'Archivist. In the county record office. Famous ancestors, old battles, boundary disputes, lost fortunes. The stuff of many a thrilling novel, except it hardly ever came to anything. People could waste *years* pursuing a crazy idea.'

'Sounds fantastic,' sighed Thea.

'Frustrating, mostly. And then they made me redundant, so that was the end of that. Out on my ear at fifty-eight, and not a hope of getting anything else. Luckily for me, my dad came to the rescue and gave me enough cash to see me through. I'm the only child, and he's kept enough for his own needs. And I can still do some freelance researching if the mood takes me.'

Thea sighed again, feeling more than a hint of envy. Why hadn't she thought of a job like that, instead of plunging into all that house-sitting? At least it answered a question she was sure to have asked Rachel before long – what's your line of work? A woman barely sixty was seldom seen out and about in the middle of the week, unless she was visibly caring for grandchildren or aged parents.

'So . . . ?' Rachel prompted. There was a hint of propitiation in her tone. 'Have I said too much? Are you offended? I don't want to quarrel with you. Perhaps I was too quick to assume we'd been bonded by what happened yesterday. Have you read that book, *Enduring Love*? It's by Ian McEwan.'

'I have, actually. Where the man gets carried up by the balloon, and then it all changes into being about a stalker.'

'Sort of. Anyway, I'm feeling a bond born of the shared trauma. Do you see what I mean?'

'I suppose so.' Thea frowned. 'You know what it is –

when I was house-sitting, I would meet people and have chats like this, and then never see them again. Now it's different, and I haven't adjusted properly yet. I can't quite believe that I can make friends here, and nobody's going anywhere, and I might still be their friend in ten years' time. I mean – I had friends like that in Witney, but once Carl died, most of them seemed to fade away. It was probably me – I didn't give them much of a chance. The only constant friend I had was Hepzie.' She indicated the spaniel, who was slumped in her basket, the plastered leg sticking out incongruously. The dog looked up, hearing her name, and grinned briefly. 'She's had to cope with an awful lot of change for most of her life.'

'What happened to her leg?'

'A silly accident. She's been very stoical about it.'

'Okay. So you think we might manage to be friends, then? Or at least we can press on with this idea about Ashbee and all that? I really am thrilled at the prospect. It's *exactly* what I need, and I think there are plenty of others who'd feel the same. Pity about Hillie,' she finished, as if the thought had escaped from her unbidden. She looked shocked. 'She's really gone, hasn't she? We'll never see her again.'

Thea had heard similar sudden realisations before, many a time. They came to people of all ages, all kinds, often much later than was happening here. She simply nodded.

'I've lost a good friend. Everything's going to change. And Graham's . . . well, things are never going to be the same for him now, are they?' Rachel looked down at the book still in her hand. 'And here I am, idiotically behaving as if things could go on as before, because it wasn't *me* who died.' She blinked rapidly. 'What a fool you must think I am.'

'I don't at all,' said Thea, trying not to come over as a patronising know-all. 'Of course I don't.'

'Thanks. Anyway, with all this, I'm cancelling my trip to Bristol. It's a little job I was going to do for my father, but it can wait. The police are going to want to talk to both of us, aren't they? I mean, *again*. Did you get a visitation yesterday?'

'I did, yes. Do you go to Bristol often? Do you get the train?' Curiosity about details was never going to go away.

'Sally takes me as far as Gloucester and I get the train from there. She goes every Thursday to look after a grandchild. We have a standing arrangement that I can hitch a lift any time I want.'

'Useful.' It was, after all, a dull subject and Thea quickly lost interest.

'The police questioned me too. Whether we like it or not, we're at the heart of the whole business, aren't we?'

Before Thea could reply, Hepzie, in her basket, gave a yap. A second later, Thea heard footsteps at the front of the house, and then the bell ringing. 'Oh God, it must be somebody for Drew,' she said. Then, 'I wonder what he's doing. He doesn't usually stay in the office as long as this.' Had her husband tactfully left her to deal with her visitor, despite a probable desire for a drink?

Men's voices came next, one much louder than the other. 'Surely that's not Mr Bunting?' said Thea in a whisper. Rachel shook her head.

The voices carried on, evidently still on the doorstep, until Drew finally came to the kitchen door. 'It's a man called Hemingway. I think he said *Oscar* Hemingway.' He frowned. 'He wants to talk to you about his mother's dog. And his aunt: the woman you found yesterday in the freezer.'

Chapter Eight

'Good grief, that's Caroline's son,' said Rachel, rather loudly.

'The man himself,' confirmed the newcomer, edging around Drew and coming into the kitchen. 'Sorry to barge in, but I need to get some things straight.'

Thea met Drew's eyes, widening her own to convey bewilderment. The newcomer was big and wide and young. Under thirty, anyway. His felted jacket bulged with muscles around the shoulders. His hair was very dark, and longer than might have been expected. It looked to be in need of a wash and a good brushing. Thea switched her attention from one man to the other and back again, almost ludicrously conscious of the differences between them.

'We'd be happy to help if we can,' Drew said, with an affability that did not conceal his ruffled nerves.

'Good. Thanks.' The big man sighed, and seemed lost for words. His gaze fell on the spaniel, and a little frown appeared between his eyes. 'Oh dear! What happened to you, then?' he asked her.

'She had a bit of an accident,' said Thea. 'She's almost better now.'

'Accident,' repeated the man. 'There's so much danger everywhere, isn't there? Awful things happening, even to a sweet little dog like that.' He gave a sudden frown. 'And Biddy! My mother's beloved Biddy. Where *is* she? Nobody seems to have any idea.'

'A man called Ant has got her. Rachel knows where he lives. Outside the village somewhere.'

Rachel spoke up. 'The surname's Frowse. They live on the Dunholme estate. It's easy to find, but not so easy to get in, apparently. The new man's got electrified wire around the perimeter.'

'What?' Everyone looked at her as if she was joking.

'It's true, but it doesn't matter now.'

The man nodded. 'I came about the dog, partly. What's going to *happen* to her? I can't have a pet where I live. Why has some man with a stupid name got her, anyway?'

His mother was dying or dead, Thea reminded herself. And his aunt had died horribly. He could not be expected to reveal his usual self under such circumstances. 'Well, she's all right for now,' she assured him. 'What else can we do for you?' she said, echoing Drew, only in a louder and firmer tone.

'Oh, yes. Sorry. I know I shouldn't have come. But they told me you found Auntie Hillie, and now Uncle Gray's under arrest, and the whole family has fallen apart. There's nobody I can talk to about it. The police lady said I could probably get a little word with you in a few days. I decided to come now, though.'

'The police gave you my name and address?' Thea was horrified.

'Oh. No, they didn't. That was the woman next door. I phoned her and she said it was you who'd called the police and must have found Auntie. She knew who you were. Everybody knows who you are,' he finished, with a flash of reproach.

'It's a mixed blessing,' murmured Drew, who was standing at a distance from them all, clearly hoping to make an escape.

'How *is* Caroline?' asked Rachel, from her seat at the kitchen table. 'I'm Rachel Ottaway,' she added, when Hemingway simply stared at her. 'I'm a friend of Hillie and Graham.'

'Yes, I know who you are. But what do you mean – how's Caroline? She's dead, isn't she. She died on Tuesday night. Or was it Wednesday morning? In the middle of the night, anyway. Uncle Gray was with her.'

Everyone fell silent at this indignant outburst. The death of Caroline had been so overshadowed by the much more dramatic demise of her sister that the news of it had not reached Broad Campden. Though why should it, wondered Thea in confusion.

'So they died more or less at the same time,' said Drew, eventually. 'What a terrible thing for the whole family.'

Thea gave him an admiring look for the way he'd kept abreast of events that scarcely concerned him at all.

'Not so much terrible as a complete catastrophe,' Hemingway corrected him. 'There are three of us sons, as well as Uncle Gray, floundering about, with no idea what

100

to do. It's like being in a ghastly nightmare, and not being able to wake up. People say that, don't they – and it's exactly right. The police are all over us, obviously.' He put a hand to his head, covering his brow and much of his eyes. Only the lower lids were visible. Thea thought he must be weeping.

'You poor thing,' crooned Rachel. 'Sit down and have some coffee.'

You make it for him, why don't you? thought Thea rebelliously. *Whose kitchen is this, anyway?*

Drew interpreted her thought and hurried to the kettle. Judging it to contain enough warm water for at least one more mug, he clicked it on. So unselfish, thought Thea, when he must be gasping for a drink himself. She was panting to ask this Oscar a whole string of questions, whilst knowing it would be wrong to do so. He had his own very understandable desire to know the details of what she and Rachel had found in the Buntings' kitchen, in an effort to make some sense of the family catastrophe that had befallen him, and his needs obviously came first.

'You've got two brothers?' she allowed herself to enquire, even as she knew she had it wrong.

'No, no. It's just me. Cousins. I've got cousins. Tom and Edward. Tom's getting here later today. He'll be staying at our place. Ed's trying to get back from Japan. It's just me,' he said again, with a forlorn little shake of his head.

'What about your father?' Thea knew she was pushing her luck with a second question, but nobody tutted at her, which she found encouraging. Drew was pouring the coffee, and Rachel was clasping the visitor's hand in an excess of female sympathy.

'What about him?' Oscar lifted his head and gave her a bleary look.

'Well, I just thought . . .'

'He's on his third wife, and they've got two little children. What would he care?'

'Sorry,' Thea muttered.

Drew went to her side, and put a hand on her shoulder. 'I think Mr Hemingway needs to just sit quietly for a minute,' he said. 'He's had a lot to deal with.'

But Oscar surprised them all by smacking the table, slopping his coffee and raising his voice. 'No! I need *explanations*. Did Uncle Graham kill Hillie? That's what the police seem to think. They won't let me talk to him. He can't go home – not that he wants to, I imagine – and they listen to his phone calls. Then they tell me that's breaking most of the rules, and is being done with his best interests in mind.'

'Gosh!' said Thea. 'He's under arrest then, is he?'

'I don't know what they call it. They're certainly keeping him under supervision. The woman told me they couldn't legally hold him beyond the middle of today, but I got the impression she thinks she can persuade him to stay until one of his sons shows up. She does seem reasonably kind.'

'That must be Gladwin,' said Thea. 'She's a bit of a maverick at times. She'll be doing whatever she thinks best.'

'Graham *was* in a dreadful state,' said Rachel. 'Maybe they've just got him under observation for his own safety.'

'That must be it,' Thea agreed, pleased to have evidence of a thoughtful and concerned piece of police behaviour.

'You saw him, did you? Yesterday, I mean.' Oscar's

expression was pathetically hopeful, as if his need for explanation might actually be fulfilled.

Thea leapt to reply. 'Yes – he came home just as the place was full of police and ambulance people, about an hour after we found your aunt. He was completely distraught.'

'He would be. He'd just watched his sister-in-law die. My mother. He was so kind about it. I know people think he's always angry and out of control, because of the loud voice. I know he can't help it. I shout quite a lot myself.'

'Must run in the family,' said Rachel.

'Of course it doesn't. We're no blood relation, are we?' He stared at her as if wondering about her competence. Then he took a deep breath. 'But that's not him at all – he's never really angry or violent. He's a perfectly nice man. He wanted to give me a break. I'd been sitting with Mum for ages and he offered to take over. Then she died and I missed it.' He covered his eyes again.

'You couldn't have known,' said Drew, who had heard the same story a hundred times. 'People very often seem to wait until their family are out of the room, for some reason. They just slip away.'

'But that might mean that the family keep them hanging on. When I left her, she must have felt there was nothing to keep her. I went off and left her to die.'

'But your uncle was with her. She wasn't alone.' Drew was sliding into full undertaker mode, which Thea suspected might not be quite what was needed.

'And now he's accused of murder,' said Oscar with bitter force. 'The last person in the world to do such a thing.'

A dreadful thought struck Thea. Graham Bunting had

been with Caroline when she died. Had he put a hand over her nose and mouth, speeding her demise? Had he somehow murdered *both* sisters? Would the police conceive an identical suspicion? It seemed inevitable that they would. And perhaps it was true. Nothing else, on the face of it, made any sort of sense.

'So your aunt must have died at about the same time as your mother,' said Rachel, repeating Drew's earlier remark as if only now grasping the full significance. 'As far as we can tell.'

Oscar shook his head. 'It's a nightmare,' he said again. 'How could such a thing happen? We're just an ordinary family. No vendettas or fortunes to inherit. No reason for anybody to get themselves murdered. What am I going to tell Tom?' This suddenly acquired prime importance. 'He's going to blame me. He always did pick on me, when we were young. He's going to want everything explained, and he'll go on at me until he's satisfied.'

'You've come to us to help you explain things to your cousin?' Thea was incredulous. 'Why does it have to be *you*? Leave all that to the police. They'll have to talk to him, anyway.'

'He won't listen. Not if he thinks they're going to charge his father with killing his mother. He'll go wild, and I'll have to pick up the pieces.' He groaned. 'I wish I could just stay here and not see him at all.'

Another thought hit Thea: the Buntings' house was empty. Whilst the kitchen might be the scene of a crime, there need not be any veto on using the other rooms. Oscar could hide there from his cousin. Except . . . the cousin had a prior claim on it. The house was probably his childhood home. He'd very likely have a key to it and know where everything was kept. She echoed Oscar's groan. 'It's all a horrible mess, isn't it,' she said. 'But I still don't see why you should worry about Tom. He's not your problem.' Then she realised something. 'Does *he* shout all the time, like his father?'

'Not so bad, but yes, he's quite loud. He's the oldest of us, and can be quite nasty. We used to fight. I might be big, but I could never defend myself from him.'

Just an ordinary family, then, thought Thea ruefully. In her own childhood home there had been squabbles and subtle torments inflicted by the siblings on each other, which had left minor scars ever since, but nothing like the anxiety that she could see in Oscar Hemingway.

Rachel patted his hand reassuringly. 'It'll be all right,' she said fatuously.

'It won't,' said Oscar, with a flash of anger. 'How can it ever be all right?' He squinted at her, as if seeing her for the first time. 'Why are you here, anyway? You're just one of the bridge people, aren't you?'

The woman recoiled as if burnt. 'I told you. I'm a friend of your aunt and uncle. You said just now you knew who I was. I visited them every week, for bridge and lunch, and we all knew each other for years. Hillie and I went on walks together. We sometimes went for a swim, as well.'

'I'm sorry. Take no notice of me. I know you're the person who found my aunt.' He suddenly switched topics. 'Have you got a husband?'

Thea leant forward in an instinctive eagerness to learn more.

'I have not. What does that have to do with it?'

'Just wondered.' He kept his eyes on her. 'It sounds to me as if you were pushing between Auntie Hillie and her husband. Why couldn't she go for walks and swims with *him*, not you?'

Good question, Thea applauded silently. Then it came to her that Oscar might have strong views about marriage, either for or against, given whatever his own experience might be. He might have instantly seen Rachel as a home-wrecker, a seductress leading his aunt into wickedly perverse ways. Anything was possible, although Thea had come to the conclusion that Rachel Ottaway was too open and straight-talking to be guilty of anything bad. *I seem to be defending everybody*, she realised. None of the people involved were conceivably capable of murder, in her view.

'Don't be ridiculous,' Rachel responded. 'They're not joined at the hip. Hillie didn't play bridge with us, and Graham didn't come for walks. There's nothing remotely unusual or suspicious about that.' She spoke hotly, defensively, leaving a heavy silence on the air when she stopped. Then she added, '*Weren't* joined at the hip, I mean.' The use of the past tense generally took a while to become automatic, in Thea's experience.

'All right,' Oscar said flatly. 'And you still haven't told me exactly how you found my aunt. What were you both doing there in the first place?'

'We'd been there on Tuesday, which was the first time Rachel and I met,' Thea began. 'We'd come up with an idea for a new group, and I guess we both went back next day to carry on with planning it.'

'You guess?'

'Well, I don't think we actually told each other that's why we were there. Did we?' she appealed to Rachel.

'I can't remember. Did I tell you Graham phoned me and I went round to say there were no hard feelings?'

'Oh, yes. You did.' She sucked her lower lip for a moment, thinking that with hindsight, this seemed a slightly strange thing for Rachel to be doing. 'I'm not sure you want every detail, do you?' she asked Oscar. 'Why would you? Hilary was in the freezer, naked, with ice on her already.' She had begun the sentence confidently, taking a run at it, but before it was halfway uttered, she had begun to shake. Her insides fluttered. Her voice faltered. 'I don't think I need to say more than that, do I? It was a huge shock, finding her like that.'

'Naked?'

'Yes.'

'Were there any wounds on her? I mean, had she been attacked in some way first, and then the body disposed of in a panic?'

'I don't think so. We didn't look very closely. Did we?' Again she appealed to Rachel, who mutely shook her head.

'They were both very shocked,' Drew interrupted, with a faint tone of reproach. 'Traumatised, in fact.'

'He made me drink hot sweet tea,' said Thea with a watery smile. 'It works, you know.'

Rachel made a sound that suggested impatience, if not outright contempt. Thea looked at her. 'What did *you* do?' she asked, wondering whether she'd been remiss in not giving the woman more thought at the time. She couldn't even remember how they'd parted, once the police had told them they could go.

'Cycled home and put the telly on.'

'Cycled?'

'Of course. That's the way I always travel.'

'Haven't you got a car?'

'Nope. Lost my licence a while ago, and still have a year or two to run before I can have it back.'

'Oh dear. So where's the bike now? You walked down the lane, didn't you? I assumed you'd left a car by the church.'

'As it happens, something's gone wrong with the gears this morning, so I'm not using it until it's fixed. I got the bus to Campden and walked from there.'

That explained the necessity of hitching a ride with Sally Taylor when she needed to get to a station, Thea concluded, with a little twitch of satisfaction.

Somehow it seemed as if a line had been drawn under the conversation. Oscar pulled himself to his feet, gave an unfocused smile to the room in general, and mumbled that he ought to be going. He extracted a business card from a wallet and put it on the table. 'You might want to get hold of me,' he said vaguely. Drew seized his chance and ushered him briskly to the door, telling him he hoped things would quickly be resolved, and he was really sorry for the double loss. Thea was left with Rachel and the disappointed spaniel, who had received rather less in the way of blandishments than she would normally expect.

'Well, I suppose I should go as well. You must have things to do,' said Rachel, when the men had gone.

'I suppose I have, although I can't think what they are. It's all turned upside down, isn't it?'

'We're both on the outside, when it comes to it, aren't we? You don't know any of these people at all, and I'm just a friend – one of many.'

Something snagged in Thea's head. 'Really? I'd rather gathered that the Buntings were a bit . . . well, *unpopular*, in the village.' Hadn't that been the gist of Mr Shipley's original remarks to Drew, far back on Tuesday morning?

'Graham, maybe, but everybody liked Hillie. You saw for yourself how friendly and open she was. She was like that with everybody, always willing to stop for a chat, or join in any activity. And Graham was all right when you got to know him. I think "unpopular" is far too harsh. The Taylors would say just the same thing. They always looked forward to the bridge with Graham.'

Thea had forgotten the Taylors. The couple who had been there on Tuesday, whose names she had also forgotten, might well find themselves on the list of witnesses to be questioned by the police. They had, after all, been granted privileged insight into the Buntings' marriage. 'Have you seen them?' she asked. 'Since . . . you know. You and Sally are close friends, aren't you?'

'Oh, no, not really. I don't socialise with them very much, except for the bridge sessions. I'd say I was closer to Hilary than I am to Sally. But women with husbands don't make very reliable friends, especially at my age.'

Thea silently thanked her stars that Drew wasn't in the room to hear that. It was bad enough having to process it for herself. 'But you all live in Blockley, right?'

Rachel didn't answer, but picked up the Ashbee book and her shoulder bag and headed for the hallway. Even from the back, Thea could tell that she had transgressed once again. *Too many questions*, she realised with a sigh. 'Sorry,' she said. 'I'll see you soon, I expect.'

'Are you sure you want to?'

'Why? Don't you?'

'I don't know. Give me a few days. I'll phone you. What's your number?'

Thea could still remember a time when the answer would be, 'It's in the book,' in the knowledge that she'd be readily found under 'Slocombe'. Now it seemed a lot more complicated. 'Well?' Rachel prompted.

'You mean the landline? You've got my mobile number from Tuesday, surely? When we were looking for the dog. We all got each other's, you, me and Hilary.'

'Of course the landline. I only use the mobile when I have to, and I guess you're the same.' She glanced around the kitchen where no smartphone or iPad was visible.

'Okay.' Thea recited the number, which Rachel apparently committed to memory.

They parted on the doorstep, where trees were still thrashing about in the wind. They had to shout their final farewells.

Drew had disappeared when Thea went back into the house. It was half past eleven, and she felt drained of all energy.

Chapter Nine

Despite the continuing gales, Thea was driven outside by an incurable restlessness. 'Come on, Heps. Let's see what it's like in the fields.' She recalled the spaniel's apparent pleasure in having her ears blown inside out and her feathering ruffled by the wind that morning in the garden.

They set out like intrepid explorers, Thea wearing a woolly hat pulled down firmly over her ears. As she reached the lane, she noticed a light in Mr Shipley's house, opposite hers, was flickering. 'There'll be power cuts next, I suppose,' she muttered. So far, since coming to Broad Campden, there had been no electricity failures. It was an event she dreaded more than was rational. She worried about the contents of the freezer, and the effect on the computer.

Once she and the halting dog reached their usual field, she led the way in a diagonal trajectory towards the hedge at the upper end. The ground rose gently, and the going was easy. Surrounded by trees, it was noisy, but the effects of the wind were lessened. Thea stood still, and then turned in a circle, enjoying the wild effects on the vegetation. One or two evergreens were being dramatically shaken back and forth, as the one in the next-door garden was.

The walk was doing very little to clear her mind, but she found it invigorating. She kept going in the same direction, and was perhaps twenty yards from the hedge when there was a strange creaking sound. Looking up, she saw that a substantial branch from an ash tree that had perhaps been unwell for some time was parting company with its central trunk. It looked to be a gradual process, impeded by a pair of electric cables that ran along the edge of the field. There were three poles in a row supporting the wires, and the trees had mostly been kept trimmed back out of reach. Except for the ash tree, and one or two others, which rose high above the lines. The broken branch was resting firmly on them, and as Thea watched, it finally broke away, and took one strand of cable with it. The effect was horrifying. Torn away from a nearby pole, the snaking black line came flying down, its end landing about a yard from Hepzie, who was idly sniffing the ground, oblivious to the danger.

Thea screamed and rushed for the dog. Grabbing her up, she scooted backwards, falling over a tussock and landing on her back, the dog still in her arms. Sparks were flashing, arcing – whatever they did – over an area of grass that was already making a very strange smell. Hot and unnatural, it conjured notions of the fires of hell. Then it all stopped, as presumably some kind of fail-safe mechanism kicked in.

Thea got to her feet, feeling shaken and rather foolish. How much danger had she and the dog been in, really? The cable did look dreadfully perilous, and there were blackened spots where the grass had been electrocuted.

Such a random, unpredictable thing to happen! It made her shudder to contemplate the 'what ifs'. Her dog fried to a crisp by all those volts, for a start. And now, of course, the power would be off for as long as it took for the damage to be repaired. She ought to report it right away. She could take the workmen to the exact spot, if required.

Carrying Hepzie, she hurried home. 'Drew!' she called. 'I assume the power's off?' She flicked the hallway light switch to check, and her assumption was confirmed. 'I saw the line come down. It almost hit me and Heps.'

Drew did not respond. He did not emerge from his office or call back that he had heard her. She wondered whether a family had unexpectedly materialised and he was arranging a funeral with them. In that case, her yelling through the house would not be seen as appropriate. Slightly better would be if he was on the phone. With belated caution, she went to the office door and listened.

Silence. She opened it and found it empty. 'Drew?' she shouted, louder than ever. 'Where are you?' He was not in the house. His absence was a palpable thing, just as the Buntings' had been the previous day. The echoes were unsettling. 'For heaven's sake, I was only gone twenty minutes,' she muttered. How could she lose a husband in that time?

She went into the kitchen, which had more daylight than most of the rooms. On a January day there was very little light anywhere indoors, and the power cut was already irritating. She couldn't make coffee or listen to the radio. The heating would fail to come on at three as programmed, and there was only a sliver of battery life left in her phone. And she didn't dare open the freezer, for a number of reasons.

On the somewhat slovenly table, where debris from breakfast had not yet been removed, there was a sheet of paper on which a note had been written: 'Summoned by school. Stephanie damaged. Doesn't sound too desperate. I'll phone you.'

'For heaven's sake!' said Thea again, quite loudly. The spaniel took it personally, and hopped worriedly into her basket. 'Not you, Heps. Not anybody, really. Just life. Fate – whatever it is that's obviously determined to get us, one way or another.'

The note had diverted her from her intention to call the electricity people. With every passing minute it was more likely that one of the neighbours would already have done it, although with several of the houses only used for weekends that could not be relied on. So she rummaged for a recent bill and called the number it gave for such situations. It was answered immediately by a robot, which told her they were aware of an outage and it was estimated that power would be restored by 5 p.m. that day.

'That was quick!' Thea told the machine in astonishment. It could not be more than twenty-five minutes since the line had come down, and was probably a lot less. Perhaps they could tell via some electronic messaging system exactly where the damage was and what needed to be done to rectify it. That seemed unlikely, but what did she know? In any case, the prospect of a cold, dark house with no hot drinks for the rest of the afternoon was very unappealing. Combined with the suspense of not knowing what had happened to

Stephanie, she was left feeling jangled and apprehensive.

Drew had obviously taken the car, leaving the hearse and the elderly van that he and Andrew used for removing bodies from homes, hospitals and private houses. Thea was not authorised to drive either vehicle. Every time she thought of doing so she was reminded of the daughter of the undertaker family in *Six Feet Under* who regularly drove herself to college in a hearse.

Where did she want to go, anyway? Who could she run to for a warm welcome and some hot soup? She had a mother, daughter and two sisters, all living many miles away and therefore of no use in a crisis. The lack of any local friends suddenly struck her as a very serious omission. What had she been thinking, to let it come to this? She knew dozens of people in the area, encountered during her many house-sitting commissions, but none could fully qualify as a friend. There had been friction, suspicion and outright hostility in her dealings with some of them. Others had painful associations that Thea could not avoid stirring up. Rachel Ottaway was liable to be added to their number, after the previous day's events, when she stopped to think about the associations there were with Thea Slocombe. A woman who had shown such promise as a potential friend was sure to keep her distance, once she had realised that every time she saw Thea, she would also see the frozen face of Hilary Bunting.

And Hilary herself might well have turned into another local pal, given the chance. It felt as if some malicious hand was plucking every prospect of company away, the moment it became possible.

She drifted restlessly from room to room, waiting for Drew's promised call with news of the damaged Stephanie, and wondering whether she'd overlooked some crucial consequence of the power cut. From the living-room window she saw a large truck crawl by, almost too wide for the little lane. It was festooned with gadgetry and appeared to contain at least four men. They would simply drive it into the field through the gap at the end of the track, over the bumps and ruts to the far side. There was something primitive about the image – a mammoth saviour appearing like magic to straighten out the woes of the village. She felt small and helpless and grateful. The system was working, and that always gave rise to a flood of relief. They would perform their mysterious tasks out there in the elements, and she wasn't even slightly tempted to go out and watch them.

There was a lurking irony to the timing of the loss of power. If it had happened thirty-six hours earlier, Hilary Bunting might still be alive. Except, that *surely* she was dead before being dumped in the freezer? Otherwise, wouldn't she have fought and pushed and kicked at the lid until achieving an escape? Reluctantly, Thea let her thoughts focus on the dreadful implications. That poor woman! And that puzzling husband, so seemingly aggressive, and yet so broken and wretched. The mystery of it all would snag anyone's attention, not just nosy people like Thea. The village couldn't fail to be buzzing with it, in the pub and any other gathering place. Except there *were* no other gathering places. The church held services on a rota basis, the Quaker Meeting House was open every Sunday for a handful of people who sat in silence and probably refrained from gossiping about a local murder.

It wasn't such a daft place to hide a body, on the face of it. The defrosting contents on the worktops had been the only clue that something was amiss, and that did seem like a foolish oversight. But then, there was little reason to expect two women to go barging into the kitchen uninvited, and find the evidence as they did. Perhaps Graham Bunting – if it was him – had every intention of returning quickly, and tidying all the soggy peas and ready meals away. Possibly – gruesome thought – popping them back on top of his frozen wife.

And if it *wasn't* Graham, then who could it possibly have been? Automatically, Thea ran through everyone she'd encountered in the past two days: the Taylors, Oscar Hemingway, Rachel Ottaway, Antares Frowse – it was a short list. There were also the two Bunting sons, both apparently far away at the time of their mother's death, and an assortment of neighbours. In fact, the neighbours might well find themselves under suspicion, if only because there had already been a degree of animosity towards the Buntings, if Mr Shipley had been correctly understood. Had somebody gone to remonstrate with Hilary, while Graham was out, and managed somehow to kill her? Things *did* occasionally get out of control, with violent swings of household objects, or reckless pushes that led to cracked heads on hearthstones. A respectable Cotswold worthy might be so appalled by what he'd done that he hurriedly stuffed the result of his action into the only place large enough to conceal a body. It was a wild scenario, but not completely impossible to believe.

Still standing by the window, in a confused idea of finding some sort of social contact out there, she was doubly rewarded when a male figure appeared at the gate and came purposefully up the path. Rewarded, that is, by the materialisation of one of the very village worthies she had just been mentally slandering.

She met him at the front door. 'Mr Shipley!' she greeted with grimly excessive enthusiasm. 'What awful weather!'

'The power's off,' he said, as if it were very much her fault. 'I only got back from London an hour ago, and now everything's in darkness. My lights were flickering at first, and then the whole thing went off. I came to see if it was just me, or a general power cut.'

'It's not just you. I was out there and saw it happen. A cable was torn down by a falling branch. It almost killed me and my dog.'

'Have you contacted the helpline or whatever they call it?'

'I tried, but just got a recording that said they're dealing with it. I saw a team of men in a big truck go past two minutes ago. I hope it's not too boggy for them.'

'They'll send a helicopter if so,' he said, as if party to inside knowledge.

'Will they? With loose cables everywhere, and this awful wind?'

'I don't honestly know. Did they say how long it would be off?'

'They estimate it will be back by five o'clock this afternoon. That's not so bad, really, is it? Although, if your lights were flickering, that might mean you've got a separate problem, maybe. But more likely it was because of the branch resting on the cable – or something.' She heard herself prattling and stopped.

The man gave an exasperated roll of his eyes, and then turned his back on her, scanning the few properties he could see. 'Looks as if it's most of the village. All of it, possibly. I could try the pub, maybe.'

'They'll have sandwiches and lamps, I expect.' Thea felt wistful at the thought of lunch in the friendly Bakers Arms, which had made such a point of welcoming her dog when she had visited a few weeks before. A change of ownership had brought a big improvement in that respect. 'It's not really *dark*, though, is it? It's the middle of the day still.'

The man was dithering, although he would never have accepted the term as applicable to himself. Indecision made him frown and pout. Then he gave Thea a big surprise. 'I've got some smoked salmon. Salad. Beer. Bread. Would you care to come over and share it with me?'

'Oh! That does sound tempting. Are you sure?'

He nodded. 'Of course. What are neighbours for?' he added fatuously.

She abandoned every worrying domestic responsibility and followed him across the lane, in through a freshly painted wooden gate, up a weed-free path, and through a doorway she had never entered before. Mr Shipley had made himself known to her and Drew months before they finally moved in, but his approach had been more suspicious than neighbourly. His house was constructed of the ubiquitous honey-coloured stone, with a tiled roof. Dormer windows, a generous porch and small but perfect garden all fitted with Thea's impression of the man. When he produced a key and unlocked the door, having remained literally in sight of the house for the whole of his five-minute absence, this further confirmed her notion of a fussy, anxious, rather brainless individual.

Indoors was initially no different. The hallway was papered with a William Morris design and carpeted with something oriental. A living room, barely glimpsed, revealed a pair of armchairs and a long-pile rug in front of an open fireplace. Even in the gloom of a cloudy January day it shone. A mirror sparkled over the fireplace and there was gilding on a good-sized rococo coffee table.

However, in the kitchen, to which she was being led, there was suddenly another aspect of Shipley's character. The room was at least twice as big as the equivalent one in the Slocombe house, and had a high ceiling. A wall must have been knocked down at some point to achieve such a size. French windows at one end opened onto a garden that was mostly lawn. There was no Aga or Rayburn – an omission that was close to subversive in the Cotswolds. Worktops flanked the sink on each side, but the majority of the wall space was occupied by open shelves. On these shelves stood an extensive and motley collection of glass, which looked antique to Thea's amateurish gaze. Glass decanters, vases, drinking vessels, jugs, tankards, and more. Many were engraved, some had gold decoration. Every one looked impossibly fragile. 'Oh!' she gasped.

'They look better when the lights are on,' he said, pointing to an array of spotlights set in the ceiling.

'They look absolutely gorgeous,' she said. 'You're a collector, then?'

'For my sins,' he admitted. 'I inherited four or five pieces from my mother, and somehow they demanded company. I can't really explain it.'

Thea had met one or two other barely sane collectors during her time in the Cotswolds. A woman in Snowshill was especially memorable. Compared to her, Mr Shipley was perfectly normal, almost to the point of modesty.

'Sit down,' he invited, pulling out a wooden chair. The table, she noticed, was of modern geometric design, in a pale wood she suspected was oak. The chairs matched, in a subtle harmony with the style of the table. They looked hopelessly expensive.

'Thanks.' She tried to swallow back the many questions that persistently rose to the surface. 'How long were you in London?' she couldn't resist asking. Surely an innocuous enough question?

'Two days. I had some meetings. I'm on a few committees and so forth,' he said vaguely.

'And you haven't heard what happened here, have you?' It had been obvious from the first moment that he was in blissful ignorance of the Bunting calamity. Unless, of course, he was pretending, she told herself. After all, he could hardly claim to feel any affection for the Buntings after his talk with Drew on Tuesday.

He cocked his head at her, pausing halfway between the table and the fridge. 'Happened?'

'Oh dear. I'm not sure quite how to tell you.' She was indeed finding it difficult. Describing the events would

121

bring them back in more vivid detail than she was prepared for. Words could be so painfully powerful, as she had come to discover. The mere mention of a name could bring tears. But she took a brave run at it. 'Mrs Bunting is dead. The police seem to think it must have been her husband who killed her.'

'Somebody killed her?'

'So it seems. She was naked in their freezer.' There – she had said it. Those words were growing familiar, and therefore easier to articulate. She'd said them to Oscar Hemingway, and now they came almost trippingly to her tongue.

'How did they find her? The police, I mean.'

'Ah – well, that was me. And Rachel Ottaway. Do you know her?'

He shook his head, as much in disbelief at the news as in answer to her question, from the look of him. 'Hilary Bunting can't be *dead*. Not like that. Naked, you say? Had she been . . . *attacked*?' It was impossible to mistake his meaning.

It was the first time such a thought had occurred. Hilary's nakedness had displayed nothing remotely sexual to Thea's eye. But men almost invariably seemed to associate the word 'naked' with sex, to the point of tedium. This one was evidently no exception.

'She might have been, I suppose. I really have no idea.' She spoke coolly, hoping to convey reproach. 'I hardly think her husband would rape her before killing her, though.'

'Graham Bunting wouldn't kill anyone,' said Mr Shipley with utter certainty.

'How do you know? Especially after what you said to Drew on Tuesday morning. He says you were talking as if the couple had violent fights all the time, and the village was trying to decide what to do about it. I'm surprised that you're surprised, actually, given all that.'

'Oh.' He seemed nonplussed. 'I'd forgotten about that. I suppose the police will get to hear about it, and that'll make it look much worse for Graham.'

Thea tried to assess the extent to which the man was shocked. He had asked reasonable questions, gone directly to the core of the matter, and was still inattentively collecting items for a cold lunch. But he was pale, and his hands looked unsteady. 'You're *not* all that surprised, are you?' she accused him.

He ignored the question. 'Was Graham in the house at the time? Were there witnesses? How could she possibly be in the *freezer*?' He placed a plate covered with tinfoil in the middle of the table. 'Salmon,' he muttered.

'Lovely,' said Thea numbly.

'Graham Bunting would never do that. He's boorish and antisocial, I admit, and he treated his wretched wife very badly – but this is much too *gothic* for him. It's just impossible to imagine.'

'You sound as if you know him quite well. That wasn't the impression you gave Drew on Tuesday. If you're so well acquainted, why didn't you go and remonstrate about all the shouting, instead of trying to get Drew to do it?'

'Believe me, I did my best. He told me to get stuffed, or words to that effect.'

'Well, I blame you,' she said flatly.

123

'What?' His colour turned from white to grey. '*What* did you say?'

'Oh, I don't mean you killed her. But you got me involved, to the point where I actually found her dead body. It was horrible. The most horrible thing that's ever happened to me, just about. I'm going to have nightmares about it for the rest of my life.'

She had been looking down at the table as she spoke. Now, when she looked up, she saw the man flourishing a long kitchen knife. She yelped, before realising that he was about to use it to slice cucumber and tomatoes. 'Sorry,' she mumbled. 'I'm a bit jumpy.'

'You've had a seriously traumatic experience,' he said. 'Although not for the first time, as I understand it.'

Here we go, she thought. 'Never anything like this,' she said, not quite truthfully. The Snowshill experience, for one, had been very nearly as bad.

'Have the police interviewed you?'

'Of course. I found the body.' She repeated this last with some force.

'All right. Did you mention me?'

'I can't remember. Probably not. No – I don't think I did. They weren't interested in why I went there on Tuesday.'

'Was it Tuesday you found her?' He had his back to her as he spoke, rooting once again in the dark fridge. The absence of electrical power gave everything an air of unreality. Fridge lights went on when you opened the door. Things pinged and hummed. Radios chuntered in the background. Little red lights glowed in corners. None of that was happening in this mysterious house.

'Yesterday morning. Don't ask me to explain it all. The fact is, I went because you suggested it to Drew. That's why I said it was your fault. It was. I'd never even *heard* of the Buntings before that.'

'It was a spur of the moment impulse, which came to me in the night. I was going off to London that day, and wanted to get everything straight first. Mrs Thackery and Mrs Yacop both kept insisting that something had to be done, and I suddenly had the idea that your husband might be the ideal person to get involved. He's obviously very good with people. We wanted to bring you in, so to speak. I know there's not a great deal of community activity here – we tend to go to Chipping Campden for that sort of thing – but we're not completely antisocial. There's the village hall committee, and a few other things like that.'

'And bridge,' Thea murmured.

'Pardon?'

'Surely you know about that? The Buntings – well, Graham, anyway – plays bridge. A couple called Taylor, and Rachel Ottaway come every Tuesday to play.'

'Oh, yes. I did know that.' He shook his head as if despairing of his own forgetfulness, then put an untouched loaf of brown bread in front of her, followed by butter, plates, a small salad and a fork. 'Help yourself,' he invited.

'You're well supplied,' she remarked. 'Considering you've been away.'

'Long habit,' he said. 'I wasn't away for long this time, but I like to have the essentials here for when I get back. There's nothing worse than arriving hungry and tired, and having to go out to the shops for something to eat.'

The salmon was not in the usual thin slices, but much thicker chunks. The implication that it was on at least its third day did not much concern Thea, but it made her wonder about the trip to London. For a man so dedicated to advance planning, it struck her as incongruous that he would leave something so highly perishable in his fridge, even for forty-eight hours. 'Was this a whole fish?' she asked.

'Sorry? How do you mean?'

She laughed. 'That was a daft question, wasn't it? I meant, have you already eaten the rest of it?'

He obviously found this both impertinent and irrelevant. 'As it happens, I did buy a whole salmon on Saturday, for a dinner party I gave that evening. We managed about two-thirds of it, and yes – this is what's left. Does that worry you? I assure you it isn't the least bit spoilt. As you saw, I kept it well covered and chilled.'

'I'm not at all worried,' she said, and reached for a large piece of the fish to prove it. 'Even if that makes it five days old.'

'What would you like to drink? I've got bottled ale – Rev. James or Bass, I think. And a can or two of Coke somewhere. I would suggest opening a bottle of wine, but . . .'

'No, no,' she said quickly. 'Beer would be perfect. Thank you. Bass for preference.'

'Excellent. I like a woman who knows her own mind.'

The way this was said, with a kind of archness, brought a sudden revelation that Mr Shipley really didn't like women very much at all. The dinner party acquired a new character at the same time – a group of men, relaxed over their poached salmon, swapping anecdotes and gossiping about acquaintances. She scrutinised him slowly – did that image fit with the man in front of her? His fussiness suggested that he seldom really relaxed. His concern for peace and quiet, and the very fact that he lived in the Cotswolds made him a sympathetic character. But he went to London perhaps more frequently than she and Drew realised, and she found herself entertaining silly speculations about clubs and bars and other men's beds, which she quickly stopped. *Stick to the matter in hand*, she told herself.

The man was opening bottles, casually taking two glass tankards down from one of the shelves and filling them with beer. 'You really *use* them?' said Thea.

'Sorry?'

'All those glasses and jugs and vases. You actually use them, do you?'

'Of course. They were made to be used. Not one of them was ever intended to be merely ornamental.'

'Nice,' she said, with complete sincerity. 'I like that.'

At last they were both seated at the table, eating and drinking in a friendly silence. Thea found herself watching the scene as if from a point outside herself. A man approaching sixty, providing a highly civilised impromptu lunch to a neighbour fifteen years his junior, discussing a very recent and very local murder with a notable lack of passion. It was both bizarre and strangely normal. Only when Thea had implied that Mr Shipley was to blame had the atmosphere grown prickly, and that was hardly to be wondered at. Without even thinking about it, she had adopted a matching tone to his, forgetting her horror and confusion of the previous day in this oasis of good-mannered calm.

'They've had nearly an hour to fix the broken cable,' she said. 'I wonder how long it can take?'

'That depends, I suppose, on whether they brought the right equipment and were able to get into the field. Those cables are likely to be quite heavy and cumbersome. They wouldn't want to leave it half-finished, and not fully secured. From past experience, I wouldn't be surprised if it's tomorrow before we're on again.'

'Help! Don't say that. I've only got a couple of candles and the battery in the torch is almost dead.' Then she remembered. 'Oh, and Drew's daughter has had some sort of accident at school. She'll want to be warm and coddled when she gets home.'

'Accident?' He looked at her as if this must be an invention. 'Really? You haven't seemed worried about it.'

'Drew can cope with whatever it is. You know how schools overreact these days. It's probably just a grazed knee.'

'But you don't know?' He scanned her body, rather as Rachel had scanned the kitchen table that morning. It took Thea a while to understand that he was looking for a phone.

'Oh, Lord! I left the mobile in my bag, didn't I? He might be trying it if I don't answer the house phone.' She chewed her lip. 'God, I hate phones. Don't you? I'd be so much happier if they'd never been invented.'

He smiled. 'I do. Every time I see one, I want to snatch it away and stamp on it. The mobile variety, I mean.'

'But I really should go. I'm hopelessly unprepared for the blackout.'

'You should probably go and get a new torch battery for a start,' he agreed. 'And some pies or something for those children. You do have an open fire, don't you?'

'A wood-burning stove. It has a flat top, so I could boil potatoes or rice, if necessary. There aren't many logs, though. We used most of them over Christmas. We generally keep the stove for special occasions.' She took a final mouthful of salad. 'I will have to go,' she said again.

'You haven't lived in the countryside before, by the sound of it.' He had got up as she did, in an old-fashioned protocol, and was waiting for her to make the next move.

She bristled. 'I lived in Witney all my married life. On the outskirts, actually. It was every bit as rural as this is here. But we almost never had power cuts,' she admitted. 'And my first husband was very efficient at keeping us well stocked.' It still felt slightly treacherous to refer to Carl in this way. It seemed to diminish him, and consign him firmly to the past.

Mr Shipley gave a little shrug, as if this was none of his business. Which it wasn't, thought Thea. She had no intention of disclosing her personal history to him.

'Take an apple for dessert,' he offered. 'There are some nice Galas in the bowl.'

'Better not, thanks.' She looked at her watch. 'Nearly two! I've only got an hour and a bit before the school bus gets here. Even if Drew brings Steph back, Timmy's going to be on the bus. I'd better take your advice and go shopping.' She sighed inwardly. The complete lack of any retail outlet whatsoever in the village always meant a trip by car to Chipping Campden or further afield. In Witney she could walk to any number of shops in the long and busy main street.

Only then, with a lurch of frustration, did she realise she could only go out if Drew had come back with the car. 'Oh God!' she wailed. 'This is a ridiculous situation. I'll just go home and wait for something to happen. We can muddle through with what we've got.'

'You don't actually know for sure what happened to the little girl, do you? It could be something serious.' He gave her a look that said he doubted her performance as a mother.

'It didn't sound very serious from the note he left me – but he is going to be very upset when I don't answer the phone. He'll think something's happened to me, as well as Stephanie. Oh Lord, I don't know *what* he'll think. How long have I been here, anyway?'

'A little over an hour, I think.'

'We wouldn't have heard if he'd come back, would we? And he'd never guess where I was.' She looked him full in the face, unable to credit her own weakness. She had let herself become distracted by curiosity about this man, with his beautiful glass and intriguing character. She had neglected her family in the distraction of talking to him, and keeping up appearances as a worthy resident of his precious village.

'You were thinking about the power cut,' he said, with a welcome infusion of tolerance. 'That drove everything else out of your head.'

130

It was true, or very nearly. 'Thank you,' she said. 'Thanks for rescuing me and feeding me, and everything. Sorry to dash away, but you can see how it is.'

'Your worst sin was leaving the phone behind,' he smiled.

'I know. And I feel awful about it. Poor Drew! He's going to be so worried. And he's busy. There are funerals . . . Oh God. I'm sorry – I really shouldn't have come.'

'All my fault, again, then,' he said, with a look that was not entirely benign.

Chapter Ten

She was back in the house barely three minutes before Drew drove up with Stephanie beside him. He and Thea looked at each other, rendered speechless with all the questions and information and relief and anger that filled their breasts. They scrambled into the house, where Drew tried to switch on the hall light.

'There's a power cut,' said Thea. 'It might last until tomorrow.'

'You didn't answer the phone. I called the landline and your mobile. Where were you?'

'Over the road. Mr Shipley gave me lunch.'

'And you didn't take your phone?' They had moved into the kitchen, where the messy table still presented a silent reproach.

'I forgot. The power cut sent everything out of my head.'

'You forgot about me and Stephanie? How is that possible?'

'I don't know. Maybe I'm still in shock from yesterday.' She rubbed her head. 'That might explain it.'

'I was at the *hospital*,' Stephanie interrupted. 'They had to *stitch* me.' She waved a thickly bandaged hand in demonstration.

'Really? Did it hurt?'

The child shook her head. 'It was quite nice, really,' she said. 'The doctor made lots of jokes.'

'So where was the damage and how did it happen?'

It was deceptively easy to sit with her arm around the little girl listening to the jumbled account of her accident. It had happened in the classroom, when a jam jar fell off a table and broke. Ever helpful, Stephanie had rushed to pick it up, and sliced an impressive gash across her palm. Inside the jam jar there had been three big snails, collected by a certain Simeon FitzJames, who belied his superior name by spending all his time crawling around on the family acres gathering molluscs and insects. 'Mrs Leather *told* him to stop bringing them to school,' said Stephanie. 'But they were very beautiful snails. I wonder what happened to them,' she finished woefully.

Drew made a tutting noise and went to phone Andrew, who would be waiting for instructions for the following day.

'What about Timmy?' asked Stephanie.

'What about him?' said Thea. 'He'll come on the bus as usual, won't he?' She looked at the kitchen clock, which announced the time as ten past three.

'He'll wonder where I am, and what happened to me. He'll think everybody's forgotten about him.'

Which they sort of had. 'We'll go and meet the bus in a minute, and tell him the whole story. I'm sure one of the teachers will have explained it all to him.'

Stephanie looked dubious. 'Why is it so *dark*?' she wondered next.

'The electricity has gone off. I had rather an adventure myself, this morning. So did Hepzie.' She realised that Drew knew nothing of the flailing cable and the narrow escape of his wife and her dog. Maybe he would be more forgiving when he heard it. The day had been full of drama, with danger narrowly averted, and all sorts of questions hanging unresolved over their heads. Her own transgressions were already beginning to pale into mere oversights, born of a crowded day and a host of interruptions.

'When will it go on again?'

'Nobody knows. Possibly by teatime, but it could go on all night. The men have got quite a big job to do, to get it all fixed.'

The child looked around, as if in search of these men. 'Where are they?' she asked.

'Out in the fields, where the electric wires are. The ones that run from pole to pole – you know. The wind blew part of a tree down onto a wire, and it broke.'

'How do you know that?'

'I was there. I saw it happen. Listen, Steph – you must *never* touch one of those wires if you find one on the ground. They can kill you if you do.'

'Okay,' said Stephanie carelessly. The world was impossibly full of things that could kill her or frighten her or offend her, or invade her space or make her feel uncomfortable. The only thing to do was to lump them all together and put them out of mind. She was fairly sure she wouldn't be tempted to touch a dirty big black wire anyway.

'I'm going to meet Tim now,' said Thea, a short while later. 'There's no need for you to come. You can stay here with Dad. I won't be long.'

'Okay,' said Stephanie.

Outside, the wind was slightly less violent, but the sky was as grey as ever. 'Damn, I forgot to look for the candles and batteries,' she groaned to herself. What was the matter with her head? One thing after another just dropped out of it, at the slightest distraction. Drew was no help, either. He had spent hours tending to his lacerated daughter, on a day that had been full of plans and procedures for funerals. As he repeatedly told her, he could only keep the family fed and clothed if he worked a full forty hours a week. If no funerals materialised, then he would have to find other means of earning money. 'Or I could get a job,' Thea always said, with the predictably mixed feelings this idea gave rise to.

The only job she was likely to find was in a shop or museum, with part-time hours to fit with the children. 'I might be able to do the filing for a GP or in a hospital,' she suggested once or twice.

Drew would always laugh, and shake his head, and say, 'We can't spare you from the house. I need you here to answer the phone, for one thing.'

That wasn't true. They both knew there were other reasons why it suited everyone for her to be on the spot. Even the dog would strenuously vote against the idea of Thea going out to work, given the opportunity.

The lack of a shop in the village was a regular irritation. It automatically limited the sort of people who lived there, for one thing. The very elderly, anybody with no car, the disabled or house-sharing youngsters were all unseen in Broad Campden. There was something deeply uncivilised about it, in Thea's view.

She stood waiting for Timmy's bus, willing the electricity to go on again before it got really dark. The houses that were visible were all unilluminated, most of them empty anyway, their occupants at work or in their city homes during the week. What had it been like, she wondered idly, in the days of Charles Ashbee and his friends? There would be gaslight, as well as lamps and candles. Half the buildings would have been for horses, the traps pushed indoors as well, out of the rain. Feedstuff, manure heaps, harness and spare parts would all take up space. Children would have been running free with cheap home-made toys, or walking to and from the village school. It was a picture that gained in detail as she let her imagination roam. Dogs would have joined the children in their freedom to play in the lanes and fields. However unsentimental she tried to be, the whole thing couldn't fail to seem pleasanter than the present day. Everywhere now there was the danger of traffic, so that animals and children had to be confined. The necessities for survival were scarcely more easily obtained now than they had been a century ago, if you considered the huge distances over which they were transported. Ashbee had built his reputation on such considerations. He insisted on having as many objects handmade as possible – which amounted to almost everything. Carpets, furniture, crockery, decoration – it could all be created in a local workshop with local materials. It was an aim that found great favour with Thea, as well as with Drew. Wasn't that the underlying principle of his business, after all?

At last the bus came, its lights on, and the woman driving it waving gaily at Thea. Before the door opened, she turned off the engine, which was unusual. Then she was leading Timmy down the steps, with that distinctive expression of apology and concern and reassurance that every mother knew all too well. It meant the child had not had an ordinary day. Something had gone wrong. There had been tears or violence or loss or misbehaviour. The little boy's face showed clear evidence of the first in the list. 'Hey, Tim! What's the matter?' Thea asked, looking from him to the bus driver.

'He's worried about his sister,' explained the woman.

'But surely somebody explained it to him?' Thea was indignant.

'I don't know much about it, but it seems not. He said his teacher told him Stephanie had gone to hospital with their father, and nobody knew any more than that.'

'Oh, Tim!' Thea crooned, pressing his face into her middle and gently swaying him from side to side. 'Stephanie's all right. She just cut her hand, that's all.'

'I expect they thought you'd phone to let them know.' Reproach was unmistakable.

'Yes, we should have, of course. But there's been a power cut, and Drew's very busy, and I . . .'

'Never mind. It's all right now. Better get on. Power cut, you say?' She looked around. 'I *thought* something was funny. Everywhere's so dark. I hope it's not off in Blockley as well.'

137

'Probably not.'

The bus drove off, with the scattering of remaining children aboard, to be dropped at the further end of the village.

'It's okay, Tim,' Thea repeated. 'You didn't need to get in a panic.'

'Mrs Leather was cross,' he mumbled, still rubbing his face against her jumper. 'She came to our room, and said Stephanie Slocombe had been taken to hospital by her father, but they didn't know any more than that. She said I'd have to go on the bus by myself.'

'You've done that before, haven't you? When Stephanie had a bad tummy. You went both ways without her then.'

'Mmm,' he said doubtfully.

'And the driver's really nice and kind, isn't she?'

He didn't reply, and Thea was aware that she was missing the main point. Timmy had felt abandoned and obscurely blamed by the school for his family's sloppy ways. 'We should have phoned the school to tell them everything was all right, so you'd know what was happening,' she said clearly. 'We were wrong not to do that. I'm sorry, darling. It must have been worrying for you.'

'What if she was *dead*?' he burst out with dreadful intensity.

Like his mother, thought Thea with a cardiac thud. Why did adults so quickly forget how it was to be a child? How the connections between events were so confusingly obscure that you could only make wild guesses based on very limited previous experience? If a sister could vanish so easily, what else might happen, given that your mother had

138

already died by inches throughout your early childhood?

'She's absolutely fine. I really am very sorry you got so worried. Now, listen – there's no electricity in the house. No lights, no telly, no cooking, no bath. I should really go and buy some candles. We've only got one or two. And the torch's batteries are running out.'

'Can I come?'

'Yes, if you want to. We'll just drop your bag and tell Dad where we're going.'

It was soon accomplished, and they were back in the house by half past four. Drew had lit every candle he could find, which turned out to be a grand total of five. He reported that he and Stephanie had walked up to the field and watched the men working on the broken cable. 'They seemed to be doing everything possible. I dare say it'll go on again any time now.'

The house was cold, so Thea made a big production of finding the warmest jumpers they possessed and dressing everyone in them. The neglected woodburner, which could have improved the situation dramatically, had almost no wood left to burn. The log pile was down to about five items.

They had banana sandwiches and juice for their tea, surrounded by the soft yellow light of the candles.

'I wonder how Mr Shipley's managing,' said Thea. 'I forgot all about him.' She proceeded to describe his house, with the lovely collection of glass in the huge kitchen.

'What a busy day we've all had,' said Drew with a sigh. 'And even worse tomorrow. For me, at least. I'll have to spend an hour or so out there this evening, as well.' He shivered at the prospect of the chilly little room holding two dead women. 'I might well get frostbite.'

Thea had a suspicion he'd been about to say *I'm sure to freeze to death*, before he remembered the fate of Hilary Bunting.

'Miss Temple at eleven,' said Thea, proud that she remembered. 'And people about trees on Saturday. And Tuesday's new person on Monday. What's her name?'

'Mrs Mary Lavinia Johnstone – with a "t" and an "e". There's another new person, as well, don't forget. A Mrs Card on Tuesday. We had to take her to Cirencester, just for tonight.'

'Mrs Card?' giggled Stephanie. 'That's a funny name.'

'She must have loved Mr Card very much to marry a man with such a name,' said Thea.

'It's not so bad. What about Mrs Pitchfork?'

'And Mrs Ramsbottom,' said Timmy.

Nobody could think of any more names, so they fell silent. The sound of footsteps up the path was therefore unmistakable, even to Hepzie, who was a very poor guard dog. She yapped half-heartedly.

'What now?' said Drew with a sigh. 'Shall we pretend not to be here? Easy enough with the lights all off.'

'They'll have seen the car, and the candlelight,' said Thea. 'Maybe it's somebody from the electricity board.'

'Hah!' scoffed Drew, as he got up to answer the knock. 'Kids – go into the living room, will you? I'll bring whoever it is in here, assuming they want to come in, and can stand the cold.'

'Look who it is,' he announced half a minute later, bringing the visitor into the romantically lit kitchen.

'Hello,' said Thea, with scant enthusiasm.

'Hi, everybody. Sorry to barge in,' said DS Sonia Gladwin. 'What's with the candles?'

Chapter Eleven

'There's a power cut,' said Thea. 'We're improvising. You'd better come into the kitchen and have a glass of orange juice.'

'I won't stay long,' the police detective promised, sitting down at the table with Thea. 'I'll get right to the point. Just thought you'd like to know that we've charged Graham Bunting with the murder of his wife.'

'Oh,' said Thea. 'Didn't he have an alibi? Wasn't he in Oxford?'

'He was, yes. But only from 11 p.m. on Tuesday. Then he stayed there all night. But the time of his wife's death is impossible to pinpoint accurately. She hadn't eaten anything solid for ages, and the havoc caused by her body being half-frozen makes it mostly a matter of guesswork. It's perfectly feasible that she died sometime on Tuesday evening, when he was at home.'

'Oh.'

'What's the matter?'

'I don't know. It just feels a bit too *easy*, I suppose.'

'It's usually pretty easy. You've had a very unusual set of experiences, mainly thanks to your unusual line of work. Nearly all the murders I've had to investigate have taken about ten minutes to solve. This is one like that. We could maybe do with a few more bits of hard evidence, but taking everything into account, it's a reasonably straightforward case. Although there is one awkward aspect to it.'

'What?'

'Caroline Hemingway. They can't say for sure what she died of. They've referred it to the coroner, and I have a nasty feeling they might find something potentially sinister.'

'Like what? You think it was Graham doing something to her?' Again she had an image of the man stifling his sister-in-law with a heavy hand over her face.

'Well – nobody's saying anything yet. But she wasn't expected to die quite as rapidly as she did, and she said some disturbing things in her final days. I gather the word *poison* passed her lips.'

'Blimey! Like in Victorian times. Do people get poisoned these days?'

'Officially, no. But this case makes you wonder. I mean, whether it happens more often than we know. It's still very tempting, I imagine – if you've got an annoying spouse that needs to be disposed of, for example.'

'So you really think Graham Bunting killed his wife's sister, as well as his wife?'

'Steady on! I never said that.' Gladwin's Geordie accent acquired full rein. A slender woman in her mid forties, she was energetically restless, plain-speaking, highly intelligent. Mother of twin boys and wife of a man who remained firmly in the background, she appealed to Thea on a number of levels.

'Isn't that what you think?'

'Not yet, it isn't, no. Far too soon to even contemplate such a thing. All I'm saying is that there's a bit of a question mark still hanging over it all. And the Bunting woman's stomach wasn't entirely empty.'

'Oh? I thought you just said it was.'

'I really shouldn't be telling you, but I can't see the harm. She'd had no food, but quite a bit to drink. Whisky. Probably neat. And the tox chaps found codeine mixed in with it.'

'What – literally mixed in? Or just taken at a similar time?'

'The former, as far as they can tell. And they can, pretty much.'

'So she was doped before going into the freezer. Thank goodness for that.' One small section of the cloud that had hovered above her since the previous day began to lift. 'I couldn't bear to think of her banging on the lid, knowing what was happening to her.'

'Mm,' said Gladwin.

'Would it have even *killed* her? The codeine? Isn't it pretty dangerous in large doses?'

'Seems the dose wasn't as large as all that. Just enough to make her woozy, if it's mixed with booze. It adds to the case against her husband. We found his fingerprints all over the glass, and the whisky bottle, and the pill container.'

'Well, he did live there,' said Thea, instinctively putting the counter-argument.

144

'True. But the glass especially is hard to explain. The wife's prints are on it as well, on top of his. That suggests he doctored it and then handed it to her, and she innocently drank it. The pills were put back in the bathroom cupboard.'

'So he just slipped it to her without her knowing, then when she'd dozed off, he dumped her into the freezer to die of hypothermia. And maybe he killed Caroline as well, at the same time. That's incredible. When will you know something definite about what happened to her?'

'Not for a day or two. There wasn't going to be a post-mortem. The coroner is still thinking about whether one's needed.'

'So where did the poison idea come from? Not her son, surely? He came here today. He didn't seem to suspect anything.'

'Aha – there you are, you see.'

'Pardon? What am I supposed to see?'

'That it could all be quite innocent. I mean, not *all*, but the sister's death, at least.' The detective looked pained, as if under some sort of duress. 'You're right – it's too incredible otherwise. There's no hint of a motive, for a start.'

'The permutations get complicated,' said Thea. 'Two men – Graham, and Oscar Hemingway – with the means and opportunity, and two dead women – but not much in the way of motive for either of them.' The cloud lifted a little more. The arrival of Gladwin had successfully returned her to earlier times, when murder was primarily a puzzle, and not something she needed to take personally. 'And I can't believe you've got enough real evidence against poor Graham.'

'*Poor* Graham?' Gladwin's wide eyes were dark pools in the dim light. The candle had started flickering. 'What do you mean, *poor* Graham? As far as we can see, everybody hates the bloke.'

'You mean the people in the village? Do they, though? I'm not sure that's right. You ought to go over the lane and talk to Mr Shipley.' She thought of the way the man had recanted, backing away from the original impression he'd given Drew and admitting he'd known the Buntings considerably better than the Slocombes had assumed. 'I think they found him alarming, with that horribly loud voice.'

'Didn't you?'

'Only at first. I can't say he was very *nice*, but . . .' She stopped, seeing again the man's face, the previous day. 'I think he must have been fond of Hilary. I think he was absolutely appalled when he came home and understood she was dead. I don't think anybody could act that well.'

'You'd be surprised,' said Gladwin dourly. 'He'd had all night to practise, after all.'

'But he wouldn't come home just like that, knowing he'd be the main suspect.'

'Double bluff. Where else could he go without cementing himself as the perpetrator? His best chance was to act normally.'

'Cementing' struck Thea as an odd word, but she got the idea. 'So you've got enough evidence, then?' she repeated.

'We will have. The house is still being examined.'

'Oh. Well, thanks for coming to tell me. That was really good of you. It's nice to see you again.'

'Is it? One of these days, we should have lunch or

something, without any mention of murder or evidence or finding dead bodies.'

'There's no escape from dead bodies,' said Thea, with a little wave of her hand towards the rest of the house. 'I'm married to an undertaker.'

Gladwin laughed. 'And a very fine man he is, too.' She looked around the shadowy room. 'How's it going with the kids?'

'Mostly okay. At least, none of the problems are the ones I expected. They're very affectionate, trusting even. They're pretty normal, amazingly. Except – sometimes I forget about Karen, and what it must have done to them, deep down inside. Timmy, just now, was terrified that his sister was dead. That can only be because of his mother. It pops up without warning.'

A cry suddenly went up from the living room: 'It's on!'

Thea blinked, uncomprehending. Nothing had changed in the kitchen. 'Oh, look,' said Gladwin, pointing to the lane outside. 'Lights!'

Thea had not closed the curtains. 'Oh!' she said, and got up to test the switch by the door. The central bulb was blinding. 'So it is.' She grinned. 'Isn't it ghastly, compared to a candle?'

'There's nothing to stop you carrying on with candles. Except they're dangerous. You might set the house on fire.'

Thea shuddered. 'Don't,' she begged. 'There's enough danger all around us as it is.'

'Danger? Like what?'

'It sounds silly when I put it into words, but everything feels fragile all of a sudden. Even the electricity going off

147

shows how dependent we are and how little we can actually control. And Stephanie cut herself at school today. The dog's got a broken leg. We're just much too complacent these days, don't you think?'

Gladwin spoke carefully. 'Not when you're in the police. Every bag or box is a potential bomb. Every driver is likely to crash into a crowd of little kids. We have to have special sessions to help us get it all into perspective, and stop expecting Armageddon every day of our lives.'

'I suppose you do.' Thea thought of her daughter Jessica, a sunny-natured young woman currently employed as a police constable in Manchester. She hoped Jess didn't expect Armageddon every day. She had never looked at it quite like that before. 'That's pretty horrible,' she added.

'Yeah, well . . . Apparently human beings are hard-wired to expect disaster. If everything's going along happily and peacefully, we don't feel right. We look for trouble. It's all those sabre-toothed tigers out there, I guess.'

'My mother would agree. She says climate change is just made up to frighten everybody.'

'My mother says the same thing.'

They laughed indulgently, until Gladwin said, 'I saw the son, Tom, just before coming here. He's all over the place, not surprisingly.'

'Why did *you* see him? He can't be of any use in the investigation.'

Gladwin gave her a stern look. 'Of course he can. If his father killed his mother he's fairly likely to have some idea of the reason for it. Background information is crucial. Even little hints like which parent he seems to prefer are useful. We have to build a case, assuming the man pleads not guilty – which I'm sure he will. For the moment, the son's going to be very useful, given that his dad isn't speaking.'

'Pardon?'

'No. He just sits there looking ravaged. His eyes dart all over the place, and he moans now and then, but other than that, he's schtum.'

'Did a lawyer tell him not to say anything?'

Gladwin shook her head. 'He hasn't seen a lawyer. It's unnerving, I can tell you. And it means we can't proceed properly.'

Not for the first time, Thea felt nauseated by the intrusive nature of a murder investigation. Families were forced to reveal their secrets, their ancient feuds and shameful moments. Except that Graham Bunting would not be forced, it seemed. Another irony, then – the shouty man rendered silent by desperate events. 'He must be in shock,' she said. 'Catatonic.'

'That's what some of us think. Others are a lot less charitable. Including his son.'

'I was going to ask you – which parent did Tom prefer?'

'His mother, of course, like any normal lad. At least, that was my impression. I didn't ask him directly. And it might not be quite as simple as that.'

In spite of herself, Thea was drawn into the story. Coming from a large family, she imagined herself to have a degree of insight into the undercurrents and mendacities that never entirely went away. She had been a normal daughter, apparently, in having a preference for her father. 'Not so simple, how?' she queried.

'He had no hesitation whatsoever in declaring his father's innocence. He insisted there was no way in the world the man could ever kill anyone, least of all his wife. They've been married for thirty-odd years, always done everything together—'

'Well, that's not true,' Thea interrupted. 'He played bridge and she didn't. She went for walks without him. She had her own friends.' Another inconsistency struck her, as she recalled Oscar's remarks about Tom and his mistrust of his father. On that point, she opted for discretion, at least until she had a better picture.

Gladwin nodded knowingly. 'You have to allow for a degree of exaggeration at times like this. They generally tend to tint everything a bit on the pink side. The point is, he is absolutely certain it was a happy marriage.'

'Hmm,' said Thea.

'You don't agree?'

'Neither of them struck me as being exactly *happy*, especially her. But I only saw them together for about ten minutes – maybe a bit more. I'm in no position to judge.'

'So Tom says people misjudged his father because of the loud voice. He says that was an increasing problem over the past year or two, and really bad from around last summer. It made it hard for people to see the real man. Even old friends had begun to avoid him. He said the last time he visited them, a few days before Christmas, the house had felt rather sad.'

'I thought you said he was all over the place. He managed to say quite a lot, by the sound of it.'

'Between sobs, you mean? Come on, Thea. He was choked, yes, but he could still talk.'

'Right. Sorry.' Thea was abstracted, rendered almost mute by a startling new idea. 'Is Graham going to be given bail?'

'Hardly. He'll be remanded, given the circumstances.'

'Where?'

'His best hope would be Leyhill, but he's much more likely to be sent out of county.'

'Where's Leyhill?'

'It's low security. Just off the M5, a fair way south of here. I've only been there a couple of times.'

'How long would he be in there?'

'Usual sort of time. It's mostly close to a year these days.'

'A *year*? Waiting for the trial, you mean? All that time when he might turn out to be not guilty. Isn't that a scandalous breach of human rights?'

Gladwin rolled her eyes. 'Don't tell me this is news to you.'

'I suppose I must have known. But I read a lot of fiction from the nineteenth century. They had the trial about a fortnight after the arrest and charge.'

'I know. And inquests were the same week. And funerals were two days after the death. We still use the same system now for a population that must be three or four times the size, and it's not coping.'

'Yes, but – he'll be completely institutionalised by then. And have picked up all sorts of horrible habits from the others. What if he *isn't* guilty? What terrible damage will have been done to him?'

'Stop it. It's not *my* fault, is it?'

'Can I visit him?' The question burst out with no conscious thought behind it. It hovered in the air, almost visibly. 'What are the rules about visitors?'

151

'Slow down, for heaven's sake. You're about four steps ahead of yourself.'

'But you said he'd been charged.'

'Yes, he has. At least, we went through the motions, but it's still very early days. We still have to convince the CPS, and for that we need a lot more evidence. It's all ongoing. That's why I'm here. You and Mrs Ottaway will be material witnesses. We've got your initial statements, but there are details still outstanding. Doors, for one thing. Lights for another.'

'Lights! The power's back on – I should start the supper. And take the dog out. You don't want to go all over my whole statement again *now*, do you?'

Gladwin sighed. 'The sooner the better, before you forget. But tomorrow will be fine. It's best done at the station. Can you come down in the morning, do you think?'

'If I have to. I could give Rachel a lift. It's rather a long way by bike, even if she's had the gears mended, and the buses are sure to be at the exact wrong times.'

'Bike?'

'Yes. She lost her driving licence. I don't know how she manages this time of year. It must be freezing. You don't see many cyclists around in January, do you?' As she spoke, she was thinking that in a proper murder investigation, there'd have been background checks on Rachel Ottaway and her driving misdemeanour discovered. It all pointed to a virtually instant conclusion that Graham Bunting was the one and only suspect in the case.

Before Gladwin could reply, Drew came in, followed closely by the children. 'Are we going to have some supper tonight?' he asked, with a probing look at both women. 'If so, the cooker needs resetting. I don't know how to do it.'

'We are,' said Thea calmly. 'What time is it now?'

'Quarter past five.'

The family ate together at six-thirty most days, with Timmy's bedtime barely an hour later. The routine was more relaxed than Drew thought desirable, his gentle nagging only marginally effective in achieving his wishes. Thea had never rated cookery as one of her skills, and could not bring herself to regard the evening menu as of much significance. At weekends she made more effort, though usually baulking at providing the traditional Sunday lunch.

'I'll do scrambled eggs and sausages,' she said. 'That won't take long.'

'We had sausages yesterday,' he reminded her, without a smile.

'Gosh – so we did. That seems so long ago now. Okay, then, we'll have spaghetti bolognese. There's lots of sauce in the freezer. How's that?'

'Lovely,' he said, still without enthusiasm.

'I'll go,' said Gladwin, who was already at the door. 'Sorry to keep you.'

'See you tomorrow, then,' said Thea. She went out with the detective, pleased to see lights glowing in Mr Shipley's house, as well as the one next to his. She would have liked to tell Gladwin about her odd little lunch with the man who she still felt had set the whole Bunting business in motion. Some tenuous bond had been formed between him and her, which she worried about. Had she been cavalier and ungrateful, rushing off the way she had? Had she told him

153

too much about the discovery of Hilary's body? Wasn't his instant resistance to the idea of Graham Bunting as a killer of some relevance?

'I haven't met anyone who thought Mr Bunting could have killed his wife,' she said, with some urgency, as Gladwin took a few steps into the lane. 'I still think you might have got it wrong.'

'If we have, we'll put it right. But who else could have done it? I know that's not proof, and is dubious logic, but you have to take it into consideration.'

Thea had to let it go at that. She went back into the house and tried to obliterate thoughts of the Bunting tragedy with mundane family concerns, such as where in the freezer the bolognese sauce might be hiding. But this was never going to work, she realised, as she finally withdrew the errant plastic box, with numb fingers. Despite her freezer being of a quite different design to that in which Hilary Bunting had been dumped, the associations were impossible to ignore. Would it *hurt*, she wondered, as your extremities ceased to function, and your heart and brain fought valiantly to keep working against all the odds?

Drew remained quiet and very slightly pained throughout the meal, his mood even darker after being told that Thea was required in Cirencester the next day. He remained quiet throughout the evening that followed. His day had been as bad as Thea's – worse, he might justifiably claim. Stephanie's bandaged hand had begun to throb, and there were no junior aspirins in the house. Tim remained large-eyed with bewilderment at the swirling events that had made his father look so stern, and his stepmother so distracted.

'I think I ought to say sorry,' Thea tried, once they were sitting together in the living room. 'For forgetting all about Stephanie when I was at Mr Shipley's. I can't explain it any better than I have already. It was awful of me.'

'It's okay. I understand how it was. You've had a horrible couple of days. All these people coming to the door, and the power cut – and you didn't even know the Bunting people. It does seem awfully bad luck.'

'Yes.' She gazed fixedly into his face. 'Is that what you really think?'

He met her gaze. 'Pretty much, it is, yes. I'd like to believe you should never have gone there on Tuesday – or Wednesday. But it was well intentioned. I thought it was nice of you, even if just a little bit nosy. I think the local history idea is great and I hope it continues. But I worry for you, Thea, to be perfectly honest. You never seem to be able to steer clear of people who might not be all right. I mean – they might not have the same good intentions as you do. Do you see what I mean?'

'I suppose I do. Which people do you mean, exactly?'

'That Rachel woman, mostly. I keep thinking everything about her seems just a bit too neat and tidy and convenient to be true. I still don't understand why she was there yesterday, just at the same time as you were. Did *she* suggest going round the back and into the kitchen? Were you some sort of stooge? A witness to the discovery you made together?'

'You're saying she knew we'd find Hilary? Does that mean you think *Rachel* killed her?'

'I was just wondering, that's all. She knows all these

people, and you don't. That makes you vulnerable to being exploited and manipulated. Haven't we learnt by now that just about everybody lies when it comes to murder? This Rachel woman seems to me to be decidedly untrustworthy.'

'Oh, Drew,' she sighed happily. 'So you're not cross with me. You're *worried* about me. What a relief!'

'Why would I be cross with you?'

'Because I'm a pathetic wife and hopeless stepmother – or the other way round. I can't even cook you all a proper supper unless it involves sausages.'

'I'm not complaining,' he said. 'I feel bad for expecting you to suddenly cater for four people, just because you've taken up with me. I should do a lot more of the cooking myself.'

'We'd eat better if you did.'

'We're still finding our feet here, don't forget. It's a lot less convenient than Staverton, which I didn't quite realise until we moved here. No shop. Nowhere to grow food. The field out of sight, and the neighbours a lot more picky about how things look.'

'Somerset has a lot going for it,' she agreed. 'Maggs got the long straw, or whatever the saying is.'

'Poor old Greta meant well, of course.'

It was a conversation they'd had before. Without the gratitude of one of Drew's customers, they would never have contemplated living in Broad Campden. She bequeathed her house and field to Drew, on condition he opened an alternative funeral service there. He had dithered for a year or more before concluding he could not afford to reject the proposition. Not so much for financial reasons as for honouring the intention, and spreading the gospel of environmentally benign burials. The population of the Cotswolds was younger than he would have liked, with fewer deaths than elsewhere, but for those who did get old or ill the notion of an individual grave with almost no rules was appealing.

'Early night for us,' Drew ordained. 'Who knows what tomorrow will be like?'

'You've got to bury Miss Temple, whatever happens,' she reminded him.

'And you've got to spill the beans to the cops.'

She laughed, and followed him upstairs with a much lighter heart.

Chapter Twelve

Rachel Ottaway was unenthusiastic about accepting a lift from Thea. 'I can get there on the bus quite easily,' she said. 'And I don't imagine they want to see us together, do they?'

'Probably not,' said Thea, thinking that seemed an odd reason for declining a lift. Drew's suspicions about Rachel returned to her with some force. The woman always seemed to have a complicated agenda directing her actions, to which Thea was far from privy.

On the way to Cirencester it struck Thea then that there had been no incident room set up in the village, as generally happened after a murder. So that must mean that they were entirely satisfied that they had their killer and no further disturbance of the peaceful Cotswold countryside was required. She ought to be glad, of course, that everything had been resolved so quickly, but her sense that it was all much *too* quick and easy had only strengthened overnight. The sheer malice behind Hilary's death kept forcing itself into her thoughts. She tried to go through what appeared to have happened, step by step, finding it very hard to credit that Graham would have stripped his wife naked, garment by garment, as part of his homicidal procedure. And were the clothes neatly folded up somewhere, or strewn around the house? Had Hilary co-operated, thinking something quite else was going to happen? Gladwin had been careful not to reveal the precise cause of death, and the question of whether the woman had been conscious when slammed inside the freezer was not completely resolved. That made an enormous difference, Thea realised. Surely the combined whisky and codeine would have knocked her out? It showed a degree of mercy, perhaps.

She drove fast south to Cirencester, unconscious of the road in front of her. Other vehicles passed by unseen. Instinct ensured that she obeyed the basic rules and stopped in the right places. Her mind's eye was entirely filled with images of bare skin turning blue and eyes frosting over. It had become considerably less horrible since Wednesday, but still made her feel sick. Her own face felt sympathetically cold, and her toes were going numb on the accelerator.

Would she really visit Graham Bunting in prison, she asked herself. It seemed a rash thing to do, on reflection. What could she possibly say to him? Would it all be listened to by warders in a big room full of small tables where visitors sat one side and their prisoner the other? She had recently watched the unhappy Shirley Henderson in the film *Everyday* doing exactly that. Perhaps it would be better to go to Graham's trial when it eventually took place. Then she remembered that Gladwin had said she would be required there anyway as a witness. Did that mean she would not be allowed to watch the proceedings before and after her testimony? That would be frustrating, if so. And would it interfere with her duties at home? It was all impossible to imagine. Despite being involved in numerous murder investigations, so far she had never set foot inside a courtroom. The prospect of having to stand up and answer a lot of questions in front of a crowd of onlookers was far from inviting. She had never done any public speaking, other than giving brief papers as a student, and had no wish to begin now.

When she got to the police station, she did not see Gladwin. A detective inspector questioned her, with her original statement in front of him. He placed particular emphasis on where she and Rachel had gone in the house. 'Only the kitchen,' she repeated.

Was the door through to the rest of the house open or closed? Closed. But the door onto the back garden from the kitchen was unlocked? Yes – unlocked and closed. Why did the two women go into the house? Hard to explain. They just meant to shout for Hilary. But they'd already rung the front doorbell? Yes. So – why persist? Hard to explain. Rachel had come all the way from Blockley. She didn't want to go home without seeing Hilary. Probably. Perhaps. Thea didn't really know. So Mrs Ottaway had been the leader? She had gone in first? More or less. It had felt like a joint exercise. But she had been into the rest of the house the previous day? Yes. Why – were her fingerprints on anything? That remained to be seen, since they did not have her prints on file.

And so it went on, meticulously, even tediously, but

it was in no way alarming. The DI made small notes, underlinings and ticks on the paper in front of him, smiled a few times, stared at a corner of the room in thought, and finished with a sigh and a stretch.

'Thank you very much, Mrs Slocombe. That's all for now.'

She did not see Rachel anywhere as she left. There was no reason to worry that the woman would say anything to contradict Thea's account of events. Minor discrepancies were to be expected anyway. Major contradictions were out of the question, unless Rachel turned out to be a total liar, intent on incriminating Thea somehow. That wouldn't work, Thea inwardly scoffed, trying to ignore the inner flutterings that the idea produced. *Stop it*, she told her overactive imagination. It was, she insisted to herself, fortunate that the two of them had made the discovery together, confirming each other's observations as they surely must. The niggles that persisted were nothing more than foolish fantasy. But they wouldn't go away. Why *had* they been so persistent in pursuing Hilary, when nobody came to the front door? Her answer to that was feeble. Wasn't it just something that women did? They made free with each other's houses, calling 'Coo-ee!' up the stairs with gay abandon. Rachel regarded herself as Hilary's friend, after all. Nothing had seemed out of order to Thea at the time. But now, reliving it, she recalled the whole thing being rather rushed. She had felt almost *bundled* around to the back by Rachel's haste. Other interpretations were possible, if searched for. But the police wouldn't search, would they? Because they were quite sure that Graham Bunting had killed his wife.

Then she connected that part of the story with the previous day, when Rachel had vaulted over the fence during the quest for the missing Biddy. The woman was energetically athletic, always on the move. Cycling everywhere, intent on the next thing, brisk and capable – how could anyone do anything else but trail obediently in her wake? Wednesday morning's behaviour probably hadn't been any different from her usual manner.

There were still legions of unanswered questions. Had Oscar Hemingway found Ant, and his mother's dog? Had Mr Shipley consulted his fellow villagers as to how they should respond to the horror in their midst? Was she, Thea, ever going to meet Tom and Edward Bunting? Would her proposed local history group ever materialise? Could she, indeed, be entirely sure that such a group did not already exist, quietly meeting in somebody's house, and discussing the glory days of the Arts and Crafts Movement?

She was driving slowly through the streets, wondering whether there was any big shopping she could usefully do before going home. The prospect was not appealing. Broad Campden was calling to her with surprising insistence. Not just the dog, left alone while Drew buried Miss Temple, but more abstract matters demanded her presence. Vague perils kept threatening her peace of mind, most of them completely improbable. But then, hadn't a broken electricity cable been off the scale of probability, before it actually happened? There were no guarantees against landslides, multiple traffic pile-ups, spontaneous fires breaking out, psychotic gunmen . . . She found herself actively inventing dangers for herself and her family, which she quickly recognised as bordering on the insane. It was definitely neurotic. And completely out of character.

She saw Rachel Ottaway on the pavement without immediately identifying her. A bus was pulling out in front of Thea's car, and she understood that here was her fellow witness, arrived in town on public transport, over an hour later than she would have got there if she'd accepted Thea's offer of a lift. Automatically, she stopped the car and found the button that opened the passenger-side window. 'Hello!' she called.

The woman ignored her until she tried again. 'You got here, then,' said Thea fatuously.

'As you see.' A smile was formed with visible effort. 'You must think I was very churlish, but I thought it better if the police didn't think we'd been colluding about what to say to them.'

The awkward bending necessary to speak to a person in a car was plainly not to her liking. And yet she had quickly delivered her little speech as if it had already been at the front of her mind. Thea could only work her jaw in a fruitless effort to reply coherently. The idea of collusion had not entered her head. What did they have to collude about? 'What?' she stuttered.

'Doesn't matter. It sounds daft, put like that. But you can never underestimate their suspicious minds, in my experience.'

'Oh. But we've had plenty of chances to get together since Wednesday, haven't we? They're just as likely to think it strange that you opted to use the bus instead of coming with me.'

'Have you been seen already? Did they say anything like that? What did you say about me?'

A car hooted irritably behind her, and she realised she was causing an obstruction. 'Sorry, can't stay,' she blurted. 'Phone me or something this afternoon.'

Or something? She asked herself what that could mean. Did she really want the woman showing up on the doorstep again? For a person without a driving licence, she certainly got around. After all, she could *walk* the three miles from Blockley, if all else failed. She probably did it all the time. And she had not needed an invitation thus far; why would she hesitate to do whatever she wanted in the future? Again the difference between being a house-sitter and living somewhere permanently became stark. On earlier occasions, Thea could always tell herself – *at least I won't be here this time next week*. Now she was going to be in Broad Campden for ever, and anybody could find her whenever they liked.

She drove home, every bit as lost in thought as she had been on the drive out. She had encountered women like Rachel Ottaway before – educated, decisive, strong-minded. The Cotswolds seemed to be a rich breeding ground for them. Often with murky pasts involving unsatisfactory men and estranged children, they had discovered the joys of the single life and set about making the world a better place, as they saw it. Rachel definitely fitted the formula – and yet it was unwise to make assumptions based on previous experience. When it came to a closer examination, everybody turned out to be quite different from everybody else. They wanted different things, and held very different views and ideologies.

She wondered about Hilary Bunting, and how closely

she matched the stereotype. For a start, she had a husband, which put her in a minority. It was a maxim Thea had heard more than once from the police that if a woman was going to get herself murdered, the husband was by far the most likely person to do it. And here was the very obvious villain in the shape of the loud-voiced Graham. Nobody else with any realistic claim for the part had crossed Thea's vision. But then Thea did not know the characters involved: the Taylors, or the neighbours, or the members of the Blockley Bridge Club. And plenty of others as well. Presumably the police questioning had failed to throw up any names of people with a grudge against poor Hilary, which left the original obvious suspect standing under the spotlight all by himself.

But Rachel Ottaway was only just outside the ring of light. She was behaving strangely. She said bizarre things. When she might be expected to be shocked and scared, she remained calm; then when she was requested to give the police a detailed account of finding the body, she was defensive and nervous. Something wasn't right with the woman, and in the absence of any other avenues, Thea could only focus on her.

She caught herself up. Why did she need an 'avenue' at all? What did she think she was doing – again? She was the wife of an undertaker, the stepmother of his children. She had tasks to perform, lives to take care of. Let murder look after itself, she thought irritably. It was not for her to intrude and annoy, as she had done so often before. This time, she had to remain on good terms with the locals, because she was now living amongst them, one of them herself.

'Maybe I should get a job,' she muttered aloud to herself. She could almost certainly find something in Chipping Campden, and walk there every day across the intervening fields. The money would be useful, and she would become distractingly busy. Every day would have a firm structure, with cooking and housework fitted in around the edges. 'It would keep me out of mischief,' she said to her invisible listener. 'And everyone would be grateful for that.'

Chapter Thirteen

It was half past twelve when the inevitable knock came. Thea had known somebody would disturb her uneasy peace, sooner or later. If not Rachel Ottaway, then Mr Shipley, or some concerned neighbour of the Buntings. When she got back, Drew was still conducting Miss Temple's funeral in the burial ground. The hearse was absent from its discreet parking area, and the phone was set to give its apologetic message to the effect that the call could not immediately be taken, but please be assured that no delay would result, and attention would be quickly forthcoming.

Thea had snuggled onto the sofa with her dog, reading about Charles Ashbee and trying not to feel like an idle Victorian matron. The book was absorbing and had already taught her a lot. There were moments when she found it so stimulating that she wanted to jump up and run around Broad Campden demanding that people wake up and celebrate the fabulous history beneath their feet.

She went to the door expecting Rachel. But a man stood there, with a shaggy dog at his side. 'Good-o. This must be the right house?' he said. 'They told me it was down here.'

'Hello, Biddy,' said Thea. 'That really is Biddy this time, isn't it?' She looked closely. 'I'd forgotten about you.' She looked into Ant's face. 'How's she been?'

'Confused. Scared. Nobody's told me what I'm meant to do with her. I thought you might know.'

Thea had considerable experience of scared and confused dogs. 'Poor thing. Has Oscar found you? I don't remember what he said, but the responsibility must rest with him, to decide what happens to her.'

Ant frowned. 'You've lost me already,' he said.

'Come in, then, and we can try to bring you up to date. You know Hilary's dead, don't you?'

He followed her through to the kitchen, the dog's nails clicking on the stone tiles. 'I feel as if I've gone through a portal into a different world,' he said, his face serious. 'All I did was find this animal and offer to look after it for a bit. That Rachel woman seemed to think I was the answer to a prayer – which was over-egging it more than somewhat. She asked me all sorts of questions, but I still don't really understand. Hilary is the dog's owner, right? And she's dead? How? When?'

Thea waved at him to sit down. He did so, with the dog between his knees. Hepzie limped up to them, giving an affable greeting to man and dog. Biddy reared back for a moment, before relaxing with a slow wag of her tail. Ant stroked the soft spaniel head, and made no comment on the plastered leg. Then he returned his attention to Biddy, idly fondling her ears and neck, instinctively calming her and maintaining the precarious new bond he had with her.

'Actually,' said Thea, 'her owner was called Caroline, but she's dead as well. She's got a son, Oscar, who was supposed to contact you. Now I think about it, I remember he said he couldn't have a dog where he lives. Can't you keep her permanently?'

He ducked the question, and produced one of his own. 'Has there been an epidemic or something? Two women dead seems a bit much.'

'Where do you live?'

'Not far away. Midway between here and Ebrington, more or less. I live in a cottage on a big estate, where my father used to be the gardener and general factotum.'

'Rachel said something weird about an electrified fence round the whole property.'

He groaned. 'That's right. We can't get in or out without a special key card. The postman can't come to the house.'

'Who's "we"?'

'Me and my parents. It's a long story, but there's a crisis coming any time now.'

'But you live in a detached house with lots of land. So another dog would be okay, surely?'

'It might if it doesn't chase pheasants, or freak out when guns go off, or scare the peacocks.'

'Blimey! Where *is* this place?'

'I told you,' he said. 'It's owned by a chap who made his fortune by the age of fifty-five and now has nothing to do but spend it. Usual sort of thing. He bought the whole estate, but hadn't reckoned on a stubborn little family sticking to their guns and refusing to be evicted. We're a thorn in his side and he doesn't like it.'

'That must be horrible.'

'You get used to it. It's a game – that's how we look at it.' He gave her a rueful smile, and said, 'So why don't we turn this around and let *me* ask some questions for a change? All I did was find a missing dog on Tuesday evening, take it home, and mind my own business ever since then. So who's dead? How did it happen? And who the devil is *Oscar*?'

'Percy!' Thea suddenly remembered the name of Ant's dog. 'He looks like Biddy. How are they getting along? Where is he now?'

'They're not getting on too well. I left him out in the van. Neither of them seems to know what to make of the other. Don't change the subject.'

'Sorry. I'll see if I can explain, but it's a pretty long story. Rather nasty as well.' She frowned at him. 'Are you *sure* you haven't heard anything? It must have been on the local news. Everybody must be talking about it.'

'I'm rather a loner, and I certainly don't follow local news.'

'Okay. Here goes, then.' And she blurted out the tangled tale of the woman in the freezer, her sister in the hospital, the arrested husband, and three assorted sons. 'There's more,' she concluded, 'but that's the basics.'

'So where does my mum's old friend Rachel come into it?'

'She plays bridge with Mr Bunting, and she was with me when I – we – found Hilary. That was Wednesday morning. It made us forget all about you and Biddy, sorry to say.'

'I'm not surprised. What a thing!'

'I was sick all over the floor. I've never done that before.'

'Anybody would be. I don't suppose you'd ever found a dead body before.'

170

'Well, I *have*, actually. Quite a few, one way and another. But I've never been so . . . startled, I suppose. It never even crossed my mind there might be anything like that about to happen. Before, there's always been a bit of warning: somebody missing, or a noise or something. This came completely out of the blue. And there was something horribly vicious about it. Her being naked, and her *eyes* . . .'

The man said nothing. Thea looked at him, thinking that here was another example of a Cotswolds stereotype. Nicely spoken, slightly self-effacing, but unable to conceal his rootedness in the area. He exuded an air of belonging, as if descended from shepherds, with a wealth of rural wisdom. He would be good with animals and plants, and wary of human beings.

Or perhaps she had got him completely wrong in every single detail.

'The trouble is, I don't actually *want* to keep the dog. I only want the one I've got. I hate to do it to you, but I'm going to leave Biddy here with you. Your spaniel doesn't look as if it would mind.'

'But you seem so *fond* of her,' Thea protested. 'Look at you both. You're made for each other.'

'Rubbish!' His face darkened. 'I'm just trying to keep her calm. I'd do it with any creature that was under stress.'

'She can't stay here. We've got children – and funeral people. She wouldn't get enough attention.'

'Then I guess it's the dog pound,' he said without a flicker of humour.

'Like in *Lady and the Tramp*?' said Thea. 'No way.

Rachel might take her, I suppose, but I doubt it. Or one of Hilary's sons.'

'Right, then.'

'No, it's not right, then. There's nobody who'll take her on. Oscar came here yesterday, and said there was no chance of him having a dog. There are two Bunting sons, his cousins: Tom and Edward. They live miles away, and I can't imagine either of them would spare a thought for their aunt's dog.'

'Friends? Neighbours?'

She rubbed her face. 'I guess so. At the start of all this, *our* neighbour came over to tell us the Buntings were causing concern and annoyance in the village, and did we want to . . . I'm not sure what. Join a campaign or something. We had no idea who they were, until I went to their house to find out for myself.'

Ant pulled a face, indicating distaste, and a flicker of *Well, what do you expect, then, if you're as nosy as that?*

'I can see you think you're well off out of all that sort of stuff,' she accused him.

'I do, indeed.'

She laughed. 'Well, it's a bit late for me now. I'm stuck here, like it or not.' As she heard her own words, her eyes widened at the implications. Was that really how she felt? Hadn't she been serially in love with one gorgeous Cotswold village after another? Wasn't she blissfully content to be finally settled in one of them? 'Are you hungry?' she added, finding that she was herself.

'A bit. Shall we go to the pub?'

The Bakers Arms was the only pub in the village, 'under new management' as virtually every pub in England appeared to be, on a sort of perpetual roundabout. The previous manager had banned dogs, thereby offending Thea out of all proportion. Now dogs were actively encouraged with bowls of water and biscuits. 'You're on,' she said with alacrity. 'But we'll have to go slowly because Hepzie's handicapped at the moment.'

'So I noticed,' he said. 'You can tell me what happened, if you want.'

'Her leg got broken. Just before Christmas.'

He shrugged. 'Things happen,' he said.

Ant and Biddy readily adapted their pace to the spaniel's, and the little group meandered northwards to the hostelry. On a January Friday there were very few customers, and they were lucky to find that lunch was actually being provided. The plain lack of pretension, compared to some other local establishments, endeared itself to Thea, and fresh from her Ashbee reading, she realised there was an Arts and Crafts tone to the furnishing.

They chose the simplest fare, and sat at a table by the window. 'Shouldn't you be working?' she asked him. 'Poisoning foxes or something?'

He shook his head. 'I don't do that. They don't employ me on the estate. My dad worked for them, but he retired a while ago. I spend a couple of days a week on the computer, as well as picking up a bit of weekend work at the garden centre.' He sighed impatiently. 'You don't want to know how I spend my time.'

'Oh, but I do. Are you writing a novel? Or hacking into people's bank accounts?' Her impression of him altered in a flash, from a countryman imbued with the secret lore of flora and fauna to a geek with scrabbling fingers bent over a keyboard. Then she corrected herself, aware that a person could easily be both.

'I create apps,' he said. 'It's good fun.'

'And lucrative?'

'That's a gamble. Most of them sink without trace, but I've had one or two successes.'

She was disappointed, not wanting to discuss apps. But she was well aware that Stephanie was starting to lose patience with her irrational technophobia, which meant she would have to confront it before much longer. Already she'd realised that much of it went back to her first husband, Carl, who had regarded computers as sinister and destructive. It had been inconvenient five years ago to live with someone who rejected not only emails, but mobile telephony. Now, it was unthinkable.

'So it pays the rent,' she quipped.

He flushed, confusingly. 'Let me try and elaborate, so you understand. I live with my parents. It's a tied cottage. My dad was the groundsman there, thirty-five years ago, and then the whole place was sold up – twice – and now he's not needed. Hasn't been for ages, actually. He worked as a postman for twenty years, until he retired last year. But we still all live there, under siege, pretty much. The owners are desperate to get rid of us and raze the house to the ground. They never do any maintenance on it, so it's cold and damp. My mum's incredibly stubborn, and keeps a low-level war going between us and the landlord.'

'Sounds incredible,' said Thea, aware that he earnestly wanted her to get the whole picture. 'But why are you still there? How old are you?'

He flushed again. 'Thirty-four. I did leave for about seven years after college, but things went wrong, and I came back. Now I feel as though they need me to stay. I said there's an electronic gate between us and the road, which causes every sort of trouble. I can override it with a bit of judicious hacking, so we can come and go as we like. They only let us have two key cards for three people, and they don't always work. It's programmed to open for their car, but not my van. The situation is close to impossible – my mum and dad could never cope with it on their own.'

'But they can't keep you locked in.' She was bewildered. 'What do you mean?'

'It's a long and ridiculous story. They're harassing us, while being careful not to break the law – which is pretty strongly on their side anyway. All the usual low-level irritants that landlords go for. Our mail doesn't get delivered; the bins don't get emptied; the boiler's never serviced. But it's still a great place to live. Loads of woodland, long walks in every direction. I'm not sure I could ever leave it again now. My mother feels even more strongly. She says she could never live anywhere else.'

Thea sighed happily, despite sharing Ant's outrage at the situation. Such glimpses into other people's lives were meat and drink to her. She mulled it over, wondering how she'd feel in the same situation. 'Do you inherit the tenancy when your parents die?'

'I doubt it. But we like to pretend we believe so, just to wind them up.'

'Is the house really worth fighting for, though?'

'My mum thinks so. She had us kids there, and she

doesn't like change. But I can see that it's an awful eyesore. The landlord ships in by helicopter with his rich friends, and there's us, bang in the middle of the estate, with my old van, and a battered set of garden chairs and general mess. My dad tinkers with bits of carpentry, and there's always something lying about. He does it on purpose, and Mum's just as bad.'

'Well, I'd never have imagined such a thing,' she said.

'I expect it's quite unusual these days. The council took a brief interest, but we don't fit any of their categories, so they've given up on us.'

She looked at him, thinking he certainly didn't fit the categories she'd been trying to put him in. He was a distraction from the unhappy business of murder, at the very least. Biddy nudged at him, reminding them both of her existence, and the problem of what to do with her. The pub landlord had made a fuss of both dogs, asking solicitously about Hepzie's leg, plainly disappointed at Thea's brief and evasive response when he asked how she'd done it.

'What's going to happen to her?' Thea asked worriedly. 'I can't bear rejected dogs. It's the thing that upsets me most in the world.'

'You exaggerate,' he said, without emotion. 'There are countless things that are far more upsetting. A woman being dead in a freezer must be one of them, for a start.'

'I suppose so,' she said, inwardly disagreeing. Did that make her a monster, she wondered. Biddy was alive and in urgent need of love. Hilary was beyond all that.

Two people came in, bringing January chill with them. When Thea looked up, she knew she'd seen them before, but could not immediately remember where. A large man with white hair and a woman wearing a sheepskin coat. They saw her, and performed a similar where-do-I-know-you-from? reaction. Then the man saw Biddy, frowned fleetingly before more complicated facial messages passed over his features.

'The lady who came to see the Buntings,' he said. 'With the sister's dog, unless I'm much mistaken. Biddy – right?' He cocked his head invitingly and the shaggy creature gave him a submissive smile. 'I'm afraid I can't recall your name,' he told Thea. 'Tuesday seems a long time ago, with all that's happened since then, doesn't it?'

He was asking not just Thea, but everybody in the bar; only his wife replied. 'Yes, it does.' She grimaced, but Thea was unsure that any real emotion lay behind the look.

The man – Barnaby Taylor, Thea finally recollected – bent down to stroke Biddy. 'Poor old girl. What's become of your people, then?' he crooned. 'Who's going to look after you now?'

'Good question,' said Ant with feeling. 'I've had her since Tuesday, but it can't go on. My mother's never been much good with dogs, and this one barks far too much for comfort.'

The wife, whose name eluded Thea, detected something the others did not. 'Oh, no. Barney – no,' she said.

He ignored her, intent on his caresses and blandishments. 'Such a nice dog. So misunderstood. That horrid Graham always shouting – wasn't that awful, eh? And everything different from home.' At last he looked up, managing to meet the eye of the pub landlord, who was watching him

177

in undisguised amusement. 'Her owner died, you know. We only heard about it last night, didn't we, Sal?'

Sally! Sally and Barnaby Taylor. Got it.

'Really?' said Thea. 'The police didn't want to talk to you, then?'

'No. Why in the world should they?' asked the man.

Thea felt wrong-footed, while at the same time noticing a further confirmation that the police had little interest in pursuing an extensive investigation into Hilary Bunting's death. They saw no need for extraneous input from fellow bridge players, even if they'd become aware that such people existed. She ignored the question and focused on the problem of the dog. 'She's got nowhere to go,' she said, being only marginally behind the wife in deducing what was in Barnaby's mind. 'We'll have to take her to the rescue place, I suppose.'

'The dog pound,' added Ant, with the slightest of winks at Thea.

'Over my dead body,' asserted the man. 'We've got quite a thing about unwanted dogs.'

'We've got three already,' said Sally tightly.

'She won't be any trouble. It's the least we can do for poor Hillie. Look at the poor thing, she's shivering.'

It was true. Biddy was gazing raptly into Barnaby's face, her whole body quivering.

'She loves you,' said Ant.

'They always do,' the man smiled. 'I think I must have been a dog in a previous life.'

'Like in *Dean Spanley*,' said Ant, receiving nothing but blank looks in response.

Thea was reminded that she had already relinquished concern for the dog once, when Rachel Ottaway told her that Ant had adopted it. Perhaps this was another false hope. After all, Sally Taylor might be in charge of such matters, and she remained patently unconvinced.

'Sally, we can just take her for tonight – for the weekend, maybe. We can let all the trouble die down a bit, and give the poor thing a bit of TLC, while they decide what's to happen to her.'

Mrs Taylor had obviously heard it all before. 'They won't give her another thought, will they?' she said with more than a hint of resignation. 'I mean – who do you think is going to care what happens to her? That son of Caroline's, whatever his name is – he doesn't sound as if he'd be interested. If we take her now, we'll be stuck with her.'

'And would that be such a bad thing? Eh?' Her husband twinkled at her, with an expression that Thea assumed any wife would find exasperating. But amazingly Sally seemed to find it unobjectionable. She grimaced fondly and patted Biddy's shoulder.

'There!' crowed the man. 'All sorted. Now, who's drinking? It's on me.' He waved a twenty-pound note at the man behind the bar. 'So long as nobody asks for a double Scotch,' he added.

Ant and Thea exchanged glances. 'We're fine, actually, thanks,' said Thea. 'We've nearly finished. I should get back. It's great about Biddy. Someone should tell Oscar what's been decided.' She waited for somebody to offer to take on the task, only to be met with silence. 'Oh, well – I suppose I can do it,' she said, wondering why in the world she should. What did it have to do with her? And then it hit her again, for the tenth time at least that week, that she could now permit herself to be included in the social circle on a permanent basis. She was no longer an outsider. When would it feel real, she wondered. When could she simply stop thinking about it and get on with being a normal person with normal friendships?

'You've got his number, have you?' asked Sally, noticing something of Thea's state of mind. 'I suppose you've been questioned by the police and all that stuff. Can't have been much fun.'

'And this poor little wounded soldier is yours, is it?' added Barnaby, belatedly showing solicitude towards Hepzibah. 'What a quiet little thing you are, eh?' He reached out a hand to caress the spaniel, who gave him the most perfunctory acknowledgment. She usually liked pubs, but this one had required an annoyingly long walk, and provided nowhere soft to sit. Then all the attention had gone to the shaggy orange animal who emitted worryingly neurotic vibes. Hepzie had crept under the table, in the hope of averting any unpleasantness.

'Yes, that's Hepzie,' said Thea. 'Come on, Heps. Time to go home.'

'Interesting name,' said Sally, with a faint hint of a sniff.

Thea gave her a probing look. Here was an intriguing woman, she thought. Did bridge players have the same skills as those who chose poker? Straight faces, ability to deflect assumptions, bluffs and quick-thinking. Murderers needed much the same talents, she supposed. And wasn't

180

there a suggestion of diversionary tactics in all this business with the dog, when their good friend had only just died in horrible circumstances? There had only been the most oblique reference to it, which might accord with the old British habit of avoiding painful topics, but was definitely not natural in current times. 'I found her body, you know,' she said, slightly too loudly. 'Your good friend Hilary, dead in the freezer. *I* found her. With Rachel.'

Both the Taylors glanced nervously around the bar before replying. The barman had retreated to a corner, where he was polishing glasses. Ant gave a sound like a stifled laugh. Hepzibah sat down and sighed. 'It must have been ghastly for you,' said Sally. 'We thought you might not want to talk about it.'

'I don't. But neither do I want to pretend it never happened.'

'Of course. Right. Yes.' The woman tipped her head in a gesture of helplessness. 'Poor Hillie. The whole thing is just *incredible*.' For once Thea found the word appropriate to the situation, unlike most of the times it was used. Sally was still talking: 'I can't bear to think about it, to be honest. I really can't. I know that's feeble of me, but it's true.'

'Seems to me it's best not to chatter overmuch,' said Barnaby. 'The police have enough of a job without speculation and so forth. Best just to let them sort it out. It's what they're paid for, after all.'

Now *he* was being supercilious, Thea thought irritably. They were both putting her in her place, with the greatest politeness. Another familiar factor she'd encountered in the Cotswolds a number of times: everyone was so damned complacent, so sure of their rightful place in the scheme of things. Her thoughts and feelings churned, and all she wanted was to go home. Ant was sitting empty-handed, showing no sign of wanting to say anything, even more of an outsider than Thea was. His extraordinary lifestyle was going to give her something new to report to Drew. She might even be tempted to say something to Gladwin about the harassment from the plutocrat landlord.

But she had lingered on the threshold long enough. 'Come on, Heps,' she said again, pulling open the door and heading back along the cold country lane that led to the house that still didn't entirely feel like home.

Chapter Fourteen

Drew had finished the funeral of Miss Temple, and had ducked out of the reception afterwards at the hotel in Blockley. 'They only ask me out of politeness,' he had told Thea many months earlier. 'It's a kind of convention. I hardly ever show up.'

It had struck Thea as rather sad, this image of himself as a kind of spectre at the feast, but she could understand it. The undertaker had not come to the post-funeral party when Carl had died, nor after her father's funeral. But Drew was different. He was a perfectly pleasant person, carrying no aura of embalming fluid or corruption, as far as she could detect. She felt the rejection by association, and it saddened her.

'I had lunch at the pub,' she told him, having found him in his office. 'With two men, two dogs and a woman.'

'Sounds like fun.'

'Well, I lie, a bit. I only actually ate with one man and the dogs. The good news is that Biddy's found a new home. It's almost too good to be true.' It was, she realised. People did not so readily adopt a big needy dog, these days. Just as human adoptions required all sorts of bureaucratic involvement, didn't a dog have to be certified and registered and generally kept track of?

'Who's Biddy?' asked Drew, his eyes still on the sheet of paper in front of him.

'Mrs Bunting's sister's dog. Keep up. You heard us talking about her with Oscar Hemingway yesterday.'

'Did I?'

She sighed. He was often like this immediately after a funeral, and she often forgot to make allowances for it. Relief that all had gone well, combined with a residual respect for the passing of a human life, and the association with raw emotions at the loss were all more than enough to render him quiet and contemplative for the rest of the day.

'Yes. And I said I'd tell the Hemingway man that she was okay. He must be her official owner now. Did he give us his number on Wednesday? I can't remember.'

'Um . . . he left a card. It's on the side somewhere.'

The side was a corner of one of the worktops where papers accumulated as they waited in that limbo land between first arriving and finally being thrown away when deemed to be no longer relevant. Important letters or documents were filtered out bit by bit, leaving a growing stack of flyers, letters from school, jotted notes and occasional postcards from friends in distant parts. Thea's mother had taken to going around Europe on coaches, and sent a lot of postcards.

Thea found Oscar's business card very close to the top.

'I could send him a text,' she said. 'If I phone I might get him at a bad time. I always seem to do that, every time I call anybody.'

Drew merely nodded, so she set about composing a text. *Biddy has found a new home, so no need to worry about her* was her first effort. Then she wondered whether the man was going to even remember the dog's name. Surely it was obvious from the context? But was there a subtly implied criticism in the second part? There was every chance that he hadn't been worrying at all. She amended it to *Just to say your mother's dog is okay. She seems to have found a new home. Call me for more details.* That would have to do. She sent it, with the realisation that Oscar now had her number, and might call, and so she ought to make sure the phone was charged and kept on.

'There,' she said. 'Mission accomplished.'

Drew got up. 'I need to get started on Mrs Card,' he said. 'Andrew's just brought her back from Cirencester. She won't have had anything done.'

'I thought she was coming back yesterday. Didn't you say she—'

He cut her off. 'Don't worry about it. You don't have to follow every little twist and turn of the job. I was thinking aloud, I expect. Don't take everything I say as gospel. It changes all the time. Every phone call brings something new to be factored in.' He sounded a lot more irritated than the situation warranted.

'What's the matter?'

He shook his head. 'All this business with the freezer murder, of course. It won't leave us alone. I have no idea

185

how or why you got involved again today. Why it has to be *you* who sorts the dog out, for heaven's sake. I leave the house for an hour, and here we are, right in the middle of it all again.'

'You're quite right to be cross about it,' she soothed, feeling rather gratified that their roles had suddenly reversed. 'It was a man called Ant – Antares officially – who came to the door, and said he couldn't have Biddy any more. It was only because we're easy to find, and he couldn't think who else to try. So we went to the pub, just because it was lunchtime, and he's nice to talk to. And then the Taylors turned up. You don't know them. They live in Blockley.' She paused, with a frown. 'I have no idea why they were here, come to think of it. Anyway, he's wild about dogs, and they're always rescuing them, and so they've taken Biddy. That's it. We hardly talked about the murder. They didn't want to mention it at all until I forced them.'

'He can't be called Antares. That's a star. Is he a hippy?'

'A bit. Honestly, Drew, you should hear about the way he lives. It's a scandal. We should see if we can do something about it.' She took a breath to see her through the whole story, but again her husband interrupted her.

'No, not now. I realise I should be glad you're meeting new people, and being useful and all that, but it doesn't feel like something to be glad about.'

'They're all very nice,' she said humbly. 'You'd like them.'

'I'm the same as Hepzie. I like everybody.' He sounded very gloomy about it. 'But I work with the dead, Thea, and that sets me apart. It's not as bad as if I was a mainstream undertaker, and I'm sure the village will take us to their hearts eventually, but not if we get embroiled in the nastier side of things. Not if we never show any signs of the lighter elements. And it's not just you and me, is it?'

She began to glimpse the real source of his trouble. Or she thought she did. 'But isn't it exactly the same as before, when you and Karen were in North Staverton? How is this any different? I mean – you can't get much nastier than having your wife shot by a criminal, can you?'

'You're right, of course. But somehow it *is* different. The whole set-up down there was far more transparent than it is here. People passed our burial field and house, seeing them every day, all as one unit, with the kids playing in the garden. Tucked away down here, crammed in amongst all these smart homes, with the field just a patch of forgotten grass on a different road – it feels as if we're *hiding* something. As if we're ashamed of ourselves.'

'Oh.' This was going to be difficult, she told herself. Her instant reaction was that he was trying to say he wanted to move. That Broad Campden wasn't working for him. That they would have to uproot and make huge decisions and argue and panic and get into tangles with bureaucracy. But she swallowed all that back, and clung to a fragile calm. 'Yes. I can see it is a bit like that. But we're *here* now. We *decided*. There must be all sorts of things we can do to make it work better.'

'Remind me what they are, then.' He met her eyes without a smile.

He thinks this is all down to me, she thought. He was blaming her for her reckless engagement with unsuitable people and their exasperating tendency to get themselves murdered. 'Well, for a start, we could ask Mr Shipley over for a drink or something. He's perfectly nice, and he could introduce us to more local people. And I could press on with the history stuff. There must be ways that could work, assuming I wouldn't be treading on any toes if someone's doing it already.' She spoke bravely, in a rush to reassure him. Her mind darted through every local encounter she'd had in the past few months, searching for more likely characters who might help them to put down roots. The mere idea of moving again made her stomach clench.

'We could do a lot of things, but I'm not sure any of them would be any good. I think it might already be too late. If we weren't already tainted by the work I do, then this business with the Buntings is going to really put people off. Nobody's ever going to forget that it was you who found her.'

'I couldn't help it,' she said, feeling every bit as childish as she sounded. 'You must see that.'

'I do. I've been over it a dozen times and I can't honestly blame you. You need local friends, even more than I do. I mean – that isn't my main worry. Not at all. I've got plenty to keep me occupied. It's *your* interests I'm thinking about, don't you see? I can't think how we can carry on as we are, because you're always going to be out there looking for distraction. And somehow that always seems to lead to somebody getting killed.'

He waved away the incoherent protest that sprang to her lips. 'No, no. I didn't mean it like that. I'm sure the

188

people would get killed with or without you. But you just manage to *be* there, somehow. It's like some sort of crazy curse. And I really want it to stop.'

'So do I!' she shouted. 'Even more than you. I can't bear it, all over again. But I can't just ignore it, now it's happened. And I'm not going to be scared away from here by it. That would be even worse.'

He stared at her unblinking. 'Who said anything about going away? What do you mean?' His face turned grey. 'You're not *leaving* me, are you?' he choked.

'Of course I'm not. Of *course* I'm not, you idiot. I thought *you* were saying you wanted to move. All of us, to another house. Isn't that what you meant?'

'No. No, it wasn't what I meant at all.' He got up and went to her. 'Come here. Don't panic. We'll be all right, so long as we don't panic. And never ever even dream of doing anything or going anywhere without me.'

'I never ever did,' she said. 'Not for a single second.'

They clung together, squeezing each other too tightly for comfort. Thea's heart was somewhere just under her chin, and her stomach down by her kidneys. Everything had turned upside down in the past few minutes, and was crashing around inside, as it tried to get back to normal. 'I don't think I've ever felt so frightened,' she whispered, after a few minutes.

'Nor me,' he said.

The arrival of the children, half an hour later, saw them still in the kitchen, holding hands and trying to construct a plan of campaign for the future. Stephanie and Timmy stood

189

wide-eyed in the doorway, trying to gauge the atmosphere. 'Did something happen?' asked Stephanie.

'Oh, no. No more than usual,' said Thea, which made Drew laugh.

'You do like living here, don't you?' he asked his offspring. 'Tell the truth, now.'

The children exchanged looks, silent communication a well-established knack. 'It's okay,' said Timmy. 'Some shops would be good. And a place to go bowling.'

'And a movie house,' added his sister, who was currently using American terms whenever possible, for reasons nobody understood.

'But it's okay really,' Tim summarised. 'Bowling's lame, anyway.'

'You've never been bowling in your life,' said Drew, bewildered.

'I know. But it's always in films, and they have popcorn and Coke.'

'Do they?' Drew looked from face to face for an answer, but none was forthcoming.

'We'd better stay here, then,' said Thea. 'Because it sounds as if you two want to live in the middle of a big city, and *that's* not going to happen. Hepzie would hate it, for a start. And the schools would be dreadful.'

'This is okay,' said Timmy again. 'Why? Have the neighbours tried to make us go? Ned McGragh at school said they'll force us out because nobody wants to live near an undertaker.' His face was a picture of anxiety and hurt.

'Oh, Tim, he didn't, did he?' Thea pulled the little boy

to her and hugged him close. 'He's completely wrong about that. The neighbours don't mind us at all. We'll soon have a whole lot of proper friends – all of us. We haven't really had enough time to get to know people yet. It's all been so busy. But we will. I promise.'

'I've got a friend,' said Stephanie, with a thread of resentment. 'She's called Abigail. I *told* you about her.'

'There you are, then,' said Drew with patriarchal finality. 'Now let's all stop being so serious, and go and watch some telly for a change.'

Both children groaned. Try as they might, they could never convince him that nobody ever watched telly any more.

'Can we play a game instead?' begged Stephanie. Christmas had seen them obeying tradition and working through a stack of neglected board games. Thea's sister Jocelyn had given them one called 'Agricola', which only Stephanie had really been attracted to at first, given its extreme complexity. The precocious little girl had persisted, and the game had lasted into a third day and ended up with three more converts. Even Timmy had mastered it, making a mockery of the age guidance on the box.

'There isn't time,' Drew objected. 'Now you're back at school.'

The ringing telephone took him away, thus making his point for him. Stephanie growled fiercely at the intrusion. 'Why does he never have any time off?' she complained. 'He works *all the time*.'

'It's not really work,' said Thea. 'He just has to be available for people who want him. It doesn't happen as often as we'd like, actually. Our survival depends on it, don't forget.'

Timmy's head came up. 'Survival?' he said thoughtfully. 'We survive because somebody dies, then.'

It was a startlingly mature remark. 'Gosh, Tim,' said Thea. 'That's very deep.'

'It's right, though,' said Stephanie. 'We're like carnivores or vampires, needing to eat something dead so we can live. Except we don't eat them, of course,' she conceded.

'We perform a very important service,' Thea told her. 'As you very well know.'

It was still a puzzle to Thea just how much the children understood about dying and funerals and the fate of the physical body. The death of their mother had forced them to confront the whole question, but before that their father had buried people just outside their house. Stephanie had often found herself with her father in the little office where he arranged the funerals with the bereaved families. Thea wondered sometimes whether there might be something slightly unwholesome about this; something that might be damaging them more than Drew would acknowledge.

They all seemed to be waiting for this uncomfortably intense intermission to be over. For Thea and Drew it had lasted all afternoon, and was decidedly draining. It felt like a counselling session without the counsellor. And on their own, they didn't know how to bring it to a close. The notion of a can of worms was all too fitting, a great writhing mass of fears and dangers, seldom confronted, and now crawling all over the house and beyond, refusing to go back into its tin and have the lid pressed firmly down. Not so much

192

worms as black prickly things that could bite and sting.

Drew came back from the phone. 'We're really talking about what happened on Wednesday, aren't we?' Thea concluded hesitantly, addressing the children after a glance at Drew. 'You two probably know by now – some of it at least. And it upset me quite a lot, because it was really horrible, and now I want to try to make it at least a bit better for myself and everybody else who's concerned. I found a dead woman in her own kitchen, and I can't make that unhappen, however much I want to. I can't just carry on regardless, now I've seen her husband and friends and even her nephew. I just can't leave it. You see that, don't you?' She appealed to all three of them.

'You're right,' said Drew. 'That is where the trouble mostly lies. All the rest of it can be put right, but if you keep walking into other people's desperate lives the way you do, we have got trouble.'

'I know. I'm sorry,' she said. 'But I really don't seem able to help it.'

She pulled an exaggerated face denoting apology and chagrin, which made Timmy giggle, at least. Drew and Stephanie looked equally lost for words. Then he gave a quick shrug and said, 'Well, it is what it is, I suppose,' which felt to Thea like some kind of absolution; probably the best she could hope for.

Stephanie had the last word. 'Well, most people would say it's good to care about your neighbours' troubles, wouldn't they? The vicar came to do assembly today, and he said everybody should love their neighbour as much as they love themselves. Didn't he, Tim?'

Timmy made it plain that he had entirely failed to absorb the gist of the vicar's words, and had nothing whatsoever to say on the matter.

'Well, good for him,' said Drew, in a parting shot as he left the room.

Chapter Fifteen

Friday evening was usually a very relaxed point in the week for the Slocombes. No school the next day; no funerals, either, unless Drew had been persuaded to make an exception. But this Friday was different. The revelations of deeper feelings left them all wary about what could and could not be safely uttered. The air was scarcely clearer than it had been four hours earlier, and Thea found herself almost dreading the coming weekend.

So she was relieved, and not unduly surprised when somebody knocked on the front door at eight o'clock. Even though visitors in the hours of darkness were very rare, and generally disconcerting, the whole week had been so topsy-turvy that anything might happen. Drew was still upstairs doing the bedtime stories, which left her free to rush recklessly to respond to the summons. *Let it be a murderer, if that's what it takes to teach him that it's not my fault*, she said to herself, with a singular lack of coherence.

She switched all the lights on, including the one over the front door, and chirped at Hepzie in the hope that she might at least try to act protectively. The dog gave her a long stare of incomprehension. 'All right. Point taken,' said Thea.

The man standing on the doorstep was Oscar Hemingway, looking even bigger than before against the dark sky, with random shadows dancing across his face and body. 'I should have phoned,' he said quickly. 'This is awful of me. I hope I haven't frightened you? You're not here on your own, are you?'

What would she have done if she had been, she wondered. Almost certainly let him in and allowed events to take whatever course the gods had planned for them. Logically, there was a fair chance that this man had actually killed his aunt, and even perhaps his mother. He definitely had had the opportunity to do so, and there could easily be a good old-fashioned motive like greed or resentment of some kind.

'No, no. Drew's just putting the kids to bed,' she said. 'Come on in. Did you get my text about the dog?'

'I did. Thanks for that. Poor old Biddy.'

'I know. She must have been so bewildered. But she's landed on her feet, apparently. Barnaby and Sally Taylor, the people your uncle plays bridge with – they've taken her. They're very keen on dogs – or he is, anyway. I think she'll be all right.'

'Thank goodness for that. She has been on my mind, now and then. The truth is, I never managed to like her very much, and the feeling was mutual. My mother got her for all the wrong reasons. It was very selfish of her.'

'Oh dear.' You really ought not to speak ill of the dead,

Thea thought. It was very bad taste, apart from anything else. And probably bad luck as well.

'Sorry. Anyway, I came about Uncle Gray, actually.'

He was following her into the living room, where it was chilly and poorly lit. The heating was kept as low as they could make it, to be augmented by the woodburner, in theory, at least. But nobody had lit the fire that afternoon. One of the light bulbs on the wall had expired, leaving a gloomy corner where the sofa was.

'I hardly saw anything of him,' she began, in an instinctive attempt to distance herself. It was a necessary disclaimer, especially given Drew's firmer-than-usual stand on the matter.

'You saw enough to know he'd never commit murder. Didn't you?'

'Quite honestly, no, I didn't. What I saw was a man who sounds permanently angry and who can't have been at all easy to live with. I thought Hilary looked frazzled and rather cowed by him.'

'Oh.' He slumped onto the sofa and rubbed his face. 'Oh,' he said again. 'I didn't get that impression from you yesterday.'

'That's the trouble, isn't it? Everything's just *impressions*. I don't know any facts. Nobody ever really knows what's going on in a marriage, at the best of times. All I did was follow Rachel into that damned kitchen, and now *my* marriage is suffering as a result. And we've only been married a few months,' she finished sadly.

'Well, Graham didn't do it,' said Oscar, suddenly loud and emphatic. 'It makes absolutely no sense to think he did.

They might as well have arrested me. That would be every bit as logical. But who's going to listen to me? I wasn't here. I was concentrating on my mother – who everybody seems to have forgotten, by the way.'

'I haven't forgotten her.' That wasn't entirely true, she admitted to herself. Hadn't there been something disconcerting about that death, according to Gladwin? 'Did I hear that she's had to have a post-mortem?'

'Oh, that,' he waved the notion away. 'They weren't going to tell me, you know. I had to get shirty with them before they'd explain what was happening. They referred her death to the coroner, sometime yesterday, but this morning they called me to say everything's going through after all. Some overcautious young doctor did it, apparently. I tracked him down, and he was very apologetic. He said one of the nurses, Latvian or Lithuanian, misunderstood what Mum was saying, and raised the alarm over it. She heard the word "poison", according to this doctor, and told the staff nurse, who told one of the doctors, and it all kicked off from there.'

'So what was she actually saying?'

'Probably it was poison, but she used the word all the time, about everything. She told me the hospital coffee was pure poison, for a start. You have to be so careful these days.' He sighed. Then his face cleared. 'It'll make a good anecdote for the eulogy, if I can keep myself together enough to deliver it.'

'That will take courage,' said Thea, a trifle absently. She was thinking about the matter of poison, and whether or not it was right to let Caroline go unexamined to her grave – or furnace. Then she thought of Drew. 'Where are you having the funeral?' she asked.

'The crematorium outside Oxford. It's handy for most people, and she didn't like the idea of burial.'

Oh well, thought Thea. *You can't win them all.*

'You ought to speak to Rachel, not me,' she said. 'She knew your aunt and uncle quite well. She must have a far better idea of what must have happened.'

'Has she said anything to you about it?'

That required some thought. 'Well, sort of,' she said weakly. 'All rather general stuff. I think she assumes, like everyone else, that the only person who could possibly have killed Hilary was her husband. But she talked more about how quickly people get over shock, and what the police might be thinking.' In fact, when she applied herself to the question, it seemed that Rachel Ottaway had barely mentioned Hilary or Graham as people at all. 'So, no, not really. Considering she must have known them pretty well, she kept rather quiet. I suppose she still couldn't believe what had happened. The evidence of her own eyes,' she added with a frown.

He shifted his considerable weight on the cushions. 'I can't agree with her, then. It's like everybody telling you that grass is pink, when you know for certain it isn't. It's an awful feeling, especially when nobody else in the world thinks the same as you.'

'What about her sons? Tom and—'

'Edward. Right. You'd think they'd understand what I'm talking about, wouldn't you? But they don't. Tom said Uncle Gray's always been unpredictable and that makes him capable of anything. But as far as he could tell it was a fairly happy marriage. Not that he ever paid a lot of attention – he's very self-absorbed. And Edward's even worse. He's hardly seen them for years. He's not saying anything much, apart from how stigmatising it's going to be, and what his girlfriend is going to say about it. She's off on some stupid sailing trip in Africa and doesn't want to communicate with anybody, or so he says. What a family!' he ended up despairingly. 'We're probably all bonkers in various ways.'

'You seem okay to me,' she said hesitantly. 'At least you *care*. You'd be quite justified in leaving it all to the police, with your own loss to cope with.'

He gave her a momentarily blank look before understanding what she meant. 'Oh – my mum. Yes, I guess so. But she's been ill for ages. It was mostly a relief when she finally died, to tell you the honest truth. We knew from last weekend that she was in the final stages.' He made a fist and thumped the arm of the sofa. 'That's what I *mean*,' he burst out. 'There was old Uncle Gray, sitting at her side, when he really didn't have to. It was only his sister-in-law, after all, but he said it was the least he could do for us, and it was no hardship. He was really *nice*, and did his best to keep the decibels down. I really think she knew he was there and was glad. They'd been getting on so well, in the final month or two.'

Thea's antennae pricked up at that. Could there be some sort of motive hidden in this disclosure? Had Graham killed his wife hoping that Caroline would rally, and he could enjoy some time exclusively with her? It seemed somewhat extreme, unless he refused to accept that Caroline was dying. Perhaps he thought he could revive her with the strength of his love. *Fanciful*, she reproached herself. And really rather silly. But not entirely impossible.

'They will have to find actual evidence against him before they can formally charge him,' she offered. 'It hasn't got to that stage yet, has it?'

'I'm not sure. I'm hazy about how it all works. Would they bother to tell me what they were doing anyway?'

'They'd tell your cousins. Are they both staying with you? Where exactly do you live, anyway?' There were so many details she had not discovered. Didn't that mean she had been considerably less nosy than usual? Didn't that earn her some points somewhere? She had taken absolutely no initiatives towards discovering anything more about the case; everybody had come to her, knowing all too well where to find her.

'I live in Chipping Norton most of the time. Tom's staying with me, but Edward's in a hotel. He doesn't get on too well with his brother. I was hoping all this would bring them together, but it probably won't. They'll both be too sorry for themselves to spare a thought for anyone else. I've got some history where they're concerned as well, but I don't let it affect me any more. It's fifteen years ago now, at least.'

'And none of you is married?'

Oscar shook his head. 'All for different reasons.'

'You said Tom used to pick on you. And I heard from somebody that he's taken the death of his mother really badly. And Graham isn't saying anything to the police.' She

201

gave a girly laugh. 'Sorry. It sounds as if I've been listening to gossip. You probably know that I've got some friends in the local police.'

'No, I didn't hear that. It doesn't matter. Obviously we're the talk of the county. That's what Edward's most worried about. Or his girlfriend will be. No sense in letting that get to you, the way I see it. It'll die down eventually. I'm off to Boston anyway, as soon as the funeral's done with.'

'Boston? In America?'

'That's the one. I've got people there. It's cold, mind you, at this time of year.'

There was nothing she could think of to say to that. Oscar Hemingway was evolving into somebody she didn't think she liked very much. Superficial, evasive, possibly irresponsible as well. He should have more care for his mother's dog, in Thea's opinion. Not to mention the two dead women in his immediate family.

'Did you say Graham's refusing to say anything?' He had evidently been reprocessing what she had just said.

'That's right. And it makes everything very difficult for the police. It all hinges on what the suspect tells them: whether he claims to be innocent or admits to guilt. They can't assume anything from total silence. It's very rare, apparently. Hardly anybody can keep it up for very long.'

'Least of all Uncle Gray,' said Oscar, with a rueful smile. 'Silence really isn't his thing.'

Next came a trilling tune from his pocket, and an automatic response to it. 'Hi . . . Tom?' There followed a one-sided conversation, in which Oscar said little more than, 'Really? That's a big surprise. What happens now?'

Thea went to the far end of the room, fiddling with a scattering of magazines that had been left on top of the television. She had no intention of vacating the room completely, regarding phone calls as intrusive, and not deserving of any special privileges. Besides, she was eager to know what the Bunting son had to say – assuming it was the same Tom.

'He's confessed,' Oscar summarised, when the phone was back in his pocket. 'Uncle Gray has started talking, and admits that he killed Hilary. They called Tom ten minutes ago and told him.'

She expected him to get up and go home, intent on hearing more news from his cousin, but instead he settled more deeply into the sofa cushions, and started to pour out his soul.

'I just can't believe it,' he repeated. 'How could he do such a thing? And *why*? He and Aunt Hilary got along well enough. And was it before or after my mother died? Was he mad? Did Mum tell him something that sent him dashing back here in a rage? We were all together a lot as kids, you know. The two sisters were close and we were always in each other's houses, sleeping over for weekends and school holidays, going camping with Uncle Gray, after my dad left us. They were always really nice to me, even if the boys were often resentful. Three's an awkward number. It was always two against one. But it wasn't so bad, on the whole. We had good times. You know Blockley – the woods and wide open fields? We used to go there a lot, running free – that was after the Buntings moved here. They were in Evesham before that and we saw less of them. We always had a dog, which came with us. Aunt Hillie would complain about the mud, but never enough to bother us. Mum and me and the dog – that was our little family.'

'And yet you don't care a bit about Biddy,' Thea interrupted.

'I know. I never did take to her. We had a lovely little corgi, called Retty – short for Henrietta – who I adored. She was really mine – from when I was eight to well into my twenties. I could never quite feel the same about any other dogs after her. She slept on my bed and followed me around. I couldn't believe it when she died. She was sixteen and I was sure she'd last till she was about thirty.'

'Were you still at home? Didn't you go to university or anything?'

'I went to Oxford Brookes, and lived at home. We were only about five miles away then. I couldn't leave Retty – or my mother. Pathetic, I know. I did grow up eventually, more or less, but it took quite a while.'

'How old are you now?' She could hear the ghostly voice of her mother chastising her for impertinence, but Oscar clearly didn't mind.

'Thirty-one. Tom's thirty-three, and Edward's thirty. We fitted neatly together, you see. In theory, anyway.'

'I almost never saw my cousins. There were four of us, so we didn't see the need for any more kids in our lives. On my father's side there are one or two I'd have liked to have known better.'

The conversation was filled with wistful melancholy, which fitted the shadowy room very well. Where was Drew, Thea suddenly wondered. Surely he could hear their voices, and would be curious to know who the visitor was? It felt unfriendly of him to stay away. Or even worse – did he assume it was somebody associated with Hilary Bunting, and was making his disapproval clear by staying away? That was almost certainly the case, she thought. And if so, they'd be back to the terrifying discord that had assailed them earlier. 'I must go and see where Drew is,' she said aloud. 'He might want me for something.'

Oscar Hemingway merely nodded as she left the room.

'Drew?' she called, in the hallway. He could be in the kitchen or his room at the back. He might even have gone out to the coffin room – the name they had adopted for it in preference to anything else.

'Up here,' came a quiet voice. 'Don't shout. Timmy's just dropped off.'

This was very unusual. Timmy was not a baby. If he woke up, he'd just go back to sleep in the assurance that family life was going on around him and there was nothing to worry about. 'So what?' she said, at normal pitch.

'He's upset.' Drew was standing at the top of the stairs. 'I've been sitting with him for ages.'

'Oh. Oh dear. Well, I've got Oscar Hemingway in the sitting room. He's upset, as well. You can tell me about Tim as soon as he's gone.'

'How long will that be?'

The man himself came to the door of the sitting room. 'I'll go right away,' he said, making it obvious that he'd heard every word. 'You've got your own problems, by the sound of it.'

'Oh, no, not really,' said Thea quickly and treacherously,

aware that Drew had withdrawn into one of the upstairs rooms as she spoke. 'Not like yours.'

He grimaced. 'Well, it's much worse for Tom and Ed. Their father's confessed to murdering their mother. Murder,' he repeated. 'What a heavy horrible word it is. Like a blunt instrument. Ugly.'

She nodded, having come to the same conclusion a while ago. 'So we were both wrong,' she said. 'About Graham, I mean.'

He rubbed the back of his neck and heaved a deep sigh. 'Looks like it. I wonder if they'll let us go and see him, and ask him *why*. I don't think any of us will be able to get on with our lives until we understand that.'

She was acutely sorry for him. A big bulky man, like a bull or – more accurately – a Newfoundland dog. There was something cuddly about his awkward size and air of bewilderment.

'It's such an awful thing,' she sympathised.

'I suppose it avoids a trial, if he's pleaded guilty. And they might go easy on him. They can't think he's a dangerous criminal.'

'Mm,' she said, thinking again of Graham Bunting's expression on Wednesday morning. 'Let's hope so.'

Chapter Sixteen

Drew's explanation of Timmy's distress was uncharacteristically intense. 'He says he thinks you're going to get murdered. He's frightened to go to school and leave you, even though I'm here practically all the time.'

'You couldn't save his mother,' she murmured. 'The way he sees it, I mean.'

'I know. It's perfectly logical.'

'Especially when people are getting killed just down the street. And electric cables go flying around, and sisters get rushed off to hospital. It's been a very perilous week for a small boy. What did you say to him?'

'I said there are times when everything feels wobbly, like a sort of earthquake, and nobody can promise absolute safety. And wouldn't life be dull if they could. I said it's all a matter of balance, light and shade, good and bad. You can't have one without the other. I got a bit Buddhist about it.'

'Sounds more like Jung. But good stuff, wherever it comes from.'

'He's old enough to take some reality – I hope. I never

could abide bland reassurances as a child. Especially when they directly contradict the evidence.'

'I agree. People really do die, and vanish for ever. He knows that.'

'But more people stay alive and healthy until they're eighty. That's what I told him. It's important to get it into perspective. I had to go through a long list of people who are perfectly all right: Maggs, her little Meredith, all your relations. And then I realised the list isn't really long enough. I couldn't mention Hepzie, of course.'

'Yes, you could. She's a good example of getting over something bad. Not every accident leads to someone dying.'

'True. But *murder*, Thea. How can anybody ever get around the sheer horror of deliberate killing? It's a long way over a line that can be explained to a child.'

'He confessed!' The words burst out of her, as the really important development of the day hit her afresh. 'Graham Bunting has admitted to killing his wife.'

'Really?' Drew gave this a long moment's consideration, then, 'Thank goodness for that.' He exhaled like a bicycle pump. 'What a relief. So we can just forget about it now, then? Say we can.' He gripped her arm tightly. 'Say it.'

'We can,' she said. 'Or we can try, anyway. We can certainly tell Timmy there's no need to worry about a murderer on the loose.' She met his gaze with difficulty. 'It's all done and dusted, as they say.'

And up to coffee time on Saturday, it almost felt as if it really was finished with. Nobody was going to bother her about the Buntings again. If Graham maintained his guilty plea, there'd be no need for any sort of witness testimony. There would barely be a trial, just a hearing and a committal. The prospect should have been entirely satisfying and straightforward. But Thea's obstinate mind would not be reconciled with that appalled and appalling look on Graham's face. She saw it when she first awoke that morning and it hovered persistently throughout the first part of the day.

'I ought to call Rachel and make sure she's heard the news,' said Thea, as she walked around the house with a mug of coffee. She was doing a perfunctory one-handed tidy-up, which amounted to little more than straightening a few cushions and taking three pairs of shoes out into the hall, where they rightfully belonged.

Drew was waiting for the first of his tree people to arrive. 'I suggested we meet at the field, but they said they'd rather come here first. Can't imagine why,' he said, rolling his eyes. 'The other lot were more co-operative. At least it's not raining or snowing.' He was leaning against the window frame, looking onto the little road outside. 'What did you say about Rachel?'

She said it again.

'Well, maybe you shouldn't,' he said slowly. 'You're probably not meant to know about it yourself, let alone tell other people. You found out from the family, more or less by accident. It's not public knowledge.'

'It might be. How would we know?'

He shrugged, and she gave it more thought. 'Are you saying you think it might be some sort of trick on the part of the police? Something intended to flush out the real killer? That doesn't happen in real life, does it?'

'I wasn't saying anything remotely like that, you idiot. It's more a matter of protocol. That sort of thing.'

She was still in full flight. 'No, but both sons were told yesterday. Who else is there? Only friends and neighbours, and that's me and Rachel.'

'Except that nobody's bothered to tell you officially, have they?'

'Not yet. They will, because as far as they know I still think I'll have to be a witness at his trial. It's bonkers to think I should keep quiet about it.'

'One of us is bonkers, I agree,' he said. Then, 'Oh – here they are. I wonder where they left their car.'

She ignored the arrivals, trying to work out whether Drew could possibly have a point. The only way to find out was to call Gladwin and request a proper update as to what was happening. But she still wanted to speak to Rachel Ottaway. Some sort of debriefing was called for, and only her fellow body-finder would be able to supply it, preferably face-to-face. A phone call would be a pale substitute for a proper long chat.

Drew was taking his people through to the office, trying to answer questions about fertiliser and wind damage, and whether there were any guarantees about care of their precious tree. Evidently it was all very urgent and important, and she smiled at his efforts to get them out of the family area before two children came hurtling down the stairs, or a dog interposed itself in a doorway.

On a weekday, Thea could have arranged to meet Rachel over a drink, or even invited her to lunch. But Stephanie and

Timmy demanded her full attention and constant presence every weekend, and she was generally very willing to give it. After all, she had five free days to conduct her own life, when they were at school. Now it was Saturday and there was a plan to go down to Stroud and explore the old canal in the area. By dint of persistent efforts, Thea had finally succeeded in creating a genuine interest in the Cotswold canal system in both children. She made it into a game, tracking the course of the waterways through woodland and cultivated fields. It got them away from their gadgets, and gave them something different to enjoy. Drew had been greatly impressed, but not particularly involved.

It worked best in winter months, they had discovered. Thea was hoping to take them to the woods near Frampton Mansell, which would require a full day and reliable weather. And a fully functioning dog. Those woods had associations for Thea and Hepzie which were not pleasant. On this particular day, she had resolved to limit their expedition to an afternoon, leaving the dog at home. 'We can look at the shops in Stroud as well,' she conceded. 'Although I don't think there are any that you'd like.'

She ought, then, to be perfectly able to discard every thought of Hilary Bunting and everyone else she'd met over the past few days. She had quite enough to occupy her without them. This, she told herself for the hundredth time, was her life now. She wasn't a house-sitter any more. She had no need to fill the boring days with inquisitive delving into people's lives. She was a wife and stepmother, and if things went quiet she could launch a local history group that had infinite scope for diversion. And if that didn't work, she could get a job, and augment the meagre family coffers. They could have holidays, get a new car, decorate the house, if she came up with some additional cash.

'Early lunch,' she announced. 'We'll be off at half past one, with boots and coats and notebooks. And the map, of course.'

'Which one?' asked Stephanie.

'Not the new one. It might get muddy.'

The new map was the one they were constructing for themselves, based on the sections of canal they'd already located, and decorated with photos they'd taken. It was very much in its early stages, but already the source of great pride.

'I *know* that,' said the child impatiently. 'There'd be no sense in taking that, would there?'

'Silly me.'

'We need OS 179,' said Timmy with authority. 'I've got it in my rucksack already. It shows the whole Stroudwater and locks.'

Thea gazed at him with utter admiration and a good deal of pride. Where was the frightened little boy of the previous evening now? It was all her own effort that had transformed him, given him a project that would take all his attention for a few hours. 'Well done that man,' she said and he preened accordingly.

So when Rachel Ottaway appeared, pushing her bike – obviously cured of its gear ailment – at the very moment they were piling into the car, Thea experienced only the slightest of dilemmas.

'Sorry – we're just going out,' she said firmly. 'I do want to talk to you, but it'll have to wait till Monday.'

'Just give me five minutes.' It was not so much a plea as a command.

Thea hesitated. Stephanie met her eye from the back seat of the car, and frowned. But the woman had cycled three or four miles from Blockley on a cold January afternoon. Her nose was red. 'Sorry, kids. This will be very quick, I promise.'

They walked a few yards down the lane before stopping to face each other. 'Graham confessed,' said Rachel starkly.

'I know.'

'So that's that, then.' There was distinct satisfaction on the woman's face. 'We can get on with our lives. Justice will be served.'

'That's what Oscar said. It saves all the expense and time of a trial, I suppose. And we won't be needed as witnesses.'

'He did the right thing. It could have been a lot messier, as you say.'

'It was fairly messy as it is,' said Thea, with a sudden flashback to Hilary's frozen face.

'Mm. But the main thing is that justice has been done now. No need to go ferreting into it any more. It's hard for the Bunting boys, of course. Horrible. But even they can go back to what they were doing, and they'll have the house, I suppose. Graham won't be needing it.' The satisfaction burgeoned, with a definite grin.

'You're telling me to butt out,' Thea accused Rachel. 'Which is what I was going to do anyway. But now' – she huffed a brief laugh – 'now I'm not so sure. Why are you

213

so *smug* about it? It isn't something to be glad about, is it? I don't understand how anybody could do such an awful thing to another person. There are still loads of unanswered questions. And here's you going on about it being all sorted, just because there won't be a trial.'

Rachel's smile had faded at the first words. Now she was very serious indeed. 'There are no questions that *you* need to ask. The Buntings had a volatile marriage. They sniped and snarled at each other much of the time. Just ask Sally Taylor, if you don't believe me. She'll tell you that we all pretended to think everything was fine, and couples can thrive on constant arguments, but now we know better. We can see, with hindsight, that it was far worse than we ever realised. For some reason, on Tuesday night Graham snapped. Probably the stress of Caroline dying before his eyes, or lack of sleep. Whatever. And I'm not sure it was as gruesome as you think. She might have been unconscious when he put her in the freezer. It was just unlucky for us that we were the first on the scene.'

'I wanted to talk it through with you,' said Thea, with some regret. 'Debriefing, I think they call it. And then I was going to try to forget the whole business. Now you've spoilt all that. Go away. I'm taking the children out, and we're going to have a good time. I'm sure I'll see you again, but I hope it's not very soon.'

More regret ran through her at the thought that the Ashbee researches might now never happen. Because she was fairly sure she would never like or trust Rachel Ottaway again. The smile of satisfaction had made sure of that.

And then Rachel changed completely. 'Oh God, I'm

sorry. Honestly, I never realised how that would sound. The trouble is I've got nobody to talk to. Not a single person who knows the Buntings or would understand what it's been like these past few days. My father's got to hear about it and keeps asking me to explain it all to him. And I can't sleep properly. That never happens to me. It's frightening. Plus I really can't bear the thought of any more questions or interviews. I just want it all to be over. That's not so weird, is it?'

Thea paused. In the car the children were chanting 'Thea! Thea!' in a very annoying fashion. 'What about the Taylors?' she asked. 'Why can't you talk to them?'

Rachel waved an impatient hand. 'They're hopeless. All they think about is dogs and gardens and bridge. There's no way they'd listen if I tried to talk things out.'

'But that's not what you want, is it? You just said you want it all packed away and forgotten.'

The woman visibly gave up. 'All right. Go off with your children and have a nice day. I see it was daft of me to come, especially at a weekend. I lost track of the days, to be honest with you.' The early smile had vanished so totally that Thea wondered if she could have imagined it. Now she looked haggard and exhausted. 'Let me try again in a few days. Please? We can't fall out over this. It wouldn't be worth it.'

That was an odd remark. Could you 'fall out' with somebody you'd known for less than a week? But the sentiment was not disagreeable. 'All right,' Thea said. 'I expect I'm being a bit out of order myself. We're probably both still stressed by it all. Now I really must go.'

She wasn't being stressed, of course. She was being suspicious, mistrustful and deplorably reluctant to abandon the case of Hilary Bunting, after all. When Rachel Ottaway had the temerity to turn up and tell her to forget the whole thing, her perverse little nature ensured that she would do the very opposite.

Chapter Seventeen

The afternoon in Stroud went much as planned. The threesome walked along the towpath of the Stroudwater for over a mile, along a stretch that Thea had never seen before. She was delighted at the extent of the reconstruction and loving care that was plainly being lavished on the canal. Boats were moored up for the winter, their paintwork bright. Cyclists and dog walkers shared the path, throwing cheerful greetings to everyone they met. Timmy followed their progress on the map with an easy intelligence that impressed Thea. It also made her aware that she was going to need spectacles before much longer. When the child effortlessly read the tiny print, all she could make out was a blur. 'What does that say?' she asked repeatedly.

'It says the canal's disused. That's the bit that's part of the Cotswold Way, I think.' He traced lines and symbols laboriously, consulting the key at the bottom of the sheet. 'It's not really clear which is the River Frome and which is the canal,' he complained. 'There's a lock coming up, just near the station.'

Stephanie was less concerned with the detail, more engaged by the changing landscape around her. 'Can we have a holiday on a boat sometime?' she asked. 'Then we could see it all properly. It feels wrong to be walking.'

'That would be fantastic,' Thea agreed. 'But they're dreadfully expensive. And as Timmy says, most of the actual canal still isn't being used, like it was originally.'

'But there are boats here, so it must be,' Stephanie argued.

'True. It's all a bit confusing,' she admitted. 'The map might be out of date.'

'2008,' said Timmy, after a careful search.

'That's a while ago now.'

It was all very bracing, Thea concluded. And diverting. And satisfying. It was an ideal outdoor expedition, combining fresh air, geography, history, orienteering and other old-fashioned benefits of a rural upbringing. Her own passion for canals had no identifiable genesis. She just liked the idea of them, she supposed. The way their heyday had been so brief was tragic in some ways, as well as inevitable. It was a slow means of transport, after all. Much slower than a cantering horse, or even a pony and trap. Fine for carrying heavy goods like coal, and useless for getting anywhere quickly. And now the playground of holidaymakers who delighted in chugging along at four miles an hour for a week, covering ground that could be traversed in about an hour by car.

There were ducks in one place, clustered under the overhanging branches of a weeping willow.

'Will we see a kingfisher?' asked Stephanie.

'I doubt it. I've never seen one in my whole life,' said Thea.

'You need to be in proper open country for that, I imagine.'

But then Timmy gave a subdued cry, and pointed across to the opposite bank. It took Thea a moment to focus on a slender grey figure with hunched shoulders, standing motionless on long stick-like legs. 'It's a heron,' she said. 'Look at that.'

They all looked. 'It's big,' breathed Stephanie. 'As big as Tim.'

'It is, very nearly,' Thea agreed. The bird was perhaps twenty feet away. She could see the feathers of its wings and throat, slightly ruffled. The long beak pointed downwards, as if in contemplation. 'It's waiting for a fish to come past.'

And suddenly, as if caused by her thought, the bird dived forward, wings opening, neck stretching, and barely a second later it was lifting into the air with a wriggling fish caught in its beak. The sheer fluidity of the movement left them all open-mouthed. As it flapped away, it circled over their heads, low enough for the frantic fish's struggles to be clearly witnessed.

'Poor fish,' said Stephanie. 'It must be so frightened.'

The spell was broken. The calm contentment of the winter day was overwhelmed by the casual cruelty that was intrinsic to survival.

'Do fish *get* frightened?' asked Timmy.

'Probably not,' lied Thea, who knew only too well that fear and danger and constant vigilance were the basics of almost every creature's existence. 'They operate almost entirely on instinct. I don't think they have feelings, the way we understand them.'

'People are different,' said Stephanie. 'Absolutely and definitely different.'

'They are,' said Thea, wondering whether that was a good thing or not.

They got back shortly before four o'clock, the light rapidly fading and the woodburner in full swing in the sitting room. Drew was on the sofa with Hepzie, reading the local paper. At least, that was the deduction his wife and children were expected to make as they bundled into the room. Thea was not entirely convinced.

'You look comfy,' she said. 'All sorted with the tree people?'

'Pretty much. I'm charging them fifty pounds a year to keep them alive. The trees, that is. I'm assuming Andrew knows what to do.'

'So if they die, the money stops. Do you have to reimburse them?'

He frowned. 'I hope not. One's an acer, and looks awfully delicate.'

'Right. But they're lovely when they work.'

'You lot look very outdoorsy. Had a good time?'

'Brilliant,' said Stephanie, as if it mattered very much that he should believe her. 'We've got lots of photos. Can we print them in your office?'

'Not now. Tomorrow. You had a good day for it.'

'It's turned cold,' said Thea. 'My hands were frozen. I forgot to take gloves.'

'I bought more logs,' said Drew. 'Popped over in the van to that place near Snowshill.'

'Great!' said Thea. 'It makes such a difference to have the fire going.'

The inconsequential chit-chat felt false, as if everyone knew there were serious things to say but nobody wanted to say them. Thea had a sense that something had happened in her absence which had displeased Drew, but which couldn't be mentioned in front of the children. 'I'll get some tea,' she said. 'We haven't had anything since lunch.'

'Hot chocolate!' said Timmy. 'Like we had at Christmas.'

'Okay – provided we've got enough milk. I can't face going out for some now.' The perpetual need for fresh supplies of milk was never going to be sorted, she feared. If only there were a good old-fashioned milkman, who would leave creamy-topped bottles every morning on the doorstep. The association brought Ashbee to mind, followed by the window cleaner she'd seen working down the village street with his ladder. Even he would soon disappear, she supposed sourly. Ladders were far too dangerous to be allowed. Had Hilary's gutter been cleared, she wondered idly, before inwardly kicking herself for letting that particular person intrude into her thoughts.

There was just enough milk to last the evening and breakfast the next day, after making two mugs of hot chocolate, but then she would have to go and find more. Sundays were exceptionally burdensome where meals were concerned. Although he didn't insist, Drew liked the idea of a proper roast and a pudding, in the middle of the day. He liked to have the four of them around the table in a time-honoured fashion. 'You're a dinosaur,' said Thea. Even with Carl and the young Jessica, she'd resisted any such convention. A small voice in her head asked why Drew himself couldn't produce the meal he so nakedly desired. He had cooked for the family while Karen was ill, with a competence level significantly superior to Thea's. He would look over her shoulder and make suggestions while she did it, and then make a major production of stirring the gravy, as his sole contribution. The stark facts would make any self-respecting woman cringe, and yet he was always so affable and jokey about it that she couldn't justify her irritation, even to herself.

'What did you do this afternoon, then?' she asked him, when they were settled on the sofa. The children were stationed at a small table under the window, until their drinks were finished. The broken light bulb still hadn't been replaced.

'I told you. I gratified every whim of my customers, in the matter of graveside trees. It does mean we can honestly call them woodland burials from now on. In about five years' time it'll look completely different. And I got lots more logs.'

'Did you see Rachel Ottaway accost me as we were going out? We had a bit of a falling-out.'

'I did glimpse her from the window, but decided to pretend she wasn't there.'

Thea laughed. 'Very wise.'

'So what did she want?'

She glanced at the children, who were semi-comatose in the warm room. 'To tell me everything was thoroughly sewn up now, and we could all get on with our lives.'

'Sewn up or stitched up?'

She gave him a sharp look. Was he just playing with words, or echoing her own suspicions? 'What does that mean?'

He shrugged. 'Nothing really. Silly thing to say. What did you fall out about?'

'I'm not exactly sure. I think I might have accused her of telling me to back off for some sinister reason of her own. Sort of.'

'Which she interpreted as you thinking *she* killed the wretched woman herself?'

'No! At least—' She hesitated. *Had* that been what she was secretly thinking? 'Not consciously. I didn't get that far. Nowhere near. I just thought she might be rushing things a bit. She seemed so *pleased* about it. And it's not something to be pleased about, is it?' She ended miserably, unable to dodge the rush of melancholy at the very fact of one person causing the death of another. 'Hilary was only about sixty. She would have had another twenty years or more. And she seemed perfectly nice, as far as I could tell.'

'Not so nice with her sister's dog,' he reminded her.

'No – that was rather cold-blooded. But Rachel liked her. I thought she liked Graham as well, but now she seems horribly keen to get him locked up for the rest of his life.'

'Which I suppose he will be,' said Drew.

'Poor man. I can't stop seeing his face. It comes back all the time, more than hers, even.' Again she glanced at the oblivious children, slowly draining their sludgy drinks. 'That's a bit weird, when you think about it.'

'Not really. There's more of a mystery to the way he behaved. After all, she was simply dead. Not too much mystery about that.'

'There is, though. She was so near the top – lying right there, just under the lid. It was . . .'

'I know,' he said kindly.

She snuggled into him, trying to force a sense of peace and rightness to gain the ascendancy over the bitter images that kept repeating on her.

'Gladwin came,' he said, almost in a whisper. 'Just as I got back from the tree business. She wants to talk to you again. I told her it would have to wait until Monday.'

'And what did she say to that?'

'She said there was no great urgency, really. Nobody was going anywhere, and she quite fancied a quiet day with her kids tomorrow, anyway.'

'What time on Monday? I think I've already got quite a lot scheduled.'

'We didn't fix a time. You'll have to phone and get it settled.'

'She nice, isn't she? You like her, don't you?'

'She's unusual. Nobody would guess what her job is, to look at her.'

'She was wonderful when I was in Hampnett with those baby rabbits. And the poor old dog. She saved my sanity, I think.'

'Your sanity was never in any danger,' he smiled, 'even if you are a bit post-traumatic just now.'

'I am,' she whimpered, milking the moment. But then her true nature asserted herself. 'What can Gladwin want, I wonder? Didn't she give you a hint?'

'Not a clue. Try not to think about it,' he added wistfully.

'I will. I promise.' And for a few hours she managed it. Only as she lay in bed trying to get to sleep did all the same nagging questions return to haunt her. And besides the *why* and *when* there were worries about Rachel Ottaway and her actual involvement in the whole business. Had she told outright lies at times? Were there any discrepancies in what she'd told Thea since Tuesday? The cycling seemed odd, her movements around the area not quite convincing. The bike had been broken one minute and good the next, for one thing. But then, there were bicycle shops all over the place these days, since the habit had returned to Edwardian proportions. Repairs wouldn't be difficult to effect, even in Blockley. Probably. Was that what Gladwin wanted to talk about? Had she conceived the same suspicions about Rachel? Were there levels of bluff and double bluff going on, casting sand in the eyes of anybody trying to get to the truth? Were Barnaby and Sally Taylor part of it as well? What about Ant? And even Mr Shipley, who, it must be remembered, started the whole damned thing off in the first place.

'We could invite Mr Shipley over for lunch,' she said, out of the blue, just before eight the next morning. 'I owe him, and it might be useful to see what he says now about Graham Bunting.'

'I beg your pardon?' said Drew, which meant that she had said something he thought absolutely barmy. 'Are we even *having* Sunday lunch?'

'We can. There's a big piece of beef in the freezer. You can cook beef from frozen,' she assured him with a confidence that was only shakily rooted. 'It leaves it nice and pink in the middle.'

'Try selling that to the kids. They might be the offspring of an undertaker, but they're not at all keen on bloody meat.'

'It won't be bloody. I'll put it in at eleven, and it'll be perfectly fine.'

'First ask your guest,' he said. Then he shook himself. 'No – we don't *want* a guest. We'd have to tidy up. And Timmy will go all silent and embarrassed. And it's ridiculously short notice.'

'If he's busy, then so be it, but I want to ask him. You'll like him. He's got hidden depths.'

His inward struggle was all too apparent. 'I know we want to get more involved in the community, for what it's worth,' he said. 'But this is a giant leap. Didn't he give you some cheese and olives? Roast beef and all the trimmings is hardly a balanced return.'

'Yes, but I want to *talk* to him. He said there was no way Graham Bunting was a killer. He was so *sure* about it. What will he be thinking now? He might even be glad that somebody wants to hear what he's got to say. He might be bursting with frustration, for all we know.'

'I doubt it,' said Drew, with a look that indicated he still thought she might be going barmy. 'And don't forget it might not be common knowledge yet, that Mr Bunting's confessed to murder. You should check with Gladwin before talking about it all round the village.'

'Surely by now people will know? They're not even allowed to keep it secret, are they?'

'Possibly not. Even so . . .'

'Oh, pish,' said Thea.

Chapter Eighteen

Mr Shipley was transparently astonished by the invitation, when Thea popped over to ask him, and not immediately eager to accept. 'I'd be intruding on your family,' he demurred. 'And I've got myself a nice venison pie. But, of course, I'm delighted to be asked.'

Thea waited for him to finish arguing with himself. Finally, he smiled and gave a gracious little bow. 'I'd be very glad to come,' he said. 'What time's sherry?'

She hoped he was joking. She knew for a fact they had no sherry, or gin, or port, or Martini in the house. They could manage an unambitious bottle of Merlot, and that was the sum total of what would be on offer. Except, of course, she had to go for milk, and could get a bottle of something at the same time. Plus some more interesting vegetables than the carrots and peas she'd envisaged. It would have to be the supermarket, she realised, and that would take up valuable time. Unless she could send Drew . . . She wondered how he would take the suggestion.

'Oh. Shall we say half past twelve?' she told Mr Shipley. 'We might just be ready by then.'

Two hours of whirlwind activity followed: Stephanie was given a duster and set to work in the sitting room; Timmy was in charge of the vacuum cleaner, which he wielded like some sort of space weapon, swiping the nozzle across curtains and door frames in a quest for spiders. 'The *floor*, Tim,' Thea pleaded. 'Where all the dog hairs are.'

Drew was almost glad to be sent to the shops, clutching the unambiguous shopping list that spelt out exactly what sort of milk, sherry and green vegetables were required. 'Oh, and we'll have to have some pudding. Find some of those little mousse things in pots. We'll need five.'

'I *can* count,' he said mildly. 'And don't those things cost a terrible lot?'

'They do, but it's only this once. Use the credit card and cross your fingers.'

Money was less tight than they had feared it would be, now that Thea's Witney cottage had finally found a buyer. 'But we can't just *spend* it,' Drew had agonised. 'What happens when it's all gone?'

'We'll be drawing our pensions by then, so that's all right. We'll set an absolute cap on how much a year we can use of it, and make sure it lasts.' He had frowned at this, unable to believe that anybody's financial affairs could really be so simple. But so far it looked as if it might work. Thea had ventured some of the money on Premium Bonds, convinced that a huge windfall was inevitable at some point when her number came up. 'It's much better than the lottery,' she said.

Hepzie found the activity quite bewildering. Her basket was removed from the kitchen, taken to pieces and thoroughly shaken out in the garden. Then a nasty new blanket was inserted into it, which smelt of something chemical. The noise of the vacuum cleaner always alarmed her, and the complete absence of fond attention was very wounding. She nibbled ostentatiously at her fraying plaster, and turned her back on them all.

By twelve-twenty they were all ready and waiting. The roast was emitting enticing smells, the sherry and glasses were on the little table in the sitting room, the children had clean faces and matching socks. 'This is as good as it can get,' said Thea. 'Thanks, everybody.'

Mr Shipley was a discreet five minutes late and brought a box of expensive chocolates. Timmy's face brightened, which was a good start. 'Call me Bernard,' the guest said, which made Thea wonder, slightly hysterically, whether he was actually called Frederick or Walter.

'I'll leave you to Drew for a minute,' she said. 'I've got to check the Yorkshires.' The Yorkshires had been a step too far, according to Drew. 'They're tricky,' he said. 'And everybody has different ideas about what they should be like.'

'Well, let me try,' she had persisted.

Now was the crucial moment. Fat from the meat poured into shallow patty tins – which had taken a frustrating five minutes or more to locate in the depths of the cupboard – heated to destruction, and then the batter (made an hour ago and left to rest, much as the meat was supposed to) poured in carefully. She knew the theory from early days at home.

Her mother had always agonised about the Yorkshires, and seldom got them right. The sizzling sounded good, as she thrust them back into the alarmingly hot oven, and turned her attention to the meat. It would have a worryingly long rest before being carved. Would it be cold? Could she call everybody ahead of schedule? There was no law that said lunch had to be precisely at one o'clock, even on a Sunday. The vegetables shouldn't be overdone, either. There were carrots, leeks and purple cabbage, thanks to Drew's selection at the supermarket.

The table was modestly laid, given that it was in the kitchen, and therefore decidedly low class. The dining room, as originally intended by the people who designed the house, was Drew's office. There was nowhere else to eat but at the scrubbed pine table situated between sink, cooker, fridge and dog bed.

Call-me-Bernard made no demur, which was as expected, given that he'd provided lunch for Thea in his own kitchen on Thursday. Only three days ago and it felt like weeks. He carried his sherry glass to the table, and placed it carefully. He would not admire the quality of either the drink or its vessel, Thea realised. His own collection contained Georgian wine glasses, impossibly delicate, and his cellar no doubt held vintage fortified wines.

The Yorkshire puddings were adequate, but far from spectacular. Dense in the middle and scorched around the edges. Drew's perfectly stirred gravy was entirely free from lumps, but a trifle thin. The children sneered at the cabbage, which Thea found both depressing and exasperating.

'So – undertaking as a profession,' the visitor began, as soon as his plate was suitably filled. 'Must be rather a solitary existence, I would imagine.'

'Less so for me, doing it the way I do. I try to keep everything open and transparent and friendly. A lot of people respond very well to that kind of approach.'

'Hm. Well, I have to admit you've been more favourably received locally than I expected. I've heard hardly a word of complaint, up to now.' He turned his gaze onto Thea. 'And the wife of an undertaker must have similar difficulties,' he suggested.

'It's too soon to say, really. We've not even been here six months yet. The children had to be settled at school, and the house altered – plenty to keep us busy. And, of course, the burial ground opened for business almost right away. It's going very well,' she finished defensively.

'I'm sure it is. Who could fault it? The personal touch combined with low prices must be hard to resist.'

'I hope so,' said Drew neutrally.

'Will you get poor Hillie Bunting as one of your . . . what do you call them – customers?'

'Certainly not *clients*,' laughed Thea, wondering whether the children were picking up on the well-concealed barbs in the man's words.

'They were usually called *families*, at the mainstream place I worked before,' said Drew. 'Which is right, really. We deal with the whole family, generally speaking. As a unit.'

'Not in the Bunting case, assuming you'll be chosen to do the necessary.'

'We won't be,' said Drew. 'We'd have been informed by now, if so.'

'What did you mean?' asked Thea. 'There are two sons, aren't there? They're family. They'll be arranging the funeral.'

Mr Shipley shrugged. 'Presumably, yes. But neither one appears to have spared much time or emotion for their dear old mum and dad. I can't find anyone who's ever met either of them.'

'And you've tried, have you?' She was doing her best to recapture the liking she had developed for him on Thursday, but it was a struggle. What was the matter with the man? There was a bitterness to him that was tainting the whole meal.

He nodded as if to say touché. 'I'm sorry. We should change the subject.' He looked at Stephanie. 'How old are you, dear?'

'Nine,' she said shortly. 'Nearly ten. Tim's eight and a half. We go to school in Chipping Campden.'

'Oh yes, I know that much. I've seen you waiting for the bus. Is it a nice school?'

Timmy made a sound dangerously close to a snort. 'It's all right,' said Stephanie. 'But some people think it's weird that my dad's an undertaker. Like you were saying.' She smiled at him. 'You were right about that. They tease Tim about it quite a lot.'

'Ignore them,' said the man emphatically. 'All it means is they've got parents who can't face the thought of death and dying. It's their problem, not yours.'

Drew cleared his throat and everybody looked at him.

'That more or less covers the human condition, don't you think?' he said. 'With only a very few exceptions.'

'Perhaps. At least, I would agree that it's rare to be completely relaxed and accepting about your own demise. An odd thing, though. Mrs Thackery, who lives a few houses along from the Buntings, and is on most of the local committees – do you know her?'

Thea and Drew both shook their heads.

'Well, you will, I'm sure. Anyway, she was saying to me yesterday how she thought Hilary Bunting was just one of those people. Some conversation they had a few weeks ago made her think Hilary really did live each day as if it was her last.'

'In what way? How would it show?' Drew was genuinely intrigued, his cutlery at rest, his body leaning slightly forward.

'That's what I wanted to know. Apparently it began with the subject of Hilary's sister, and how she was expected to die soon, and the two sisters had talked it all through, and felt all right about it. Their father was a farmer, apparently, and they'd grown up amidst all that birth and death and primitive struggle that goes on on farms. Nothing religious about it, according to Mrs T. Just an acceptance that nothing lasts for ever. She was impressed at the time, and then she said it made it easier to cope with what had happened to Hilary.'

Everybody received this little anecdote in silence for half a minute. Then Thea said, 'I don't imagine that did much towards reconciling her to being murdered, all the same.'

'Murdered?' Timmy was first to react. 'Was somebody *definitely* murdered?'

'You know they were, dummy. What's everybody been talking about, do you think? On the bus on Friday, for a start.' His sister rolled her eyes at his obtuseness.

'I didn't think it was real,' he muttered. 'I mean, I *did*, sort of. But then everything was all right again yesterday, and I thought . . .' he trailed off.

'Don't worry, Tim,' said Drew half-heartedly. 'It's all been sorted out now. There won't be any more talk about it.'

'Don't you believe it,' said Bernard Shipley with considerable force. 'They're still a million miles from grasping the truth of it.' He looked around the table. 'For a start, there is no way in the world that Graham Bunting is a murderer. I said it before, and I'll say it again. I would stake my own life on it – that's how certain I am.'

Another pause, before Thea ventured, 'But how well do you know him? I mean – what was all that stuff on Tuesday, wanting Drew to get involved in some sort of campaign against the Buntings? If you're so passionately on his side, what was that all about?'

'It was meant kindly. It was meant to be a call for everyone to rally round and *help* him.'

'Him? Not her? Not them?'

'Him,' the man repeated. 'Graham has so many problems, I hardly know where to start.'

'Yes – compulsive shouting, lack of control, domineering behaviour towards his wife, disaffected sons, obsession with playing bridge – and a charge of murder against him.'

235

Thea was in full spate, provoked by the slippery nature of Mr Shipley's utterances. 'How come you know better than all that? Plus the man has confessed. He's admitted he did it. What more do you want?'

Her guest met her eyes in a steady inspection. 'Evidence,' he said shortly. 'Even the police won't accept a confession unless it's backed up with credible evidence.'

It was true, of course. It had been floating around the back of her mind, unvoiced but persistent. If you admitted to committing a murder, you had to give a full account of how, why, when and whether you truly did as you said. Especially when the detectives had nothing but the most flimsy circumstantial evidence against you.

'Oh,' she said.

Drew began to clear plates, and pour the last of the wine. The children had not eaten everything in front of them, and Thea was forced to conclude that the beef had been more chewy than they could manage. The Yorkshires, however, had all disappeared, well saturated with gravy. The meal had been pretty close to her average performance as a cook. It lacked flair, she knew. And imagination, dedication or commitment. It was food, and little beyond that.

'But he's not an idiot. Why would he confess if he hadn't done it?'

'Thea,' sighed Drew warningly. 'Can't we drop it now. Look, everybody – shop-bought puddings.'

He meant it affectionately, she supposed, but the laughter that followed was far from flattering. Even though it had been her own idea; even though she knew she was as bad at desserts as she was at the main course, it was hurtful.

'Lovely,' said Mr Shipley. 'I haven't had one of these for years.'

'You get first choice of flavour,' said Drew. 'Mango, blackcurrant or apricot?'

'Blackcurrant, please,' said the man, which made the children sigh with relief. They both favoured mango above all other fruit, and there were two pots, which they assumed they could have.

'Apricot for me,' said Thea, despite a great fondness of her own for mango.

The conversation was steered determinedly by Drew into the collecting of antique glass. He mentioned his erstwhile partner Maggs and her husband Den, who had recently developed an enthusiasm for flea markets and car-boot sales, and the fun of learning all about old and beautiful objects.

'It's a bit of a mug's game these days,' said Mr Shipley. 'Nobody under fifty wants to accumulate objects. Their houses are too small. All they care about is their electronic gadgets.'

'There are still plenty of people *over* fifty,' Thea objected. 'And I'm sure there are exceptions.'

The man smiled. 'I'm sure there are. But have you any idea of the sheer *quantity* of things out there? Vast mountains of porcelain, china, glass, jewellery, ivory. Not to mention all that big furniture, millions of unwanted books, hopelessly unfashionable paintings. At least you can burn all those, and keep yourself warm in the process.'

The cynicism was back. He seemed to have no source

of undiluted pleasure – even his own gorgeous glass. 'What about your glass?' she asked him.

'Good question. I love it, as I'm sure you noticed last week. But when I'm dead, what's going to happen to it? I have nephews and nieces who wouldn't give it house room. So they'll send it to auction, and dealers will pay half its value, and then struggle to dispose of it, piece by piece. The chances of it finding its way into a real home with real people are diminishing every week. It makes me sad.'

'Our possessions outlive us,' said Drew. 'People often talk to me about it.'

'We found that for ourselves in Chedworth, didn't we?' said Thea. 'Old people living in big houses full of stuff. Nobody knows what to do with it when they die.'

'Bonfire of the antiques,' said Mr Shipley dourly. 'The barbarians are at the gate.'

'On the other hand,' said Thea argumentatively, 'there are very few good-quality objects being made any more. So there'll be a dwindling supply coming through. The antiques of tomorrow are made of plastic. There can't be much gold left in the ground, for a start.'

'And what there is goes into making mobile phones,' said her guest.

'Does it?' Timmy piped up. 'Wow!'

'Nobody wants silver any more,' Mr Shipley pressed on. 'They can't be bothered to clean it.'

Drew offered to make coffee, but neither Thea nor Bernard Shipley wanted any. They all got up and moved into the sitting room, where the fire had almost gone out.

Drew fed it with dry sticks, and muttered to Thea that the new logs wouldn't last long at this rate.

'We could burn some of the big furniture,' she whispered back.

When the visitor had gone, Thea said, 'He's right about evidence, you know. That's probably what Gladwin wants to see me about.'

Drew sighed. 'And there was me thinking you were all set for a new career as an antique dealer.'

Chapter Nineteen

But Gladwin had something more specific to consult Thea about. 'This man with the dog, Antares Frowse. What do you know about him?'

'Ant? Why are you interested in him?'

'He's just one of those people that the police tend to find interesting. Never actually in trouble, but somehow not entirely law-abiding. Useful, very often. People like him notice things.'

'Have you met him?'

'Not personally, but several of the team have. His mother's quite a woman. She's complained about the landlord a time or two. Threatening behaviour. Harassment.'

'He told me about that. The landlord sounds like a monster. I think the police should be keeping an eye on him, not Ant.'

'Millionaire. Freemason. Local benefactor. Not a man to fall out with.'

Thea cocked her head. 'Sounds as if the police commissioner's in his pocket. Corruption at the highest level and all that stuff.' She felt a surge of anger at what she saw as the situation. 'You can't just turn a blind eye to the way he's carrying on.'

'Hush your mouth.' Gladwin gave a placatory laugh. 'Anyway, that's got nothing to do with the Bunting business.'

'Maybe not, but I'm not going to let you forget about it.'

They were walking slowly along the roadway that comprised Broad Campden's main street. Anything less like a street would be hard to find, despite its function as the focus for most of the housing. There were no pavements or street lights for much of its length. Pedestrians were vulnerable to traffic, safeguarded only by the fact that very few motorists went through Broad Campden unless they already knew the place, or were there on holiday and had failed to shake off their urban habit of rushing everywhere. Thea had left the spaniel at home, anticipating that her slow progress would irritate the detective.

'So, what can I do for you?' asked Thea.

'Tell me exactly where and when you've seen this Ant person.'

'Let me think.' She described the search for Biddy on Tuesday afternoon, and the impromptu lunch on Friday, to which the Taylors had appended themselves. 'It was really all about dogs,' she concluded. 'Nobody seemed very interested in talking about the Buntings.'

Gladwin's eyes narrowed in her thin face. 'That's interesting in itself. I'd have expected the entire village to be talking of nothing else.'

'It never seems to work like that,' said Thea, thinking of Blockley, Winchcombe, Lower Slaughter and others,

241

where the local people had seemed intent with carrying on their normal lives and ignoring the fact of violent death in their midst. 'It might be because so many of them have got lives somewhere else. They're not *invested* in what happens here.'

'Weird,' said Gladwin, who was a relative newcomer to the area, and had the city still in her blood.

'We had Mr Bernard Shipley for lunch yesterday,' said Thea, deliberately making it sound funny.

Gladwin wasn't slow to collaborate on the joke. 'Was he delicious?'

'The meat was a bit tough, actually. Beef.'

'Who is he, then?'

'The man who lives opposite us. He collects old glass. And it was his fault I ever went to see the Buntings in the first place.'

'Oh?' The detective scanned her memory banks for the name and address. 'Somebody must have taken a statement from him, but I don't recall the name.'

'He's away a lot. Goes to London. Anyway, he pointed out that even if Graham Bunting confessed to killing Hilary you still need some hard evidence. That's right, isn't it? So, where does poor Ant fit in?'

'Hang on a mo. How was it the Shipley man's fault?'

'I thought I explained it to you before. He told Drew there was some sort of neighbourhood watch thing, with everybody getting bothered by the way Graham shouted all the time. They thought it was marital discord. They wanted Drew to get involved.' She paused. 'It really sounds a bit ridiculous, now I think of it.'

'Sounds to me as if you were set up. Everybody knows who you are, Thea Slocombe, even if you have mutated from Mrs Osborne. Your dog alone gives you away.'

'You didn't say that before.'

'I had other things to worry about then.'

'But I'm sure I remember suggesting you go and talk to him, when you came here on Thursday – was it Thursday? Whenever, anyway.'

'Ah, yes. Now it comes back to me. You mentioned "poor Graham". That's the bit that stuck out for me.'

'Yes. And you said Caroline Hemingway might have been helped along her way by somebody. That's been niggling at me as well.'

'Forget it. False alarm. Nothing suspicious there – apart from the fact that her brother-in-law was at her bedside when she died, right after he'd bumped off his missus. That's what he says, anyway.'

'And you believe him, do you?'

Gladwin scratched her short dark hair. 'That, Thea Slocombe, is the million-dollar question. It's peculiar, to say the least, the way he kept so silent for two full days, before coming out with it. "It was me. I did it," he said. Just that, until we managed to get him to add that it was around 10 or 11 p.m., and he went directly to Oxford to sit with Mrs H. Nothing about motive, or remorse, or incipient insanity.'

'"It was me. I did it."' Thea repeated. 'Sounds fairly unambiguous.'

'And he does look guilty. He hasn't slept. His eyes are hollow. And he still hardly says anything.'

'Will he be allowed out on bail, now he's confessed?'

'Possibly. It doesn't rest with me. If it did, I might consider it, although I can't imagine where he'd go.'

Thea tried to think herself into Graham Bunting's head. Would he be able to carry on as usual in his own house, with all its memories? And would the neighbours tolerate it? 'He'd be persecuted,' she said slowly. 'There'd be a petition to demand his removal.'

They'd reached the outskirts of the village. It was still barely ten in the morning, the doors and windows of the scattered buildings all firmly closed. The day was grey and raw. Gladwin stopped and looked all around. 'Isn't there some sort of interesting history associated with this place? William Morris or somebody?'

'A chap called Charles Ashbee, for one. Haven't I mentioned him to you?'

'Nope. What did he do?'

Thea did her best to explain, but her knowledge remained patchy and it sounded thin to her own ears. 'I've got a book about him. There were several of them, all living the good life around here, having a wonderful time of it. Making things, spending most of their time outdoors. They were resisting the march of technology and sterile factory work. It didn't last long,' she concluded regretfully.

'Utopias never do. But that doesn't make them wrong. It's good to offer a different outlook. Your man sounds pretty good fun.'

'I think he was. And you're right, it was a sort of Utopia. I hadn't seen it quite like that.' She took a moment to savour the possibilities the idea gave rise to. Then she added, 'So – have you asked me what you wanted to?'

'Pretty much. I thought you might have something that would spark a few ideas.'

'And did I?'

'I'm not sure. Just have a quick think, will you? See if anything else floats up. Any little thing. You never know where it might lead.'

It was Thea's turn to gaze at one vista after another. The winding village street; the fields rising away to the wolds where she'd headed off in search of Biddy; the barely visible church spire and the roofs of the houses, one of which belonged to Graham Bunting. 'There was a man with a ladder,' she said, with a little laugh. 'I think he's a window cleaner, but he was cleaning out the gutters. Hilary was expecting him sometime soon, when I saw her on Tuesday. And I saw him again on Wednesday. I suppose he was going from house to house all week. Although he didn't come to us at all. We've probably got the same blockages as everybody else. There are plenty of trees everywhere, after all.'

'Hm,' said Gladwin unenthusiastically. 'I assume we could rely on him to report it if he'd witnessed a murder. Besides, he wouldn't be up his ladder at midnight, would he?'

'Not unless he doubles as a burglar as well.'

'We don't get burglaries around here, Thea. The houses are too well fortified. And people have state-of-the-art safes as well. Very unprofitable business, burglary. Times do change, don't they?'

'Plus nobody bothers with valuable possessions any more, anyway, according to Mr Shipley.'

'I'm not sure about that, but I expect his antique glass is safe enough.'

'Well, that's all I can think of. And you needn't worry about Ant. I don't think he's got any criminal intentions.'

Gladwin frowned. 'I never said he did. But I intend to follow my gut on this, and my gut says he's interesting.'

Thea was home in plenty of time for coffee with Drew before he went out in his suit, with Andrew, for the interment of Mrs Johnstone at noon. The coffin would be transferred to the hearse and driven the short distance to the burial ground, where the mourners would have to risk the unpaved section of the field to leave their cars. 'Maggs would have found somebody to make a proper hardstanding by now,' said Drew ruefully. 'And paths. She was always wonderfully good at paths.'

Thea had to remind herself from time to time how great a wrench it must have been for Drew to leave his long-time assistant and move eighty miles away to start a new offshoot of the business. Maggs had been around since Stephanie was a baby; a rare creature whose earliest vocation had been undertaking. She was everybody's favourite amongst the bereaved families. Natural, plain-speaking, yet slightly exotic, thanks to her mixed-race parentage. She was quick-thinking, with an eye for detail, and an amazing knack for knowing what people wanted, even before they knew it themselves.

'Lucky it's been a dry winter,' said Thea. 'It'd get muddy in that corner otherwise.'

There were still a few outstanding planning issues around parking, and even more around Drew's intention to erect a small building where people could get out of the rain, and maps of the layout of the graves be kept. According to the Local Plan, which everyone insisted was sacrosanct, nothing other than the simplest garden shed could ever be permitted.

'So what did Gladwin say?' Drew asked, virtually on the doorstep. His body language suggested that he did not really want to know.

'Not much. Except, I have a hunch that she doesn't entirely believe he did it. *Nobody* believes he did it.'

'But he's still saying he did?'

'He is.'

'Well, he should know, I suppose,' said Drew.

'Yes, but . . .' She left it there. The rest of the sentence would have been far too long, Drew's patience unequal to listening to it. She continued it silently, alone at the kitchen table, for the next twenty minutes.

Mr Shipley, Oscar Hemingway and Thea herself were the main members of the 'Nobody' group. Plus Rachel Ottaway, who was oddly also included, despite her overemphatic satisfaction at the man's confession. There was something unsettling still swirling around from Saturday's encounter. Rachel was an enigma that required confrontation. She was in too much hurry to tidy the whole Bunting business away, as if it mattered less than local history, or whatever other interests the woman might have. Thea realised how little she had actually gleaned about Rachel's past and present life. She cycled everywhere. She played bridge. She once had a husband, but never mentioned any offspring. She had an aged father somewhere not far away. There had to be a great hinterland of friendships, experiences, attitudes, opinions behind the facade so far shown to Thea.

And the Taylors. They too seemed to find Hilary's death

barely relevant to themselves. Likewise Ant, with more justification. And what about the sons? And the neighbours? Insubstantial figures, the contents of their hearts entirely obscure to Thea. Would anyone start a campaign to clear Graham's name, she wondered foolishly. Of course not, because he had *confessed*. 'It was me. I did it.' Try as she might, she could read no hidden message in the simple words. The very flatness, emerging after an inhumanly long silence, sounded like a tolling death knell. How was the poor man feeling now? Was he glad he'd come clean, or still as tormented as he had looked to be on Wednesday?

She could just leave it, as Rachel had assumed, and as Drew so obviously wanted. And yet, DS Sonia Gladwin for one had different expectations. She had opted to draw Thea in again, for no very sound reason. Anyone could have told her more about Antares Frowse than Thea had done. It had been a ploy, probably designed to keep Thea in the loop, keep her curious and engaged, because Gladwin – as did the rest of her team – valued Thea Slocombe, formerly Osborne, as a very useful asset. They knew all about her inquisitive tendencies, her bold questions and lateral suspicions.

But she had no credible theories, nothing more than a nagging conviction that the bearded and bespectacled Graham, with the loud voice and the impatient manner, had in fact not murdered his wife at all.

The new week held few enticements, and Thea remembered again the business of the Most Depressing Day of the Year, which fell sometime in early or mid January. The days remained painfully short, the air unfriendly, the next few weeks highly likely to bring unpleasant weather conditions. At least Drew had enough funerals to keep them afloat financially, as well as requests for talks or interviews, every now and then. He was anxious to see Maggs again soon, as well as pressing the council to get cracking on the various permissions still outstanding. He always had something to occupy him. Thea was not so fortunate. The fact that the world disapproved of idle women staying at home on the pretext that the children needed them was always in the background. She really *should* get a job. Mornings only, something close by, where she would meet a lot of people and involve herself in their lives. Either that, or establish some sort of small business of her own. Whilst making jams and pickles was out of the question, along with stitching decorative wall hangings or quilting cushions, she could perhaps make use of her flimsy skills as a historian. She could do online research for people; or assemble facts on a particular topic and create websites from them. If websites were still the thing, of course. She knew she was perpetually five years behind everybody else when it came to the digital age. But that sort of thing could be done at home, meaning she could double as Drew's assistant when it came to answering the phone, and earn some money as well.

It all felt eminently feasible, as she sat with her second mug of coffee, and watched the clouds get darker and heavier over the hills to the north. But she wasn't going to rush into anything. First she would scan the Jobs Vacant in the local paper, even though there were never more than a handful. It would all be online, she knew, but had little idea how to find anything appropriate. She hadn't worked at a real full-time job ever in her life. Jessica had been born only two years after she'd graduated, and that time had been spent as a dogsbody in a library, turning up more or less when she felt like it. There were sure to be all kinds of bureaucracy these days that she had no idea how to tackle.

She sighed. Every time she got into this line of thought, she hit the same annoying brick wall. By marrying Drew, she had closed more doors than she'd anticipated. Confined to one small area, expected to be ever-present for the children, what else did she have to think about but how and why a woman should be lying dead inside her own freezer?

Chapter Twenty

She hadn't listened to Drew's podcast yet. He hadn't pushed it on her, and might well have forgotten all about it by this time. She wasn't aware of any response from listeners, with no sign of increased business as a result. Perhaps he felt he'd done it badly, and actually deterred people instead of attracting them. It was not impossible, although after nearly ten years in the job, he ought to know what to say and not say.

She located the file and set it playing on the laptop. When her husband's voice came through, it was with a stab of pleasure that she heard his calm, mellow tones. His slight accent carried hints of John Arlott, she noticed with amusement. It was undetectable to her in real life. The interviewer was asking whether there was a particular kind of person attracted by his sort of funeral. 'Not really,' he replied. 'Although it's always been more of a rural thing, I suppose. Burial seems more natural than cremation to anybody accustomed to open fields and woodlands. It appeals to those interested in the environment and ecology, obviously. The way we do it, the body does return to the earth more quickly than traditional burials. People understand the way everything's composed of atoms, and their own body soon becomes recycled, in a sense, in vegetation.'

'So what happens with a cremation?' asked the woman.

'Well, the atoms are still dispersed, of course – but they go up in smoke. The rules about carbon emissions mean that much of the material is captured, and I'm afraid I don't know what happens then. But the ashes that remain and are handed to the relatives are only a very small residue. The scattering of them in a garden or a favourite spot is purely symbolic. They are completely inert and don't get taken up by roots or earthworms or anything.'

'Oh.' The voice sounded faint, and Thea muttered, 'Steady on, Drew.'

'So people can book a funeral with you ahead of time, can they?'

'Yes, they can. That happens a lot. Obtaining a natural burial can be a bit more complicated than the usual routine. It helps considerably if the wishes have been made known in advance.'

'But most people prefer not to think about their own funeral, don't they?'

'That's probably not really true. I think it is a taboo, and there's very little encouragement to face it squarely, and talk it over with somebody. I find that once they've got a kind of permission, many people are glad to discuss it. They understand that it makes it easier for their families, if they know what sort of funeral to arrange.'

'Yes,' said the interviewer.

Drew went on, unprompted. 'Perhaps not surprisingly, a lot of my pre-arranged funerals come from people in the hospice. They know they're going to die, and their families know it as well. It's okay to talk about it, which usually comes as a big relief. What I would really like to see is that same sort of attitude spreading right out across society, so that everybody feels able to talk about it, without being hushed as if they'd been blasphemous or politically incorrect. It does amaze me sometimes, the way everybody behaves as if they're never going to die, when it is the one absolute certainty.'

'Indeed,' said the interviewer, bravely. 'I understand that your first wife died very young, leaving two small children?'

Uh-oh, thought Thea.

'That's right.' Now Drew was sounding faint. 'Yes, she was injured when the children were really little, and died a year and a half ago now.'

'It must have been a very difficult time for all of you.'

'Yes,' he said.

'And she had a natural burial, I presume?'

'She did.'

The message finally got through that he was unprepared to talk about his wife and her funeral. The interviewer switched tack, while making it clear she thought he was being evasive. 'All right, Mr Slocombe, so perhaps you could just briefly tell our listeners how they can contact you, and what exactly you can offer them.'

He readily complied, making much of the transparency of all his practices, as well as costs and aftercare. 'We welcome families bringing their own trees or other plants to put on the grave, and will take good care of them,' he finished.

Thea sighed as she switched off. He hadn't said anything outrageous, of course. Or if he had it had been edited out before the broadcast. Hardly anybody in the Cotswolds would know or care that he had betrayed his own beliefs, and those of poor Karen, by having her buried in a different woodland cemetery, some distance from his own in North Staverton. Only Stephanie understood and approved of that decision. Indeed, Stephanie had been the main instigator. The biggest betrayal of all had been of Timmy, who had been promised that his mother would be just outside his window, lying quietly in the ground, not going anywhere. When she wasn't, he went silent with pain and confusion. When they moved to Broad Campden, much of his distress – which had already been fading – abated, but everyone knew that there was a fatal absence of trust in his father, which Drew could do nothing to assuage.

Thea tried to imagine herself into the heads of people hearing the broadcast and perhaps thinking for the first time in their lives about the reality of their own funeral. Local radio listeners tended to be elderly, and were not very numerous. The effect, whatever it might consist of, would not be great. It would set a few minds working at best. 'Oh, good Lord, perhaps I really am going to die one day.' Or 'That's right – burial is a lot better than cremation, after all.' Or, best of all: 'I suppose I should tell somebody that I would like one of those Slocombe funerals, when the time comes.'

She had a feeling that the first was the most probable. Hadn't that been the real message that he'd been trying to convey? *'You're all going to die!'* he was quietly shouting at them. *'Get over it, and think about what you want to happen to the collection of atoms that is all you're going to be.'*

It needed to be said, she supposed. The radio station had willingly broadcast it, after all. And Drew had dodged the potential accusation of hypocrisy over Karen.

When he came in for a late lunch, she told him she'd listened to it, and thought it very good. 'Now we sit back and wait for the tidal wave of new business,' she said with a laugh.

As if on cue the phone in the hall rang.

It was not a new customer, disappointingly. Instead, Drew quickly came back into the kitchen and said, 'For you.'

'Who is it?'

'The Otway woman, or whatever her name is.'

'Ssh. She'll hear you.'

'You asked,' he said, not unreasonably.

'Hello? Rachel? This is a surprise.'

'Is it? Why?'

'Well . . . we didn't part very amicably on Saturday, did we?'

'Oh, that. It was totally my fault. I should know by now that weekends are sacrosanct where children are concerned. I thought we could start again, if you're still interested. You did say that would be all right.'

'Er . . .' What exactly did the woman mean? Start again with what?

'The Ashbee Club,' said Rachel, with a strange enthusiasm. She'd already given it a name, the capital C somehow audible. 'I think Sally Taylor would want to be involved, as well.'

'Right. Okay. Fine,' said Thea, buying herself time to think. Was this another ploy to make her relinquish all involvement with the Buntings, couched in more friendly terms? It seemed pretty certain that it was. But why should she object, if so? Couldn't it be viewed as something benign and positive? 'That's nice,' she added.

'I honestly think you might be on to something. I popped into the museum in Chipping Campden a day or two ago and they really have very little about Ashbee, and no proper mention of Broad Campden or the Coomaraswamys at all. Your poor little village is quite forgotten, which seems a shame.'

Thea suspected that most of the village's inhabitants would prefer to be forgotten if the alternative was to bring hordes of tourists down their tortuous little lanes. But the historian in her agreed with Rachel. After all, hadn't it been her own initiative at the start? Why should she feel anxious at the level of interest shown by everyone she'd mentioned it to? Why did Hilary Bunting's response make her feel obscurely guilty? As if she, Thea, had sparked something that had led to almost instant disaster. *You fool*, she reproached herself. How could that possibly be the case?

'I gather your husband was on local radio last week,' Rachel went on, filling the gap left by Thea's silence. 'Sally heard it and told me what he said. Sounded a bit heavy, under the circumstances, but of course he couldn't have known about Hillie then.'

'What? What do you mean, *heavy*?' She tried to work out the timings, rerunning her brief exchange with both the Buntings on Tuesday afternoon, when she reported her failure to find Caroline's dog. Hilary Bunting had died perhaps six or seven hours later, after probably listening to Drew's interview. And after Graham had made a phone call to Rachel to apologise for criticising her performance at bridge. The chronology of it contracted as she thought back. On the day, there had seemed acres of time between one event and the next, but in retrospect it all telescoped together. 'Hilary was still alive when the interview went out.' She spoke without thinking, only conscious of an odd desire to defend Drew.

'Oh, yes, I know. I didn't mean anything. It's very unlikely that she even heard it.'

'Mm,' said Thea, reluctant to admit that she had alerted the Buntings to the fact of the programme, and they'd expressed an intention to listen. Why did it matter? How could it *possibly* matter?

'Anyway,' said Rachel, even more cheerfully, 'how about a meeting to talk about your ideas? Don't forget I worked in the business for ages. I know how to find things out.'

What business? Thea asked herself. 'Um . . . ?' she said.

'You know – archives and all that. I'm pretty good on the computer, searching for connections and so forth. I can track down contemporary references to the whole Arts and Crafts thing, as they specifically concern Broad Campden. I bet they were in the paper practically every week.'

Thea began to feel hijacked. 'Sounds as if you hardly need me,' she said with a forced laugh. Her ideas for self-employment were being trashed at the same time as her comparative ignorance of local history was being exposed.

'Come on. You're the inspiration, the facilitator. Without you, nobody would do anything.'

'Well . . .' It was all moving too fast. A random idea, seized for no better reason than to give an excuse to knock on the Buntings' door, was growing arms and legs and running off ahead of her. 'Well, let me finish reading the book you lent me so I can get a better idea of what's involved, and I'll get back to you. Is that okay?'

'I suppose so. But I don't think that needs to hold us up, does it? I was going to suggest you pop down this afternoon, actually.'

'Oh! Well, no, I can't. I have to be here when the kids get back from school.'

'Mornings sound to be better, then. Tomorrow? Ten-thirty? I could give you a bit of lunch after we've thrashed out what we want to achieve. I could ask Sally over as well.'

It was pushy. It was like Tigger, eagerly bouncing about and wanting to get on with the next thing. She recalled the way Rachel had vaulted over the wall on the hunt for Biddy – restless, driven. No wonder she'd been done for speeding: she was congenitally incapable of doing anything slowly or carefully, it seemed.

There was something quite endearing about it. It was

rare to find genuine enthusiasm in an adult, and gratifying that her own idea had given rise to it. If she resisted and made excuses, she would look pusillanimous in her own eyes. Missing an opportunity to expand her social circle, too. 'Yes, all right,' she said. 'Where do you live?'

The address meant nothing, and Thea realised she was hoping the woman had a flat in the old silk mill, or a quaint cottage backing onto a bumpy old field full of sheep. 'It's nothing special,' said Rachel, reading her mind. 'Pretty horrible, in fact. You'll hate it. But it serves its purpose well enough. The roof doesn't leak and the insurance is minimal.' Thea understood that this was a reference to the vulnerable old thatched roofs in Broad Campden, which were beautiful and warm, and a constant source of worry.

'I'll see you tomorrow, then,' said Thea.

Drew had gone long before the conversation had finished. Guiltily, Thea realised she had broken a rule about prolonged conversations on the landline. It blocked the phone for incoming funeral business. Although Drew had a mobile, and added the number to his cards and online directories, he knew that elderly people greatly preferred the familiar numbers that began with 01 and connected to a proper telephone. If they were thwarted in an effort to reach him that way, they were highly likely to give up and try elsewhere.

It was not yet noon. Three and a half hours before the children got back, and a restless neglected spaniel giving her mournful looks from her basket. Outside it was still inescapably January, with the absence of colour and general aura of dampness everywhere that typified an English winter. The rare sparkling frosty days were even more rare this year so far. 'Oh, come on, then,' she told the dog. 'I know you've missed out on walks for weeks now. We'll go round the block then, shall we, even though I might tell you I've already had a walk today?'

'The block' was a fifteen-minute stroll along a route that resembled an approximate oval on the map, but which had dips and bends all along the way. They turned left at the first little junction, down a hill mostly bordered by fields and trees, but concealing a handful of big old stone houses that had been constructed in the glory days of wool merchants and other prosperous types. Big families, solid investments, conservative values and generally peaceful times all came together to produce the benign complacency that continued to typify the region. There might be security systems in place now, and a fiercer level of possessiveness, but very little disturbed the tranquillity of a Cotswold village. Hepzie trundled ahead, her broken leg less of an impediment with every passing day. Obviously delighted to be free, she sniffed into every tuft of grass and under every tree root. On this stretch of road, traffic was discouraged by signs at both ends, announcing 'Unsuitable for motors' – a wording with a pleasingly 1930s character.

At the end, they emerged onto the slightly larger road where she had walked with Gladwin two hours earlier. They turned right, keeping well into the side, Hepzie attached to her lead for the short distance to the opening onto a footpath that cut straight through all the bends and bumps to arrive back at the church. It had been two or three months before Thea had explored this shortcut, and she had remained enchanted with it ever since. It too was bordered by trees and a few small fields, giving virtually no hint of the fact that it was effectively in the heart of a village. One or two good-sized gardens backed onto it, but it felt like the middle of nowhere. Not once had she ever encountered another person using it.

Liberating the dog again, Thea walked slowly, her thoughts, as so often, drawn to wondering how this exact piece of ground might have been a century or so ago. If only time travel could be a reality, she mourned – how thrilling to just slip back to 1903 or thereabouts, and find out for herself. 'Careful!' she called automatically, as the dog reached the end of the path. There was a short slope down to the point where three small roads all came together. The Bunting house was directly overlooking the spot, as was the church. A fourth lane led to the famous Quaker meeting house. Two long-distance footpaths came very close as well. 'A veritable Piccadilly Circus,' Thea murmured to herself. But there were no engine sounds, and she had no fear for the safety of her spaniel.

It was therefore a very great shock to hear a squeal of pain and fear, from somewhere just out of sight, as she ran down to the road.

'Percy! Leave her alone, damn you,' came a man's voice. 'What's the matter with you?'

Thea was confronted with a jumbled tableau comprising two dogs and the intriguing Ant. Percy and Hepzibah were both quivering, one with apprehension, the other with something closer to lust. Risking real damage to the plastered leg, the larger dog was trying to mount the spaniel, who cringed pathetically and whimpered.

'Is she on heat?' asked Ant, when he saw Thea.

'No, of course not. She was spayed ages ago.' The association of ideas happened in a microsecond. 'Oh Lord! She's due for a check-up at the vet tomorrow, and I told Rachel I'd go and see her then. Damn it.' Double-booking herself always felt like an absolute failure. It turned her into a forgetful middle-aged woman incapable of managing a simple diary. 'I never gave it a thought.'

Ant smiled warily. 'Time enough to sort it out,' he said. 'And just for the record, Percy's been neutered as well. He likes to pretend now and then, that's all.'

She liked Percy, she reminded herself. As a rule, she would just have laughed about his assault on Hepzie. But the broken leg changed all that. She bent down and pushed him away. 'Sorry, old chap, but she's in no state for flirting, however harmless it might be. You'll knock her over and hurt her leg.'

'I was hoping to see you,' said Ant. 'Just to find out what's what with the Bunting lady, and everything. That's their house, isn't it?' He pointed to the row of tall old buildings beyond the patch of green.

'You can't possibly have expected to bump into me like this,' she accused him, suspicion flaring. 'Were you following us?'

'Not at all. But I was a bit shy of turning up at your house again. I thought I might get in the way of a funeral or something. I didn't know if there might be a procedure of some sort.'

It sounded credible, she supposed, despite being the first time such an idea had been voiced by anyone. And besides, Ant had shown no such hesitation when he'd come to the house on Friday, but he had a point, that nobody wanted to interrupt the stately progress of a hearse, or find themselves mingling with mourners when wearing muddy jeans or accompanied by yowling infants.

'Sorry to sound so suspicious, then. And actually, there is a funeral today. I expect Drew will be back in a minute.' She looked at her watch. Twelve-fifteen. 'No, not for half an hour or so.'

'It's very weird, having actual funerals in this little place. I ought to go and look at the burial field sometime, I guess.' He turned to look in the direction of the field, as if hoping to see through the intervening hills and trees. 'It's not far away, is it?'

'Just over a quarter of a mile. No distance at all.'

'It *is* weird, though.'

'I don't see why. There are graves behind the church here. They obviously have funerals from time to time.'

'I doubt it,' he said. 'Or very rarely. You've got them three or four times a week. It must be impossible for people to ignore.'

She shook her head. 'What people? Haven't you noticed – there *are* no people around in the middle of a weekday? It's the same in most of these villages. This time of year, it gets positively spooky.'

'There's us,' he said perkily, and she wondered again how accidental their encounter had been.

'Come down to the house, and I'll do some soup or

263

something.' No way was she prepared for a second pub meal with him. It would become a habit all too easily, and she had no intention of letting that happen. In another life, perhaps she could have let this young man get under her skin with his careless good cheer, but not now. Besides, she was at least ten years older than him. 'It's time you met Drew,' she added.

'Why is it?' He sounded like Timmy, childish and wheedling.

'Because you might need a funeral one day,' she said lightly. 'And because it's good to know the neighbours, and you'll like each other.'

'My dad's got a touch of angina, but I think he's good for a while yet. He's only sixty-six. But when the time comes, in about two decades from now, I promise we'll consider you for his funeral.'

'Thank you. You won't be sorry.' The prospect of still being the local green undertakers in twenty years' time filled her with a rush of panic that shocked her. She would be in her sixties, the children grown up and gone, probably the dog after the dog after Hepzie would be at her heels, wandering the deserted little lanes of Broad Campden with nothing like enough to show for her life. She took a deep breath, and banished this grim glimpse of the future back to the world of fantasy where it belonged. Why should she have any more claim to making a permanent mark on the world than anybody else? She would have grandchildren one day, for a start. Jessica was sure to marry at some point, because everybody in the family married, and stayed married, and were altogether conformist in that respect.

And if she didn't, then Stephanie or Timmy would, and their children would qualify almost as well.

'What?' said Ant, watching her face, in much the same way as Drew did when she went quiet.

'Nothing,' she lied. 'Come on. I haven't told you about Graham Bunting yet. Isn't that what you wanted me for?'

'Sort of. I didn't want people to think I wasn't interested.'

'Who would think that? Who even knows you're involved? And really, you're not, are you? You were in their garden last Tuesday, but you didn't see them or talk to them. They'd lost interest in the dog, anyway, with everything else that was going on. Her sister died, you know. Did I tell you that? They both died on the same night. Isn't that terrible?'

'You're a clever girl, aren't you?'

For a moment she thought he was addressing her dog. It was a startling remark, made in a tone that differed markedly from his utterances thus far. She looked at him, half-expecting to see another man over his shoulder, but there was only Ant.

'Pardon? What did you just say?'

'Just that I've had the feeling from the very first moment that you could see what I was thinking, that you didn't trust me, or even like me much. Now there's been a murder, and I can't help thinking you might see me as a suspect.'

She swallowed down her sudden sense of danger. If she shouted, surely somebody would hear? Surely all the houses weren't as empty as the Buntings'? The pub was only a hundred yards away. But this was England, where people minded their own business and only responded to screams if they were particularly prolonged. Then she looked at the man again and her fear subsided. He didn't look threatening, after all. Just reproachful and impatient.

'I never for a second saw you as a suspect,' she told him. 'I have no idea what you're thinking, and I did quite like you. You've got me completely wrong.'

'Have I? I'm right about you being clever, though, aren't I? You don't just take what people say as the truth. You nose about, following your own agenda, asking all those questions.'

It was desperately unfair. Knowing the cry to be every bit as childish as Ant's had been a few minutes before, she still rebelled violently against the imputation. 'I'm not. I don't,' she protested. 'I was just being friendly. The fact is, I really don't care very much about the Bunting couple. I barely even met them. I've got no idea what was going on between them. Neither have you, as far as I can see. So, what's got into you? Why the sudden nastiness? You scared me,' she finished, suppressing a whimper.

'The police came to see me,' he said angrily. 'And it can only have been because of you.'

'Oh.'

'Yes, you might well say "Oh". My mother was there, and she wasn't best pleased about it. Her life is complicated enough without that. The way she sees it, we're tainted now in the eyes of the law, and that's the last thing she wanted. I told you the trouble we're having with the landlord, didn't I? Well, this can only make it worse.'

Still her mind was firing on every cylinder at once. 'But maybe if the landlord saw the police car, he'll think it's because you're complaining about him. Maybe it'll work in your favour.'

'I doubt it,' he said, but she could see the idea taking root. 'Although it's a thought, I suppose.' He heaved a deep sigh, and let it go slowly. 'Well, I'll go. Sorry if I scared you. I'm not at all scary, in fact.'

She nodded uncertainly. Behind him there was an engine approaching, and a van appeared from the larger road. It pulled up close to them, and a man got out. On the roof was a ladder. Thea thought his face was familiar, which was enough to make her want to approach him. But she didn't. She took a few steps away from Ant and his dog, which had been circling his legs as he stood talking to Thea, trying to get to Hepzie, who was sitting firmly and safely behind her mistress.

'Sorry,' said Ant again, and suddenly loped away without a backward glance.

The man was lifting the ladder down. It looked heavy, concertinaed into a third of its ultimate length.

'You were here last week, weren't you?' Thea said, before she was conscious of any such intention. 'Clearing the gutters?'

'That's right. I've had to come back to replace a section on Mrs Thackery's house. It came away in my hand. Got a bit of a rocket for it, as it happens.'

'Oh dear. Well, I think my gutters might need someone to give them a look. Would you have time for that?'

He looked at the sky. 'Got a few more hours before dark,' he said. 'And even then, I can do it with a head torch if I have to. It wouldn't be the first time. Which one are you, then?'

She told him, and he promised to call in when he'd finished his repair.

'Don't worry,' said Thea. 'Our roof is nowhere near as high as these.'

They both gazed up at the tall houses, each thinking their own thoughts.

Chapter Twenty-One

Drew got back from burying Mrs Johnstone at about twelve-thirty. Thea asked how it had gone, and he replied as he always did that it was fine, and the family were satisfied and talking about a tree for the grave. The sheer predictable repetition reminded Thea of the flash of panic she'd felt that morning. 'They always go well, don't they?' she said. 'You're very reliable.'

'I like to think so. That's all right, isn't it?'

'Oh, yes. It's very good.'

'You don't sound too happy about it.'

'I'm just being Januaryish. It was bound to catch up with me. It would be better if it snowed, or got really really cold, or something dramatic like that. This grey gloom is miserable.'

'It's going to rain tomorrow, if that helps. Just when we're out with Mrs Card, probably.'

'Rain is even worse.'

'Did something happen this morning?' he asked at last.

'Well, yes. You know the man I told you about, called Antares, with the tracker dog?'

'The one you went to the pub with on Friday?'

'That's him. Well, I saw him today. He seemed to be hanging about waiting for me, at the end of the footpath by the church. It was a bit sinister. I don't think he's as nice as I first thought. But I really don't know what to make of him. He's like two different people.'

'You can't get to know a person on a couple of brief encounters, you know.'

'But I think you *can*, usually. You know whether or not they've got their lives sorted, for one thing. Whether they see themselves as helpless victims, or whether they're bitter and twisted inside. That sort of thing.'

'Come on,' he protested. 'How often do you bump into anyone like that?'

'I know. I'm not saying it right. I suppose I mean you can tell whether or not they've got a good heart. And I thought Ant had, and then I changed my mind, and now I don't know.'

'What about Graham Bunting?' Drew asked, with a searching look. 'Isn't that really what you're worried about?'

'Probably,' she admitted unhappily. 'But I can't see what I can possibly do about it. I keep hoping that Gladwin won't find any evidence to confirm his confession, and he'll have to retract it. But that's not very sensible, is it?'

'You hope he didn't do it, or that he did it but will get away with it?'

'Yes. No. Oh, I don't know. If he didn't do it, somebody else must have, and that's worse.'

'Well, you're right – there's nothing whatsoever you can do about it.'

'Drew . . . I think I should find myself a part-time job, if I can. I'm underoccupied as things are. Now we're settled here, I can get into a proper routine, maybe walking to something in Chipping Campden for a few hours a day. Would that be okay with you?'

He rubbed his cheek. 'It's completely up to you. I wouldn't try to talk you out of it. You ought to ask Hepzie what she thinks, though.'

'Oh! I forgot all over again! We've got an appointment tomorrow at the vet, and I told Rachel Ottaway I'd go to see her at some point. She seems keen to be friends.' She paused. 'Maybe we're bonded for ever after what happened on Wednesday.'

He looked up. 'She won't mind changing it.'

'I hope not. It might give me time to finish that book she lent me, all about the Arts and Crafts Movement. I must say, there's nothing so far about Broad Campden. It's all Chipping Campden. I think I might have got the wrong idea, all along. This is just a very small satellite to the real place, with virtually no claim to fame at all. I'm going to look a bit silly, I expect.'

'No, don't worry about that,' he assured her. 'Interestingly, I was talking to Mrs Johnstone's sister after the burial. She says Broad Campden goes back further than almost anywhere around here. The pub was built in the early sixteen hundreds, and so was the Quaker meeting house. That Ashbee chapel is Norman, for heaven's sake. The place is bound to have seen all sorts of major events.'

'I know. But I can't find them recorded anywhere.'

'Keep looking. It must be there somewhere.'

'I should start with the Norman chapel, I suppose. It's the only thing that gets a mention in any reference to the village.'

He was obviously losing patience. 'Have you had any lunch?' he asked abruptly.

Before she could respond, the phone rang. Drew answered it in the hall, and Thea heard preliminaries that sounded like a new funeral coming in. But then he said, '*Both* of us? Why?'

She listened closely, moving to the doorway to catch his eye, but he was writing something down. 'Well, all right . . . I suppose we could, maybe tomorrow. It's not going to be easy. The children get home at three-thirty, and I've got another funeral in the morning. And the dog's got to go to the vet for a check-up.' There followed a conversation that was mostly, 'Yes, I think so . . . okay . . . probably . . . all right, then,' which told Thea almost nothing.

She could make no sense of this at all. The only explanation she could think of was that Mr Shipley was inviting them to some sort of event or meal, and that seemed very unlikely. Why would he need to write anything down? Impatiently, she waited for elucidation as her husband made a promise to see what he could manage.

'Gladwin,' he told her, at the end of the call. 'The Bunting man has asked if he can talk to us. Both of us.'

Her heart lurched with a complicated set of fears. 'When?' she asked faintly. 'Where?'

'They can bring him here, since we're so unavailable. In about an hour from now.'

'It must be that he wants to arrange Hilary's funeral.'

Then she caught herself up, biting her lip. 'Wouldn't that be dreadfully weird, though? Is he *allowed* to do that if he murdered her? Surely it would have to be the sons?'

'I don't think it is that,' said Drew slowly. 'I think it's mostly you he wants to see, but Gladwin insists that I be there as well.'

'As my protector? In case he tries to murder me, as well?'

'No, there'll be a policeman for that. More in case you get upset, I imagine. That's what she seemed to be implying.'

'It's the strangest thing that's ever happened to me,' she said, with some drama. 'I wouldn't have thought Gladwin would do such a thing.'

'She's never been one for the rules, has she? If she thinks it'll help the case she won't hesitate to go along with it.'

'But what does he *want*? He doesn't know me at all. I barely even spoke to him.'

'You found his wife's body. I guess that feels like a connection. Maybe he just wants to apologise to you for the trauma you suffered. In any case, you won't have long to wait, will you?'

When the doorbell rang ten minutes later, they looked at each other in surprise. 'That was quick,' said Thea.

'Too quick. It can't be them yet.' He went to the door, and Thea heard a man saying, 'Hi, I'm Mike, the window cleaner. Your wife said to come and have a look at your gutters. And while I'm at it, maybe you'd like the windows done as well? Looks as if it's been a while.' He laughed.

'Oh,' said Drew. 'Right . . .'

Thea hurried down the hallway. 'Thanks for coming.

Mike, did you say? Have you got time to do the windows as well? Do you need water? This is very good of you. What's it going to cost us?'

'Thirty-five, all told. If I could just fill the bucket. Is there an outside tap?'

'That sounds very reasonable. It's okay, isn't it, Drew?'

Drew waved a hand as if it was nothing to do with him.

'Better to use the kitchen tap. You want it warm, surely?'

'Cold's fine. I'll just get the ladder up, and come back in a minute.'

She waited by the open door, aware of cold air pouring into the house, watching as he unfolded the ladder, wondering why he hadn't carried it the short way from the previous house, instead of packing it up. His van was positioned crookedly on the narrow verge outside the house. She saw him squinting up at the guttering and windows, moving the ladder slightly away from the door. 'I thought you weren't supposed to use ladders any more,' she said. 'I heard something on the radio about it.'

'They tried to stop us, but it never really worked. We can manage windows, more or less, but when it comes to gutters and pipes, you've got to have a ladder. I'll just get the bucket.' He came back with a metal pail, and she escorted him into the kitchen. He made kissing noises at Hepzie, and stood waiting while Thea cleared a saucepan and jug out of the sink.

'Quite a business about that poor lady,' he said. 'I dare say you heard all about it. Must be nearly a week ago now.'

'Yes. I saw you there on Wednesday, actually.'

'Did you?'

'You and a couple of neighbours. When the police and ambulance came.'

'I was still doing the gutters, yeah. Tell you the truth, I'd done Mrs Bunting's on Tuesday, but didn't like to bother her for the money, so I was hoping to get it the next day.'

'I see.' She had a fleeting sense of incongruity or inconsistency to his prattle. 'I suppose you never did get it, as things turned out?' Then it came to her. 'But she said she was still expecting you to do the job, when I saw her on Tuesday.'

'She probably didn't notice me. That poor woman. It's my belief she knew what was coming to her. That day, before it happened, she was so upset, I didn't like to disturb her.'

'Upset? What time was that, then?'

'Ooh, well after dark. I was fishing about up on the roof, with a torch on my head, wishing they'd got better street lights. I was right outside her upstairs window, and there she was lying on the bed, crying her eyes out. You see embarrassing things in my job, as you can imagine, but this was one of the worst. I could hear the sobs right through the double glazing. Heartbreaking, it was. And then, next day, there she was dead. Makes you think.'

'It does. What time was it, though?'

'Well, I got home about seven-fifteen, and that's twenty minutes away. Say it took me ten minutes to pack the ladder up, and all that. So maybe half six, or quarter to seven. Around then. I remember thinking it wasn't late, but in winter it *feels* it. I mean, in June, that would still be broad daylight. I work till eight or nine in the summer, some days.'

'Was her husband there?'

'No, no. He went off in the car a bit before that. Made a sarky comment about me taking my time over the job, before he drove off.'

She looked at him. 'Have you told the police any of this?'

'They never asked me,' he said, with a disingenuous smile. 'I'd be happy to talk to them if it helped – but I thought they'd got him banged up anyway. Why'd they need me to tell them what they know already?'

'They don't know the exact timings. They need independent confirmation, as evidence.'

He shrugged. 'Well, they know where to find me.'

'Do they?'

'They do now. *You* can tell them. Mike Radford, SqueakyKleen Window Cleaner. Here – I'll give you a card.' He filled his bucket and carried it carefully down the hall and out through the front door.

Thea was left with her mind spinning. It didn't have to change anything, she insisted to herself. Graham Bunting could have gone out for an hour or two, then home again to despatch his wife, and then off to the John Radcliffe to witness a second death. The police must surely have asked the hospital staff for the precise timing of his arrival and departure. He might even have had to sign in. Oscar Hemingway would be an additional source of information in that regard.

But Hilary had been upset. More than upset, by the sound of it. Sobbing on the bed like a teenager. Had she foreseen her own death, and been distraught at the prospect? If so, why didn't she make an escape while Graham was out?

Did he have some gruesome hold over her, rendering her helpless to save herself? The frozen face came back to her, the red eyes explained by the crying, as were the glazed cheeks. The woman must have gone to her death in the same state of despair and distress as the window cleaner had witnessed.

Drew had withdrawn into his office, ignoring the window cleaner. He would have paperwork to complete for Mrs Johnstone and preparations to make for Mrs Card. Two funerals in two days was hardly a heavy workload by normal standards, but traditional undertakers had large staffs, with the various tasks allotted to different individuals. Drew did almost all of it himself. 'If we get more than three a week, I'll have to get extra help,' he would say. 'There's always me,' Thea mostly answered.

But her one determined effort to become a proper part of the workforce had gone very badly. Drew had left her to make arrangements for the burial of a young man kicked to death by a horse. It had not fully occurred to them that this might raise powerful echoes of the death of Thea's own husband Carl at a similar age. She had followed the instructions laid out for her, gone through the motions without breaking down, but had resolved never to do it again. She still didn't know the full extent of Drew's disappointment with her, but the fact that he never again referred to it was in itself a strong indication. His dreams of teamwork, joint owners of the business presenting a friendly, competent, sensitive service, had not come to fruition. Thea would answer the phone, open the door, manage his children, but when it came to the actual funerals, she remained in the shadows.

She was ashamed of herself, as a result. It became evident that she was not really very good with people *in extremis*. While she could well understand their feelings, and the reasons for them, she didn't do hands-on sympathy very adequately. She was prone to rationalise, telling herself it really wasn't so very bad, and others had worse things to endure.

So now she puzzled over the likely reasons for Hilary Bunting's tears. It felt important to have at least a workable theory in mind before the arrival of Graham Bunting. Which was ridiculous, she supposed, when there was a good chance that he would explain it all to her face-to-face. Why else would he want to see her? Or was Drew wrong to think it couldn't possibly be a visit to arrange Hilary's funeral?

They hadn't had lunch. Neither of them had even mentioned it. She went through to the office and suggested a quick soup and sandwich. Drew looked up briefly. 'I'm not very hungry, actually. Andrew gave me a sandwich after the funeral. We can offer coffee and cake or something when the people come.'

She frowned. 'I'm not sure it sounds like that sort of visit.' 'The people' was an odd way to describe Graham and Gladwin, she thought.

'Oh, well.'

'What's the matter?'

He heaved a profound sigh. 'All this, of course. I don't want to get dragged into a mess with police, and murder, and maybe having to negotiate with the coroner. It's all wrong. It's not the way I like to do things.'

She wasn't entirely clear as to the source of his trouble. A funeral was a funeral, wasn't it? He dealt with the coroner all the time. 'I was just talking to the window cleaner,' she told him. 'He says he saw Hilary on Tuesday evening in floods of tears. I told him he has to tell the police about it.'

Drew sighed again. 'There's no getting away from it, is there? We're stuck with it, like it or not.'

'It'll be okay,' she said. 'Once they've gone, everything's going to be clear and straightforward, you'll see.' Reassurance that she was in no position to provide, as she well knew. 'There's really nothing for you to worry about.'

'I think perhaps there is,' he said, once again arousing sharp stabs of terror in her guts. He was talking about *her*, them, the marriage, *everything*. She felt acid in her mouth, preventing her from speaking.

The sudden appearance of Mike at the office window, squeegee in hand, was startling enough to make her gasp, and then laugh.

'Must be fun, being a window cleaner,' she said foolishly.

'Go and have some lunch. Put the kettle on. They'll be here in a minute, and you won't get the chance otherwise,' said her husband.

Chapter Twenty-Two

She sat at the kitchen table with a mug of soup made from a packet. Fifteen minutes went by, and then Mike knocked on the window to signal that he was finished. How much had he said it would cost? Should she offer him a drink? Should she try and make him wait until Gladwin arrived?

Her purse could yield thirty-five pounds only with the help of the separate stash of fifty-pence pieces she kept for parking meters. It would mean going to the bank the next day. There was shopping to do, she realised idly. Yet again, milk was running low, as well as dog food and bread. It was relentless, she thought irritably. The trivia of daily life never went away whatever huge events were taking place alongside it. If she found a job, she'd be able to combine it with regular shopping trips, perhaps – although walking to Chipping Campden across the fields, as Charles Ashbee had done, wouldn't lend itself to that idea.

'Do you want me to come regularly to do the windows?' Mike asked her. 'Every two or three months is the usual. I come here anyway, so it'd be easy to put you on the list. It's only twenty pounds, without the gutters.'

'All right, then,' she agreed, thinking they could deduct the cost as a business expenditure. The premises should be kept respectable, after all. 'Can you give me a receipt for today?'

This proved to be more than he'd bargained for, and he spent some time rummaging in the van before bringing her a small sheet of paper torn from a notebook. 'Don't get asked that very often,' he apologised.

'Sorry. But this is our place of business as well, you see. We can claim it against tax.'

'Fine. No worries. I'll know for next time.'

She let him go with a pathetic reluctance. 'You might get a call from the police,' she reminded him.

'Fine. No worries,' he said again. He looked almost eager, and Thea imagined that perhaps this was what he'd been waiting for. Perhaps his friends teased him about his failure to observe anything salacious in the course of his work.

Five minutes later, a marked police car came hesitantly down the lane. How must it have been for Graham, wondered Thea, passing his own empty house knowing he was unlikely ever to live in it again?

She stood just outside the front door, not knowing what to do with her hands, or whether to smile. Her call to Drew had not brought him to her side. Gladwin led the way, then two men. It took Thea several seconds to persuade herself that one of them was Graham Bunting. He stumbled like an old man; his beard was gone; his skin was grey. Only the heavy black glasses identified him. Without having discussed it with Drew, she hesitated between the sitting room and the office. The latter seemed much more appropriate, with its plentiful chairs and businesslike aura. 'Better come in here,' she said, waving them past the sitting-room door and into the room at the back.

Drew emerged before she had to face a second awkward decision – whether or not to knock before going in. He could have been in the middle of a delicate phone call – she almost hoped he was, as that would comprise one of very few acceptable excuses for leaving her to cope.

'I'm sorry,' mumbled the older man. 'I really am very sorry.'

'It's all right, sir,' said the younger one, rather fatuously.

Gladwin squared her shoulders. 'This is all very unorthodox,' she said. She looked at her colleague, who was in plain clothes, aged about thirty and clearly uncomfortable with the situation.

There was no suggestion of the handcuffs that Thea had half-expected.

'So what do you want from us?' Drew demanded, his voice harsher than Thea had ever heard it.

'I'm sorry,' said Graham Bunting again. 'It's all my fault.' He looked at Thea. 'I wanted to ask you one or two things.'

His appearance and demeanour were so pathetic that Thea thought she might weep. She was still struggling to reconcile this defeated old man with the shouting husband of the previous week. Now his voice was barely more than a whisper, strained and apologetic.

'Sit down,' said Drew, waving at a semicircle of chairs placed facing the table he used as a desk. 'Everybody, please sit down.'

All four of them did as instructed, while Drew took a headmasterly position behind the table. Thea was fully aware that he seldom arranged people in such a way. He generally sat side by side with his customers, showing them everything he was noting down and letting them make amendments and additions along the way. Drew Slocombe was a lot more like a friendly vicar than a headmaster.

'You shaved off your beard,' said Thea, in an attempt at forming at least some connection with the man. Did the police force their prisoners to do that, she wondered wildly. Surely not.

He nodded, with the faintest of smiles. 'Hilary would never let me before,' he said.

What? That sounded dreadfully like an expression of satisfaction that he was now free of his wife's restraint. She looked to Gladwin for explanation, and reassurance. The detective rolled her eyes, conveying some complicated message that Thea didn't grasp. Perhaps it was something like, *Don't rush to any conclusions. Let things unfold in their own time.*

'So – how can we help?' said Drew. His impatience affected the atmosphere, turning it spiky and embarrassed.

'Thank you for your time,' said Gladwin. 'I know it's inconvenient for you.'

'Better than us having to come down to Cirencester or wherever,' said Thea. 'Much better.'

'You were at my house on the day after – Wednesday, was it?' said Graham, his voice stronger and louder than before. 'I saw you. You saw me. With Rachel.' He looked at Gladwin. 'Why isn't she here as well?'

'Because I chose not to ask her.' The reply was firm but kind. 'I don't think we need her for this, do we?'

'"O reason not the need",' said the prisoner obscurely. 'Sorry. It's from *King Lear*. One of my favourite quotes, actually.'

Something about him struck Thea as quite King Learish, and she smiled, wishing she could complete the lines. Something about beggars and their merest possessions being superfluous. Nobody else appeared to have even that much of an idea as to what came next.

'We heard your radio piece,' said Graham abruptly to Drew. 'We listened to it together.'

The ominous tone was impossible to ignore. 'Oh?' said Drew, turning pale.

'It made a great impression on us.'

Gladwin raised her head, blinking in surprise. 'You didn't know about it?' Thea asked her. Wheels within wheels, she thought confusedly. Who knew what? Who *believed* what?

'We were susceptible, of course,' the man went on. 'With Caroline so close to dying.'

Oh! thought Thea. She had almost forgotten Caroline. That, obviously, was why Hilary had been crying. Pure unadulterated grief for her sister. The relief was palpable.

'I hope it didn't distress you,' said Drew. 'It's impossible to anticipate how people will react, I know. I did wonder afterwards whether it had been rather risky. The interviewer wasn't very good, really, and I doubt whether anybody gave it quite the consideration they should have before it went out.'

'I wondered that as well,' said Thea.

'With good reason,' said Graham, disposing of her brief hopes in a stroke.

Gladwin leant forward and sideways. 'Mr Bunting, we are taking up valuable time here. Could you please say what you came to say, and we can all get on.'

The ravaged face went taut with anger. 'I want the same as you want,' he snapped. 'Justice. My wife is dead. My wretched miserable wife's life has ended – as she wanted it to. This lady here did what she could to reach out a hand, and for a few hours we thought it might have reversed the inevitable. Your idea of a group delving into local history might have worked a few weeks sooner. But you know – there really isn't very much to discover. Rachel pointed that out after you'd gone. Not one of you understands how things were with us. Our sons barely bothered with us. Neither sent us anything at Christmas beyond a token card. Oscar is a better son than they are, but that isn't saying much. We made the biggest imaginable effort with the Taylors and Rachel, giving them lunch, putting up with their poor playing in order to feel we were being sociable. I even went to the trouble of phoning her to say thank you for helping to look for the dog. But it wasn't working. Hilary still wouldn't cheer up. It all came to a head when we heard that interview – though I didn't see it coming until it was too late.' His voice had risen in volume as he spoke, until the final words came out as a shout. He swallowed and fingered his own throat irritably.

'Mr Bunting, this isn't helping,' Gladwin objected. 'It sounds as if you're blaming Mr Slocombe.'

The man said nothing to that.

'You *did* kill her, didn't you?' Thea's bold question elicited gasps from Drew and the young police detective. 'Can we just get that straight?'

'It was my doing,' he said, huskily. 'It was my fault.'

Gladwin sighed and spoke to Thea. 'That's the best we can get from him. Technically, it might qualify as a confession, but it's very shaky.'

'It's not a confession, though, is it?' Thea herself began to shout. 'You blame yourself, but you can't bring yourself to say outright that you murdered her.'

'It was my doing,' the man repeated. 'And I deserve punishment for it.'

Another silence followed. Drew was showing signs of increasing discomfort. Thea was struggling to construct a theory that fitted everything she knew, as well as explain why Graham Bunting wanted to see her and Drew.

'The window cleaner saw them on Tuesday,' she said to the detective out of the blue. 'You need to talk to him.'

Gladwin looked unimpressed. 'Right,' she said, not taking her eyes off Bunting's face.

'He didn't see anything,' said the man. 'If he had, he'd have reported to you before now. Looks like a good citizen to me. Even spared three or four minutes for a sociable little chat with Hillie, a couple of times. Your interview tipped us over the edge,' Graham told Drew again. 'I think you should know that. I'm not saying it wouldn't have happened anyway, sooner or later, but that was the first time . . .' He stopped. 'That's enough. I've said enough.' He nodded at Gladwin. 'We can go now, if you want.'

'This is completely bizarre,' said Drew, standing up and

addressing the detective superintendent. 'You come here, breaking all kinds of police rules, I shouldn't wonder, and I get accused of stirring up some sort of dysfunction between a married couple, which ends up with her dead inside a freezer. What can possibly be gained by it? I have never met either Mr or Mrs Bunting until now. I gave what I believed was an honest and frank interview, with nothing but the best of intentions.' He finished with a *tshhing* sort of sound, and a violent sweeping gesture, both of which were new to Thea. She was almost afraid of him in that moment.

'Yes,' whispered Graham Bunting. 'Dead inside a freezer. Yes, indeed. And you found her there,' he said to Thea.

'With Rachel, yes.'

'Naturally with Rachel.' A thin smile pulled his lips back from his teeth. 'That goes without saying.'

Gladwin made a groaning sound, as if this comment, or ones like it, were familiar to her, and persistently annoying. Thea felt oddly sidelined; wasn't *she* the one who could be relied upon to stumble over dead bodies everywhere she went? Had Rachel Ottaway somehow acquired a similar reputation?

Everybody had got to their feet, following Drew's lead. 'This is not what I expected, Mr Bunting,' said Gladwin severely. 'I wish you'd mentioned Mr Slocombe's radio interview before. I was under the impression that you wished to explain to Thea how sorry you felt for the distress you caused her. And her husband, by extension. And I admit I was hoping you might clarify some of the details of exactly what happened on Tuesday night.'

'I did it,' said the man. 'That's all you need to know. You

287

need look no further for the culprit.' He took a deep breath. 'All right, I'll say it. I caused the death of my wife, Hilary. Is that good enough for you?'

Nobody replied. The repeated silences were getting to Thea, who still couldn't work out the real reason for the visitation. She understood that Gladwin felt there was nothing to lose by it, and possibly something to gain, but why Bunting should make such an issue of Drew's interview, given the trouble he was in, posed a bigger question.

Outside, they all loitered briefly beside the car. Thea moved a few steps into the lane, and was the first to notice a figure standing opposite them, hanging back behind a low stone wall, watching the proceedings with intense interest.

'Oh . . .' she began, but nobody heard her.

'Excuse me,' called Mr Shipley, trotting forward. 'Is that you, Bunting? Your beard – it's gone.' His astonishment was comical. 'I only knew you from the glasses.' Then he stiffened his spine, and looked round at the group. 'So you've been set free then, have you? Thank heavens for that. I said all along you could never have done such a thing. I have to tell you, my friend, I've had some sleepless nights over this business. These are police people, are they? Good of them to bring you home. Although . . .' he looked uncertainly up the lane toward the Bunting house. 'Will you want to . . . ? I mean . . .'

'*No!!*' roared Graham Bunting at a volume that must have easily been heard half a mile away. Then he went on, only slightly more quietly, 'For one thing, you are not my friend.' He looked from Thea to Gladwin and back.

'Haven't I just been saying so? There is no friendship for me in this place, and never has been. Not a scintilla of care or concern, just embarrassment and a neighbourhood conspiracy to ostracise us. All this man cares about is a useless collection of old glass – can you believe that?' He looked round for a response, in vain. 'And no, I have not been set free. I'm to spend the rest of my life in prison, which is exactly how it ought to be.'

Mr Shipley recoiled in abject confusion. 'Oh! But surely . . . ?' He retreated to the other side of the lane again, muttering apologies as he went.

Gladwin seemed to want nothing more than to bundle herself and her prisoner back into the car, and drive back to the sanctuary of the police station. 'Can I leave you to explain it to him?' she asked Thea in an undertone. 'Who is he, anyway?'

'That's Mr Shipley. I told you about him. He lives just there. He was probably watching for you to come out of the house so he could see who you were.' She gave her neighbour a little wave, signalling that he shouldn't disappear until she'd spoken to him. 'Is there anything I shouldn't tell him?'

Gladwin smiled. 'Use your own judgement. It's probably better than mine.' Then the car was gone, and Thea was left with two men glaring at her as if every uncomfortable thing that had just happened was her fault.

'Let me talk to him for a minute,' she said to Drew. 'I won't bring him in.'

'Fine, if you must. Don't get cold,' he said, with a faint smile. The afternoon was turning even colder, which meant the lack of a coat was soon going to lead to shivering, along with numb fingers and toes.

'Five minutes should do it,' she said, thankful at least for the smile.

She crossed the lane, to emphasise the absence of an invitation for Mr Shipley to enter the Slocombe house. 'Let me explain,' she said.

'No need. I think it all became clear enough. I jumped to a conclusion, that's all. You don't have to stand out here in the cold for my sake.'

'Just a couple of minutes. You're right about the beard. I could hardly believe how different he looks without it. He said Hilary would never let him shave it off, even though he wanted to.'

'Really?' He gave this a few seconds' thought. 'That sounds as if he's punishing her, or getting his own way, like a rebellious child.'

'I know. He said something that gave me the impression he was rather more under her thumb than anybody realised. Maybe he isn't entirely sorry to be free of her at last.' Hearing herself, she added, 'No, that's putting it too strongly. But he didn't seem as distraught as you might expect.'

'But why—?'

'Why was he here? He asked for special permission to come and talk to me and Drew. I'm still not at all sure what was so urgent for us to hear. He said they were both upset by Drew's radio interview on Tuesday last week. You won't have heard it. It wasn't anything much, just the case for natural burials, and encouraging people to break the

290

taboo against talking about their own deaths. He's said it all before countless times.'

'They were so upset by it that a murder was committed? Is that what he meant?'

'Sort of, I think. Drew took umbrage, understandably. And there was me, thinking Graham might be going to apologise for the trauma I suffered when we opened that freezer lid. He asked for Rachel to be here as well, which made that seem even more likely. But the police wouldn't go that far. I mean, they wouldn't ask her to come. And now they've taken him back to the cells. Actually, I think Gladwin was hoping he'd reveal some actual hard facts so she could get some real evidence. As far as I know, it's still just his confession. As you said yourself, that's not really enough.'

'He didn't do it,' said Mr Shipley flatly. 'I'm even more certain of that now. The way he shouted at me – he was scared that I was going to say something that would show him up as a liar. I could see it on his face. He hasn't produced any evidence because he *can't*. There isn't any.'

'There's the window cleaner,' said Thea thoughtfully. 'He saw Hilary sobbing in her bedroom, and Graham going out in the car. But Graham knew that – he even spoke to the man as he left. So he can't be too worried about what he might say. I don't think he can throw much light on what happened, which is a shame.'

'Well, thank you for taking the time to talk to me. Go in now, before you get chilled. I'll see you again soon, I'm sure. But I'm off to London again in the morning, for a few days. Let's hope everything's settled by the time I get back.'

She nodded, thinking *Some hope!* As far as she could work out, things were even less settled now than they had been all along. But the very fact of the unsettled state was sparking strange notions, coming at her from all angles.

Drew was in the doorway of the sitting room when she went back into the house. They looked at each other warily before speaking.

'That was extremely peculiar,' she said then. 'Are you okay?'

'I certainly didn't enjoy being told it was my fault the woman's dead.'

'He didn't really say that. He didn't say anything very specific at all.'

'He's playing with everybody. It's all a big game to him.'

She considered this. 'No, no. I don't think so. He *looked* so awful. He had a big bushy beard when I saw him last week – it's weird that he should shave it off so quickly. As if he was just waiting for the chance. Mr Shipley thinks the same.'

Drew did his sweeping motion of dismissal again. 'How could hearing me talk about natural burials provoke anyone to murder his wife? That's the bit I want to know.'

'It didn't, Drew. That's ridiculous. Let's have some tea. I want to have a proper think.'

'All right,' he said grudgingly. 'I need to get back to work. Can I drink mine in the office?'

'I'll bring it,' she said, glad of the respite this would offer her. Her husband's behaviour during the gathering had startled her more than anything else. His anger had been far greater than any she'd seen in him before; his voice louder and his eyes harder. On one previous occasion he had appeared to sulk for a while, only for her to have him eventually explain that he was afraid for her welfare. This time, she hoped she could assume that she was not the object of his rage. She suspected that it was turned against himself, as party to that original chat with Mr Shipley, carelessly passed on to Thea and thus initiating a cascade of tragedy. At least . . . not initiating the thing itself, but involving his wife in subsequent events. Except, there was also that interview, and Graham Bunting's strong implication that it was a crucial factor in what had happened. A definite shift of responsibility was going on, and Drew didn't like it.

Several details were niggling her all at the same time. Hilary's tears, for one. And the complicated timing of her husband's movements during Tuesday evening. Had somebody else gone to the house during those hours and killed Mrs Bunting? If so, would Graham have some reason for protecting such a person? One of his own sons, perhaps? Or Oscar Hemingway, crazed by his dying mother? Or even Antares Frowse, calling about the dog, and getting into a rage at Hilary's lack of concern?

And there was something fishy about Rachel Ottaway, too, come to that. Her satisfaction at Graham's confession had been all wrong; oddly out of keeping with the moment. Rachel! She still had to phone her and postpone the date for the next morning. And check Hepzie for embarrassing lumpy hair, in preparation for the visit to the vet. Perhaps the plaster would come off, with a welcome restoration of normality in that department at least.

She sipped the tea sporadically, not enjoying its lukewarm

temperature. They always did that, she reflected – leaving it to get cold before drinking it. The sign of an overcrowded life, or simply sloppy organisation? She shouldn't be wasting time with it now, when there were things clamouring to be done. She began to rummage for her phone in the pocket of the jacket hanging on the back of the chair she was on, thinking there was an even chance that it would be there, rather than in her bag.

Everything was focusing down, as it should have done from the start, on the personalities of the Bunting couple. Graham's outburst had spoken of a painful social isolation, depression, hinting at deeper mental issues. Hilary had been miserable for some time, or so he implied. He blamed himself. So had it been a sort of mercy killing, then? If so, why not come right out and say so? The courts would probably deal gently with him when they heard his story. And if that was how it had been, in what possible way was that consistent with the horror on his face when he realised what Thea and Rachel had found in his freezer?

Her musings switched to Rachel, who was beginning to look like a lynchpin in the whole story. She knew everybody, for a start, including the Frowse family, with their murdered daughter. She might be aware of the state of the Buntings' marriage, at least to some extent. She had stuck with them, along with the Taylors, when everyone else had kept their distance. Graham had wanted her to be part of the assembly that had just taken place.

She had a sense of a teetering stack of information and observation, poised precariously for her examination. All she had to do was poke it in the right spot for everything to fall onto the floor in a perfect picture that explained the whole mystery. The poking was what she had so often done before. A searching question, a sudden connection, a remembered detail – and light would suddenly dawn. It was going to happen now; she could feel it. There were shadows obscuring vital elements of the picture, and she had a hunch that Rachel knew how to illuminate those exact elements. In fact, she was increasingly suspicious that Rachel knew a great deal more than anyone else did – in which case, hadn't it been a mistake on Gladwin's part to exclude her from the meeting?

It was twenty past three. Not finding the mobile in her pocket, she went to the house phone and called the woman she was supposed to see the next morning. But there was no reply. The automated voice invited her to leave a message, which she did, through her frustration. 'Rachel, it's Thea. I'm terribly sorry, but I forgot we've got a vet's appointment tomorrow morning, so I can't come to you. I won't get away till eleven or later, and then I couldn't get to Blockley before twelve, probably.' She stopped herself from going into further detail, realising that she could in fact still manage two or three hours at Rachel's, given that the invitation had included lunch. Why was she ducking out of it, when she thought she really wanted to see the woman again? There was something blinkered going on in her thinking, sclerotic and inflexible. 'Although . . .' she went on, 'if that was all right with you, I suppose I could still be there, just an hour or two later than planned. Let me know what you think.'

Then the children were home, and the kettle on, and the

fire was being lit, and Drew was emerging from his office with a smile that looked genuine. Thea went through the motions with a slightly raised level of resentment to that which had been lurking inside her for a week or more. She wanted to carry on with her thinking, assessing her own workings, drawing all the strands together – and poking that precarious pile of material that was still squatting right before her eyes. If Drew was hoping that it could all be packed away and ignored in favour of cosy domestic trivia, then he was wrong. He might be disappointed, or angry, or bewildered, and still she had to follow through. It was her nature, and after three years of it, it was inescapably what she did. Gladwin understood and valued the special character traits that so consistently led Thea into the heart of investigations that rightfully belonged exclusively to the police. Gladwin had some of the same dilemmas in her own life, after all. Thea had never met the detective's husband, but had simply assumed he was not unlike Drew – capable, patient, accepting. Men had finally been persuaded that women possessed brains and ambitions, and were not to be impeded in using their talents in the world beyond the kitchen.

And yet, the old ways could still be glimpsed, behind the eyes of the most correct of men. There was Graham Bunting, shouting mercilessly at his wife when she left the front door open too long. Had the woman ever had a profession, going out to work and earning decent money? Had she been a competent mother of their two boys? Thea tried to recall what Oscar Hemingway had said, implying that his aunt had been a reasonably maternal figure, with no special quirks or defects. Few of his actual words came back to her now, and besides – how much would he really know of what had gone on in the Buntings' lives?

It all swirled around her head as she went through the motions, answering questions without giving them more than a tiny part of her attention. Stephanie was on the sofa with Hepzie and a book. Timmy was shooting aliens on an electronic gadget. Drew was trying to get the fire to pull itself together. Outside, the sky was turning indigo. 'It's going to rain,' said Drew.

'Or snow?' said Timmy hopefully.

'Not cold enough for that. Maybe next week, they say.'

'Great!' said the child, returning to his game.

The phone in the hallway caused all four of them to flinch to varying degrees. Only the dog ignored it. 'I'll go,' said Thea, partly in the hope of mollifying Drew and partly because she thought it might be for her.

She was right. 'I got your message,' said Rachel Ottaway. 'Why don't you come a bit later, like you said?'

Thea pushed the sitting-room door shut, pretending it was in order to keep the warm air in. 'I could,' she said. Then went on, 'Have you seen anybody today? I mean, the Taylors or someone who knows the Buntings?'

'I've been in all day.'

'But you managed to miss my phone call,' said Thea mildly.

'Must have been upstairs,' Rachel audibly shrugged. 'I certainly didn't go out anywhere. There hardly seems to be any daylight this time of year. I'm scared of being knocked off my bike in the narrow lanes. I can't wait for spring.'

'Mm,' said Thea, doing her best to think of a way to convey the latest development with Graham Bunting, while not appearing to betray any confidences. For all she knew, Gladwin would get firmly reprimanded if it became common knowledge. 'I've been a bit stir-crazy today, to be honest. I'm driving my husband mad, poor chap.'

'Wives have a habit of doing that. Just ask Graham. I'm sure Hilary was a provocation at times. She was so *miserable*.'

'So I gather. It made me wonder whether he thought he was doing her a favour, or at least putting her out of her misery. A sort of mercy killing.'

'Could well be,' said Rachel lightly, as if the thought was not displeasing to her, but that she was not qualified to judge the killer's motives too closely. Then Thea heard her mobile trilling inside the bag near her feet.

'Oh. Sorry. The other phone's ringing. I'll see you tomorrow, then. Thanks for being flexible about it.'

'No problem,' said Rachel Ottaway.

Chapter Twenty-Three

'Debriefing,' said Gladwin. 'ASAP.'

'What? Where?'

'Can you meet me in the pub? Monday night in January – we'll have the place to ourselves.' Thea thought back to the absence of an incident room, and how if there had been one, the pub would perhaps have been the venue for it. Or else the chilly little village hall, she supposed.

'I'll have to give everybody some supper first.'

'Can't that husband of yours cook?'

'He can, but he's not going to want to.'

'Tell him it's your civic duty, or you've been summoned and can't get out of it. Tell him this is the final push, and from here on you can just get on with your lives.'

'People keep saying that,' said Thea. 'I don't really believe any of them – or you.'

'I'm in the same position as you,' said Gladwin rather sharply. 'I've learnt not to make any promises, but I do have a family and they do like me to be with them at mealtimes.'

'Yes, but you're being paid.'

'Right,' said Gladwin, in a tone oddly heavy with meaning. 'As close to six as you can manage, then.'

That gave her twenty-five minutes to root through the kitchen for the makings of a meal based on the previous day's leftovers, which she left Drew to deal with. 'Should have gone to the supermarket when I had the chance,' she muttered to herself. It was a regular refrain, born of her refusal to live according to a routine of shopping. And yet they had to eat, which was a basic fact she had trouble with. On her own she had grazed on fruit and cheese and tins of soup picked up almost at random when she found herself near a shop. Even with Carl and Jessica, she had been a haphazard caterer. *Cock-up on the catering front again?* her first husband had frequently remarked.

The pub's front door had long been closed off, requiring customers to walk through the car park and enter down a little passage at the back. She could smell woodsmoke and something being fried. In spite of herself, she felt a spasm of excitement; a flurry of importance and a coming climax to the events of the past week. 'Debriefing', Gladwin had called it, which made it sound official and personal all at the same time.

'I ordered us a meal,' said the detective, when Thea found her in the small dining room.

'Blimey! Are they cooking tonight?'

'I persuaded them. Just steak and chips. That's okay, isn't it?'

'Lovely.'

'So, let's get on with it. What do we know? What have we been taking for granted? What have you heard or seen and forgotten to tell me? I'm depending on you, Thea, to walk me through the whole business, from the very beginning.'

'I wasn't at their wedding,' she said mildly. 'Which might well be where it all began.'

'You went to the house on the very day – almost the very *hour* – when the woman died.'

'That's not right, Sonia. It was only four o'clock or thereabouts when I left. It was *much* later than that when she died – wasn't it?'

Gladwin waved a hand. 'Close enough. You were a fresh pair of eyes, walking into something that had to be rising in emotional temperature all through that day. I want *impressions*, as well as all the rest. And I want us to construct a narrative out of it all. Throw out everything we've been speculating on, and start again.'

'Okay,' said Thea slowly, finding herself feeling suddenly hungry. 'Can we do it as we eat?'

'Of course. If your stomach's strong enough. I don't want any flinching away from the nasty details.'

'I was sick,' Thea remembered. 'It seems a long time ago now. I won't do it again.'

'Thank goodness for that. I told them we want two big sirloins, medium, with onion rings and peas. I'm paying, obviously. And red wine.'

'Aren't you driving?'

Another wave of the hand. 'It'll be fine.'

'So where do we start, exactly?'

'The house. You're at the front door, waiting for someone

301

to let you in. Just stream of consciousness. Don't look for conclusions or explanations. Just what was in front of you.'

She launched in. 'They were expecting the people from Blockley for the game of bridge. Hilary didn't play. She was having trouble with her sister's dog – no idea how to handle the poor thing. She was quite tall and slim, long face, grey hair. Clothes a bit shabby, considering they were expecting company. She seemed really happy to see me, as if I'd rescued her from something. She jumped at my idea for a local history group, which threw me a bit. The enthusiasm was overdone.'

'Watch the speculation,' Gladwin warned. 'That comes later.'

'Sorry. So, then Graham shouted from the living room. Wanted her to keep the door shut. We went into the room where he was, and he was just stretched out by the fire, looking quite angry, but lazy at the same time. Leaving everything up to her. Everything he said was at the top of his voice. The dog cringed every time he spoke. But Hilary didn't. She just went wooden and resistant. Neither of them smiled once, except Hilary at the door when I told her my idea. Then the visitors arrived, and we were all introduced, and I liked Rachel. She knew about me and Drew and the funerals, and she got as excited as Hilary did about the history stuff. And then I left.'

'Great!'

The steaks arrived with a flourish, the woman bringing them conveying an air of martyrdom, combined with pride at having produced such a meal at short notice. Gladwin was effusive and apologetic, and all was gratification.

When the woman had gone away again, Gladwin asked

a question. 'Did she look as if she'd been crying – when she first answered the door to you?'

'No, I don't think so. She looked tired and sort of *flat*, that's all.'

'She's been having treatment for depression for some years, but the doctor hadn't seen her for a month.'

'And what about Graham's voice? Is that some sort of physical thing?'

'Nobody knows, but probably not. He seems to believe that nobody can hear him unless he yells.'

'Awful for her,' said Thea. 'And likely to be counterproductive. Wouldn't she just tune him out, to save her own sanity?'

'Not relevant,' Gladwin warned again. 'So then you went back the same day. Why was that?'

'Hilary was taken up with the visitors and lunch and everything. She didn't have time for me.'

'Mithered, as my mother would say.'

'That's about it. But when I went back it was even worse, if anything. The dog had run off, her sister was dying, her husband had shouted at Rachel for bad bidding. She didn't know whether she was coming or going.'

'And you offered to look for the dog?'

'Rachel as well. We both did. And in the end it was Percy who found her.'

'Remind me.'

'Ant's dog. He's a brilliant tracker.'

'Leave Ant for a minute.' Gladwin chewed her meat ruminatively. It was evidently assisting her thought processes. 'It was dark by then, was it?'

'Not quite. I told you – I got home about four o'clock, for the kids. Which was actually *ages* before she died, I should repeat. It might not matter to you, but it does to me. Mike saw her at six or half past, alive and well. Or well-ish anyway.'

'The window cleaner,' Gladwin nodded. 'I remember. That was when you reported back that you couldn't find the dog, but this Ant person was on the case? You saw both Buntings?'

'They were in the kitchen. Hilary said that now her sister was almost dead it didn't much matter about the dog. I thought that was horrible of her. I went off her at that point.'

'Where was Rachel?'

'Still out with Ant and Percy. She seemed to be enjoying it all. And she must have got home quite fast because she says Graham Bunting phoned her before six.'

It appeared that Gladwin was tempted to dismiss this as irrelevant, before changing her mind. 'Did he indeed? Do you know why?'

'She said it was to apologise for shouting at her over bridge. And maybe he wanted to thank her for her efforts to find the dog. It sounded as if he really wanted to make things up with her. That's why she was there on Wednesday morning.'

'What – just to make friends with him after being shouted at? Isn't that a bit weird?'

'She probably didn't have anything else to do.'

'Interesting. The timing of the phone call needs to be checked,' she said. 'This meat is very good, isn't it?'

'Wonderful,' said Thea, who could never get the hang of cooking steak, despite everyone's assurances that it was the easiest thing in the world.

'So it isn't possible that Rachel was still at the Buntings' house throughout Tuesday evening?'

'If she was, Mike didn't see her. And that would mean she'd told me outright lies about the phone call. You should really talk to Mike, you know. And when I went back on Wednesday, Rachel looked as if she'd just turned up, the same as me.'

'On foot?'

'I didn't see a bike. And she said there was something wrong with it. I suppose it must have collapsed on her that morning, when she tried to use it.'

'That's a lot of walking.'

'Not for some people. They do ten miles a day. Or fifteen if they're jogging. And she's very fit.'

'She could conceivably have been there all night then?'

'It's possible,' said Thea, struggling to accommodate this startling idea. 'But that would throw just about everything into question.'

'The thing is, anybody could be lying. They could *all* be lying. We can't make one single assumption.'

'Except me. I'm not lying.'

'Precisely – which is why we're here.'

It felt like a heavy responsibility. 'Ant's okay, as well,' she said. 'He's got no reason to lie.'

Gladwin shook her head. 'You can't possibly say that. He might easily be in collusion with somebody else – the Ottaway woman, for a start. Or the Taylor couple. If they hatched up a plot between them and stuck to the script we'd never catch them.'

'But none of that fits with Graham Bunting saying he

did it. There wouldn't be the slightest bit of sense in that, would there?'

'Think,' said Gladwin severely. 'If he's carrying on with one of those bridge-playing women, for example, and knows – or even suspects – that she killed Hilary, then he might step forward to protect her. I'm not suggesting that's the answer, but you have to think laterally, test every imaginable scenario.'

'In that case, you have to include Mr Shipley, and the neighbours, and the family, and all sorts of people I don't know anything about.'

'Quite. But rationally, I think we're limited to the ones you *have* met. Both the Bunting sons have solid alibis for a start, which keeps them out of the picture.'

'So where were we?'

'Wednesday morning. Talk me through it.'

Thea gave as detailed an account as she could of the discovery of Hilary Bunting's body. Gladwin waited in silence, her steak finished and her wine consumed. Then she said, 'So Rachel led the way into the kitchen? Was she the first to think of looking in the freezer?'

'Not exactly. She did lead the way because she knew the house and its layout. I'm pretty sure the freezer was a mutual thing. But I can't swear that she didn't direct me somehow. I think anybody would have had a look in it, having noticed the stuff defrosting on the side.'

'Probably.' She tapped her teeth with a finger, unselfconsciously thinking, her face working as each thought came and went. 'So let's go back to the shouting for a minute. What do you think that's all about?'

Thea allowed her ideas to range free, but they turned out to be sadly limited. 'He doesn't believe anyone's listening to him? Or he expects an argument? I don't know, really. I'm not a psychiatrist.'

'Neither am I, but I think we're allowed a bit of common sense. It occurs to me that he might be trying to drown out the other person – in this case his wife. He just doesn't want to hear her, so he makes all the noise himself. Not quite the same as expecting an argument, but along similar lines. All unconscious, of course. Fairly routine marital stuff, basically, but taken to another level.'

'Could be,' said Thea doubtfully. 'Although she didn't strike me as somebody who had very much to say.'

'Maybe she'd given up ages ago.'

'So why stay with him?'

'All sorts of reasons that we can only guess at. Not what we're here for. We've already gone into too much speculation.' She sighed. 'I thought we might be getting somewhere a minute ago, but it's slipped away again.'

'The shouting has to be relevant. He shouted at Mr Shipley this afternoon to make him shut up. He absolutely *bellowed*. It was a different sort of shouting from what he did at home. That was just talking very loudly. But it shows he uses it for his own purposes, as a weapon. Or a means of control, at least.'

Gladwin grinned. 'I thought you were going to say he might have shouted his wife to death. I suppose it's technically feasible, if he burst her eardrums or something, but we don't think that, do we?'

'He gave her sedatives, and then stripped her naked and

put her in the freezer,' said Thea. 'That's what he's confessed to, isn't it?'

Gladwin went very pale, just at the moment when the waitress came back to ask if they'd like dessert. 'Not now,' she snarled. 'Let me think a minute.'

The woman backed off, trying not to look offended. Thea threw her a look of apology, trying to convey that they were in the middle of something important.

'Naked.' Gladwin repeated the word. 'God, I've been a total fool. A careless bloody fool. I can't begin to understand how I missed it.'

'What?'

'When we asked him to describe just how he did it, he wouldn't say anything for ages, and then when we told him there had to be a formal statement of culpability, he said something like, "I wrapped her in her dressing gown and put her in the freezer."'

'Well, he didn't,' said Thea. 'Because *I* covered her with the dressing gown. It was hanging on the back of a chair in the kitchen.'

'Right. And you *told* us that, but it got lost in amongst the other details.'

'But it's not so important, is it? He could have carried her downstairs wearing it, and then taken it off her, so she'd get cold more quickly.'

'Was it just thrown over the chair, or what?'

'No, it was quite carefully folded. The way some people would arrange their clothes in the bedroom as they got undressed.' Her steak, which had gone down so easily, suddenly turned sour and obstreperous. 'Oh, Lord, not again,' she said, with a hand to her mouth. Fiercely she swallowed it down. 'I know what you're thinking.' She could hear Sally Taylor saying *It's incredible*, and Mr Shipley saying *He didn't do it. I'd stake my life on it*. She saw yet again the look on Graham Bunting's face as he glimpsed the scene in the kitchen – the open freezer and the green dressing gown over the body of his wife.

In unison, she and Gladwin said, 'He didn't do it, did he?' They looked at each other for a long moment of astonishment. Thea visualised Hilary Bunting in the kitchen, weak from the bout of sobbing witnessed by Mike, woozy with the pills she'd taken, wearing a dressing gown to come downstairs from the bedroom, taking the top layer of contents from the freezer, removing the garment and folding it over the chair, and then climbing into the cold box. Her stomach was still writhing in protest.

'It was suicide,' she said. 'Deliberately made to look as if her husband had killed her.'

'I rather think it was,' said Gladwin.

'It's so *obvious*,' Thea moaned. 'Didn't *anybody* suggest it, out of your entire team?'

The detective shook her head. 'Not to my knowledge. We all got a bad case of tunnel vision – you included.'

'Yes. But why—?' She interrupted herself. 'He confessed because he really does think it was his fault. He sat there for two days, working it all out, and came to the conclusion that she'd done it with the express purpose of incriminating him. She wanted the police to think he'd killed her, and out of some terrible sort of loyalty, he decided to go along with it. But what a *revolting* thing to do. What a vile horrible woman she must have been.' Rage swept through her. 'She committed a crime almost as horrible as murder.'

'Not quite,' Gladwin objected.

But Thea's mind was racing. 'So *she* was the dominant one in the marriage all along. His shouting was just a side issue.'

Gladwin remained pale. 'I'm not going to look too good when I have to explain this to the chief. He's going to want some evidence.'

'Ask Rachel,' said Thea. 'I have a feeling she might have known the truth of it right from the start.' She recalled the satisfied smirk that the woman couldn't quite hide when she heard about Graham's confession. 'That's why she was there on Wednesday – to see if it had really happened.'

Gladwin nodded. 'Okay.' Then she grinned. 'Graham Bunting's not going to be too happy about being released. We'll probably have to drive him out with a pitchfork.'

Thea giggled. 'I don't think we do want any dessert, do we?' she said. 'You'd better make your peace with the pub people and get back to your family.'

'Some hope,' said the detective glumly. 'This won't wait till morning. I blame you, Thea Osborne. I mean Slocombe. You and that green dressing gown.'

Chapter Twenty-Four

Drew was in the bath when she got back, tired and relaxed, and she hadn't the heart to disturb him with news of beastly human behaviour. But she was far too jangled to settle down for an early night beside him. It was only half past nine. She had the car, the address and the determination to bring everything to a conclusion in her own mind, that very evening. Gladwin would disapprove, but that seemed only a minor consideration.

She found the house with only moderate difficulty, and pressed her thumb on the doorbell for ten long seconds. A light went on in an upper room. Rachel Ottaway opened the door cautiously, until Thea pushed at it and marched through. 'I need to talk to you,' she said. 'This won't wait till morning.' Gladwin's line had been repeating in her head for the past forty minutes.

'Okay, if you must. But it's awfully late.' The tone was of a kind of forced sprightliness that Thea did not find a bit convincing.

They sat in a small crowded room, with too many chairs and piles of papers everywhere. 'Do you want coffee or something?' Rachel asked.

'No thanks. Just let me ask you some questions.'

'You know – it's very rude, the way you keep doing this. I don't believe I've ever met a person so obsessed with questions.'

'I *do* know. It's what I do, for some reason.'

'Go on, then. I don't have anything to hide.'

'Really? So, for one thing – what did you and Graham Bunting really talk about when he phoned you last Tuesday? Assuming he really did phone you, of course.'

'He did, although I wished I hadn't mentioned it, ten seconds after I'd opened my stupid mouth. I'm not sure it would be sensible of me to tell you. At least, not until you've explained why you're here now, looking so fired up and excited. That's only fair.'

Thea hesitated. During the five-minute drive to Blockley, she had run through everything again, and found herself following a thread of logic that gave alarming plausibility to the idea of Rachel Ottaway as a murderer. Perhaps the narrative that she and Gladwin had so rapidly constructed was actually all wrong. And then she realised that nobody knew where she was going. Rachel could kill her as well, and nobody would save her.

But it wasn't the first time she'd taken things into her own hands like this, with confrontation and accusation giving acute provocation to a homicidal individual. So far, she'd emerged unscathed.

'Graham Bunting didn't kill his wife,' she said firmly. 'His confession doesn't fit the evidence.'

'Ah! Well, I might remind you that I for one never said he did it.'

'You went along with it, though. You even looked *pleased* about it when he confessed.'

'Yes, because it got him out of my hair.'

'What?'

Rachel leant back in her chair, and looked as if she wished she had a cigarette. Her fingers and lips twitched. 'He's been chasing after me for over a year now. Phoning, emailing, following me around. It was as bad as having a stalker. If anybody was going to kill anybody, the most likely thing was that I'd murder *him*. He was driving me mad.'

Thea narrowed her eyes. 'But you kept going there to play bridge? Didn't he see that as encouragement?'

'I had to, for Hilary's sake. I couldn't let her guess what was going on. I just hoped he would eventually give up, if I made it crystal clear that I wasn't interested. That phone call was him pleading with me to meet up with him the next afternoon, when Hilary was supposed to go and sit with her sister. He went on and on.'

'But – how could he keep it a secret from her?' She imagined the man bellowing amorous blandishments at Rachel down the phone, audible throughout the house and beyond. 'How could that man *ever* keep a secret?'

'He can whisper when he tries. For about half a minute, anyway.'

'Why didn't you just put the phone down on him?'

'I tried that. I tried disconnecting it, too. But he just finds a reason to come over here in person, if I do that.'

'Did he come here last Tuesday? He went out somewhere at half past six.'

Rachel sighed. 'He did. He was here for ages. I couldn't get rid of him.'

'But—' Thea's head was spinning with the inconsistencies of this story. 'That makes no sense. You *must* have encouraged him. There are a hundred ways you could make him stop. Why keep it a secret from Hilary, anyway, if you weren't going to co-operate with him?'

'You don't understand. I don't want to cause trouble for him. I know he's not very stable mentally. Hilary had enough problems of her own. And they both seemed so *lonely*. I hadn't the heart just to stay out of their lives. If I did that, the Taylors would drop them as well. I thought it would work itself out in the end, somehow.'

That sounded feeble to Thea, but there was a grain of plausibility to it. 'Well, it's worked out now,' she said.

Rachel went pale, and for the first time, lost her aplomb. 'Tell me,' she said huskily.

'It would appear that Hilary killed herself. She might even have deliberately made it look like murder. We'll never know if that's true. It didn't occur to anybody that a person could commit suicide like that. It's still too awful to imagine. That must be why I was sick,' she realised. 'Deep down, I must have known the truth of it. Such hatred, of herself and her husband, the house was full of it. And misery. The window cleaner saw her crying.'

'She must have heard Graham on the phone to me. I expect she had an idea already. But he *was* louder than usual, and was saying how much he loved and needed me.

314

It was all coming to crisis point that day, after the ghastly bridge session.'

'When he shouted at you?'

'Right. He pretended it was about my playing, but it wasn't really. It was frustration. He just lost it for a minute. Hilary noticed something strange. I saw it in her face.'

'You're not surprised at what she did, are you? You haven't been, from the start.'

'Oh, but I was. I never dreamt she had it in her to do such a thing. And I did think there was a chance that Graham had killed her. He went home from here in a pretty grim mood.'

'Which he must have dumped on her, and then gone to sit quietly beside a dying woman. That doesn't seem very likely to me.'

'It's *exactly* what he would do. He went to the hospital quite often. Hilary told me he liked the atmosphere, having to be quiet, and have people thinking he was such a devoted relative. It made him see himself as a good and normal person.'

'Which he isn't.'

'He's pathetic, neurotic, cowardly and fairly stupid. I'm not sure anybody has ever really liked him, his entire life.'

'That's very sad,' said Thea, thinking that all her experiences with murder, or assumed murder, brought the same waves of melancholy as this one was doing.

'Yes, it is,' said Rachel.

'It was suicide,' Thea told Drew when she got home. He had been in bed reading, but put the book aside as soon as she entered the room. The questions were vivid on his face. 'We worked it out between us. Gladwin and I.'

'What?' he said.

'Hilary Bunting killed herself, and might even have made it look as if Graham had done it.'

He rubbed his eyes. 'That's not possible,' he said.

'Why not?'

He shivered, grimaced and rubbed his face. 'The *idea*,' he mumbled through his hands. 'How could anyone come up with a plan like that – getting into a *freezer*, of your own volition? It's as bad as walking into a fire. You couldn't do it.'

'It's true, though,' Thea insisted. 'She'd drugged herself first, which would have made it easier. It could even be that she arranged the fingerprints on the glass and pill bottle so it looked incriminating for Graham. But we'll never know that for sure, even though I think he thinks that's what happened. Anyway, she was very depressed and lonely. I've just been to see Rachel, and she's filled in most of the background. It's a nasty, sad story.'

He pulled himself into a sitting position, and rubbed his face. 'So what about the sister, dying the same night?'

'Oh!' She had been on the point of sitting down beside him when she stopped. 'Oh,' she said again. 'She's not very relevant.' She slowly completed her move, before saying, 'It was all about the marriage, you see.' And she summarised what she had learnt from Rachel.

'So the Bunting man will be set free, whether he likes it or not. He's the real victim, isn't he?'

'Poor man. He must think he deserves to be locked up.'

Drew sighed. 'If it's right what Rachel says, he might well be yet.'

'What do you mean?'

'He's mentally ill. Unstable. Pursuing Rachel like that, when she kept telling him it was hopeless.'

Thea smiled. 'You're right. I think they've both been driven crazy by loneliness.'

'And not one person tried to speak up for him, did they? They all said, *Well, that's a bit of a surprise, but it must be true if the police think so.* Even Mr Shipley, who seemed so sure he'd never have done such a thing.'

'That's not true, is it? He's been the only person who strongly defended Graham all along.'

'That man's got his own agenda,' said Drew darkly. 'I don't trust him a bit.'

She blinked. 'Really?'

'As you say – or imply, anyway – he's known the Buntings for years, so why did he try to get *me*, of all people, to tackle them about the shouting and so forth? Passing the buck, because, as the Bunting man said, nobody actually wanted to be bothered with them. They were lowering the tone, which was embarrassing and complicated to try to deal with, so they agreed to send the newcomer in for a go at sorting them out.'

'It's flattering, in a way,' she said weakly.

'It's cowardly. And I very much didn't want to do it. So I let you go instead,' he sighed. 'That'll teach me.'

She laughed. 'I hope it will. I have tried to change, Drew. You know I have. But this has shown me that I don't really want to. It has been upsetting and frightening, in lots of ways, I know. And that's pretty much how I like it, within reason. I *like* the mystery and the talks I get to have with people, hearing about their lives and everything. Gladwin thinks I'm useful. She came to me, before anybody else. And I did what she wanted. She bounced it off me, and trusted me to be telling the truth, and together we teased it all out. It gave me such a huge buzz this evening, eating steak and working it all out with her. I can't stop it, I'm afraid.'

He gave her a many-layered look, containing admiration, exasperation, resignation and unconcealed affection. 'Oh, well, then,' he said. 'I guess I'll just have to live with it.'

They settled down to sleep, both venturing to hope that harmony had been restored.

REBECCA TOPE is the author of three bestselling crime series, set in the stunning Cotswolds, Lake District and West Country. She lives on a smallholding in rural Herefordshire, where she enjoys the silence and plants a lot of trees, but also manages to travel the world and enjoy civilisation from time to time. Most of her varied experiences and activities find their way into her books, sooner or later.

rebeccatope.com